SUGGESTION OF DEATH

A SUSPENSE NOVEL

SUSAN P. BAKER

REFUGIO PRESS

SUGGESTION OF DEATH

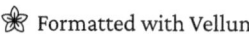

CHAPTER
ONE

S omebody was going to jail.

It was Friday. Child support Friday. At the county courthouse, Associate Judge Maria Lucia Lopez was not in a very good mood. It was springtime in the Texas hill country. By definition, that meant it was hot. And getting hotter every day. And dry. Very dry. Texas had been in a drought for a long time. For years.

And that put her in a bad mood. When she was in a bad mood, Judge Lopez put more people in jail. The courtroom was packed. It always was on the Friday nearest the first of the month. More people were scheduled because of paydays.

There was an established process that had to be followed to put someone in jail for failure to appear or failure to pay child support.

If the judge ordered a capias and set a cash bond, she would set the bond for support now owed. When the obligor was arrested, the sheriff's deputies would bring him—because it was usually the father—from the county jail on the next available docket. At that time, the judge would conduct an indigency hearing. If she found the obligor was too poor to hire an attorney, she'd appoint him one unless he waived attorney. The appointment of an attorney meant she'd have to reset the case, tell him of his right to a jury trial if jail was an option, blah blah blah. It was an arduous process that no one, except the person who failed to pay, appreciated.

On the movant's side—usually the mother—the judge would have to give comparable rights. If she appointed the obligor an attorney, then she would appoint an attorney for the obligee. Currently the Texas attorney general's office usually represented the obligee if she couldn't afford to hire her own attorney. And the obligee could never afford one any more than the obligor could.

JIM SPOTTED her the moment he entered the courtroom. Not his ex-wife who had dragged him back to court, but someone who he recognized from his experience as a reporter covering the court beat. She loomed over the right-hand side of the judge's bench, her left hand resting on some object on the bench. Cropped black hair, face devoid of expression, bulging arms in a short-sleeved deputy sheriff's uniform all caused Jim to misidentify her as a male at first. Moments later, he realized those protrusions below the epaulets, below the small transmitter affixed thereon, below the name tag bearing the name WINK, were breasts, not additional sheriff's equipment.

Something about her presence dominated the room or, per the writer in him, perhaps permeated would be a better word. After taking a seat on the front row and catching his breath, Jim noticed the other people. Subdued, they barely whispered and sat as still as novices at their first communion.

"Jim Dorman," he said to the man next to him who wore

jeans and mud-caked boots. They shook hands though Jim immediately forgot the man's name. Men of all ages, shapes, and colors clustered on the same side of the courtroom as Jim, near the door, while the women gathered on the other side of the aisle, close to the windows.

He glanced back at the bailiff and found her staring at him as though he'd committed a felony offense. His stomach felt like someone had pumped a bellows full of air into it. Jim focused on the tiled floor and wiped his sweaty hands on his pants. When the butterflies settled down in his stomach, he glanced back at the front of the courtroom. What was the worst thing that could happen the first time he attended court?

He tore his eyes away from the deputy, away from the empty, black leather chair centered high in the front of the courtroom, away from the Texas and United States flags hanging from poles standing on each side like a picture frame. He conducted reconnaissance, searching the faces of the people behind and on the other side of the room, foraging for the face of his ex-wife, Pat. The woman who apparently wanted him to suffer a final humiliation. He discovered her in the back row on the far side of the room, shielding herself behind a huge black woman. Since Pat's head remained bowed as though in prayer, he could not make eye contact with her.

"Hear ye, hear ye, all rise for the Honorable Associate Judge Maria Lucia Lopez," the deputy called, a gavel in her left hand, her right hanging down next to her gun. She pounded numerous times, wood on wood, *bam—bam—bam,* as she made the announcement.

The name on the outside of the courtroom door was not Maria Lucia Lopez. Nor was it the name on the thin plastic black-and-white nameplate glued onto the front of the bench. And, if Jim recalled correctly, Lopez was not the name of the judge in the phone book when he'd looked it up. So, who was Maria Lucia Lopez?

Jim stood with the rest of the people and watched as a dark-skinned woman, half the size of the bailiff, entered and climbed the stairs to the bench. Rather than the expected black robe, she wore a black and white herringbone jacket over a white blouse. The Honorable Maria Lucia Lopez glanced at the people in the gallery. Her eyes traveled all the way around the room, pausing briefly on a face here and there, on Jim's face, which sent a shockwave through Jim as his eyes clicked into place with hers, then moved on to light on others' until they stopped at the windows. She nodded at the bailiff.

"Be seated," Deputy Wink said in a voice that reverberated.

Judge Lopez sat down and rubbed her hands together as though to warm them. "Good morning, Mrs. Peterson," Lopez said to a tall, dough-faced woman on her right. "Good morning, Attorney Wilcox," Lopez said to a stocky woman in a pantsuit who sat at the table perpendicular to the bench. "Good morning, Ms. Baskett," she said to the court reporter. Her words held just the hint of an accent.

"Good morning, Judge Lopez," the women replied in unison.

Like a well-rehearsed play, everyone seemed to know their lines. Jim leaned forward to catch their words.

Two stacks of gold file folders stood on the counter before Mrs. Peterson. Attorney Wilcox glanced down at the hard plastic crates of files on the floor beside her chair and picked up a pen. The court reporter stared at the judge in apparent anticipation of the woman's next words.

"From the looks of things, we have a full schedule this beautiful Friday morning."

"Yes, Your Honor, a full schedule." Peterson's grim expression mirrored the judge's.

Lopez cleared her throat. "Well, let's get on with it." She picked up a computer printout, adjusted her glasses, and read into the microphone. "Number 39,404. Klein versus Klein." The words bounced around the room like a hard-hit racket ball. Peterson pulled a file folder from the stack and handed it up to the judge. Wilcox leaned down and pulled out her own file before stepping up to the bench.

Judge Lopez took the file and glanced again at those seated in the same area as Jim. She licked her lips. "Klein," she called again, her voice booming from the speakers embedded in the ceiling in various parts of the room. She leaned over the side of the bench and said to Peterson, "Am I going to have to issue a capias for Mr. Klein's arrest for failure to appear?"

She pushed her glasses up on her forehead and peered toward the group of women sitting on the benches. "Ms. Klein? That you back there? Yes, you. Come on up. I'm not going to wait all day."

A woman about the size of an elf stood and worked her way past the people sitting near the aisle, her blonde hair, in what Jim's mama would have called finger curls, bouncing around her head.

Still one more woman came through a side door by the bench and handed some papers to Ms. Peterson. Men sure seemed to be in short supply.

Judge Lopez said to the woman who stood before her, "Where's your ex-husband, Ms. Klein?"

The woman shook her head and shrugged. "He's not here, Judge."

"I can see that. I realize you're no longer his keeper, but he's usually quite prompt."

Jim whispered to the man sitting next to him. "You been here before?"

The man nodded but stared straight ahead.

5

"Who is this Judge Lopez? Where's the other judge?"

The man concealed his mouth by holding up a creased, white, number ten envelope. "She's what they call the four-D judge. Hears all child support cases."

A knot formed in Jim's stomach. He wished it was gas but knew it was fear.

Peterson stood and pushed several stapled sheets of paper at the judge. She beckoned to the attorney and handed her a set as well.

Judge Lopez took one look at the paperwork, grimaced, cleared her throat, and spoke into the microphone again. "Cause Number 39,404. In the Matter of the Marriage of Lois Klein and Oliver Klein. Let the record reflect that Mr. Adolph Eisler, court appointed attorney for Mr. Klein in the instant contempt action, filed a Suggestion of Death in this cause." She peered over her glasses at the former Mrs. Klein. The Klein woman's shoulders sagged. Judge Lopez continued her recitation. "Attached thereto is a certified copy of the death certificate signed by the county medical examiner. The Motion for Enforcement by Contempt in this cause is hereby dismissed."

"That's brutal," the man next to Jim muttered.

Jim's scalp bristled.

The judge dropped the document into the court's file and handed it back to Miss Peterson. Jim had been around courts enough over the years as a newspaper reporter to figure out that Miss Peterson was the court clerk, the caretaker of the court files.

The Klein woman stood facing the judge, but the judge didn't seem to see her anymore. Lopez took another file from Miss Peterson and called, "Johnson versus Johnson." She waved her fingers at Ms. Klein as though flicking away a fly. "You can go."

When the Klein woman turned toward the back of the courtroom, her face, white as the paper the judge had read from, appeared blank. Her eyes searched the rows of people as she wandered back toward the gallery. Jim opened the little swinging door in the bar that separated them from the front of the courtroom. She looked into his face as if hoping for an explanation. Taking her by the elbow, he whispered, "Is there someone who can take you home?"

She stumbled over the feet of the people who lined the front row. "No . . . thank you. I can make it."

Jim opened the exit door for her and watched as she walked like the dead toward the elevator. When he turned back, a black man, dressed in a dirty white t-shirt and jeans, and the huge black woman who had concealed Pat, stood before the bench.

"So, what's your story this month, Mr. Johnson?" Judge Lopez asked.

Johnson twisted a gimme cap. "I done got laid off, Your Honor. I couldn't help it. I done reapplied for a job at the employment office since then."

"They find you a job, sir?"

"No, ma'am, Your Honor. But I went on ever interview."

"Aw, he's lying, Judge." The huge woman stomped her foot. "I seen him up at the HEB grocery slugging down a beer in the parking lot with his boys."

"That ain't true, Judge, ma'am."

"It is so true. Make him give me my money, Judge. He owes me fifteen thousand dollars." Ms. Johnson repeated herself as if she thought the judge couldn't comprehend. "Fif—teen thou —sand dol—lars."

Judge Lopez glanced at something in front of her and then back at Ms. Johnson. "He did pay something in May and June."

"Yeah, a hundred dollars each time. Big deal. He's supposed to make payments like that ever week."

"I can't help it, Judge. I'm doing the best I can."

"You've been saying that ever since you started coming here, Mr. Johnson," Lopez said, licking her lips. "You know what? Your children would be better off if you were dead. At least then they'd get Social Security."

Shockwaves swept Jim's body. He couldn't believe his ears. Did the judge really say Mr. Johnson should be dead? In all his years as a reporter, he'd never heard anything like that come out of a judge's mouth.

"See, even the judge thinks you're worthless," Ms. Johnson said.

"Why you . . ." Mr. Johnson stepped toward his ex-wife.

"Bitsy," the judge said.

The bailiff quickly moved between the couple. "Go sit down over at that table, Ms. Johnson," Deputy Wink said, jerking her head toward the other side of the room.

The judge frowned and rubbed at the deep line that parted her forehead. "I'm going to reset this case for thirty days and appoint lawyers for each of you. Mr. Johnson, have your attorney notify me if you want a jury trial." She pointed at him with her pen. "If you haven't made a significant monetary contribution to your children's welfare the next time I see you, bring your toothbrush. Understand? Step over to the clerk to get your next court date."

As if to add emphasis to her words, another deputy sheriff came through the side door of the courtroom with two hand-cuffed men dressed in orange jumpsuits and scuffs. He sat them in the jury box. Jim wished he had some anti-acids to calm his stomach before his turn rolled around.

Judge Lopez banged her gavel. "Next case."

Jim watched as the ex-Mrs. Johnson tossed her head and stalked to the back of the courtroom. She pushed hard on the swinging door and sent it flying back and forth, scraping against the wood bar. The bailiff exited the courtroom through the door near the judge and went after Ms. Johnson. Jim could see them through the glass panel next to the door nearest to him. Ms. Johnson gestured wildly. Deputy Wink shook her finger in Ms. Johnson's face and pulled a card out of her pocket, showing it to the woman. Ms. Johnson said something and shook her head. The bailiff pushed the card into her hand.

"I said Dorman versus Dorman." Judge Lopez's raised voice echoed.

Jim felt an elbow in his ribs. "That you?" the man next to him asked. "Better pay attention. The judge looks pissed."

"Shit," Jim muttered. How could Pat have done this to him? Running his fingers through his short brown hair, Jim adjusted his glasses and stood. He tucked in the protruding bits of his shirt, brushed at the creases in his pants, and walked toward the bench. He stared at Patty's back as he approached. Still looked good.

"Are you James W. Dorman?"

"Yes, Your Honor." On close inspection, Jim could see that in spite of the judge's very dark complexion, she had eyes the color of ripe peaches with very dark pits. Her blonde-gray-highlighted hair looked like windblown shrubs. If he hadn't been on the defensive, he would have studied the small, but interesting, face that was older than it appeared from a distance. As it was, the writer in him had retreated and the man had charged forward.

"And you're the father of Patrick and Jeanette?"

"Yes, Your Honor." He clenched his fists to halt the quaking, hoping that neither the judge nor Pat noticed.

"What's the situation here, Attorney Wilcox?"

"Judge, Ms. Reinhart, the former Mrs. Dorman, filed with the attorney general's office several months ago when Mr. Dorman's arrears reached three thousand dollars. He hasn't paid since March tenth, and he hasn't paid regularly for the past year since the divorce."

"And just why have you gotten behind in your child support, Mr. Dorman?"

Jim rubbed his lips together. "Well, you see, Judge, I'm an investigative reporter. I lost my job when the Angeles Evening Star closed its doors." He found a nail hole in the paneling on the front of the bench and stared at it.

"How far did you go in school?"

Jim swallowed several times to wet his dry mouth. The soft patter of the court reporter's machine sounded like rain sprinkling on grass. The bailiff had returned to the courtroom and stood near Jim, one hand resting on her handgun. A strong smell of roses, as if someone had sprayed an atomizer over them, filled the air. The judge soared above him. The woman he now realized was an assistant state's attorney general stood to Patty's right. In spite of himself, his eyes met the judge's. "In school?" He glanced at Patty who clasped her hands before her and faced the bench. It was her fault that he was there in the first place. He swallowed. "I lack my thesis."

Judge Lopez's forehead wrinkled up like a Roman shade. "Your master's thesis?"

"Yes, Your Honor." Jim glanced at Patty again. She was so beautiful, her long lashes and deep-set eyes. He wanted her even now, even though he could wring her neck for humiliating him. He had told her he would pay just as soon as he got his first paycheck—which would be just as soon as he got a job.

"Then you have a bachelor's degree in what?" The judge's eyes were like armor-piercing bullets.

"Medieval literature with a minor in journalism." He shifted his weight from one foot to the other and wished he could sprint for the door.

"And can't find a job anywhere?"

"Look, Judge, I told her I'd pay just as soon as I landed a job or sold my book, whichever came first."

"So, you're writing a book, are you?" The judge smiled and leaned back, dwarfed by the overstuffed executive chair. Her gums were just beginning to recede. Her teeth were large and white, like a wolf's. Jim smiled back. "Actually, several. Which one would you like to know about?" He watched her face for signs she sympathized with him. He hoped she would be more understanding than she had been with the others. Maybe she could see that he wasn't like them.

The judge licked her lips again. "Why don't you tell me about the one that is going to provide nourishment for your children?"

Jim felt like the bottom had fallen out of the floor. He clenched his jaw and took a deep breath before answering. "There just aren't many jobs out there for English majors. I don't have a teaching certificate, none of my short stories has sold, and so far I haven't had a bite on either of the novels I have circulating."

"Have you applied to bag groceries down at the super-market where Mr. Johnson hasn't been drinking beer?"

Jim didn't appreciate her sarcasm and wished he could tell her so. "No, ma'am and I haven't applied at McDonald's, Subway, or Wendy's either. They only pay minimum wage."

The judge's eyes flared. "And how much did you bring in last week not at minimum wage, may I ask?"

He shifted his feet. "I'm still getting unemployment."

"Oh, you're still getting unemployment." The judge repositioned herself in her chair and leaned toward him. "And have you given your ex-wife any of the unemployment you're still getting?"

Pat fidgeted with her purse strap and kept her eyes fixed on something unfathomable. How could she be so unsympathetic?

"Mr. Dorman, I asked you a question."

"Yes, ma'am. Child support is being withheld from my unemployment." He put his hands behind his back and scratched at the callous on his palm. What would the judge do if she found out he worked off part of his rent in manual labor?

The judge cleared her throat. "That's good, anyway, though I don't suppose it amounts to much."

"No, your honor." He frowned when he thought of what he'd let go since he lost his job. A quarter of his unemployment might not make much difference to the judge, or even to Pat, but to him, it meant the difference between having a cell phone, buying a new pair of socks when his toe poked through the ones he had, or even having a cup of coffee when the spirit moved him.

"I'm resetting this case for thirty days." The judge pointed at him with what looked like a Monte Blanc pen. "I want you to get a job that pays a lot more than your unemployment, you understand? And start making regular payments before the next court date, Mr. Dorman, or you're going to become a guest of the county." She gestured at the clerk. "Step over there and the clerk will give you the time and date of your next hearing.

After Jim took the slip of paper from the clerk, he followed Pat to the door and held it open for her, trailing her outside into the hall. "Dammit, Pat. I can't believe you put me through this. I'm doing the best I can."

"Your best isn't good enough then." Her dark eyes glinted

in the fluorescent light. Her hair formed an oval frame around her face.

Jim might be a fool, but to him, she looked better than ever. He'd take her back in a New York minute, if she'd just give him any indication she still loved him.

"The kids need summer clothes and when school starts again, they'll need supplies." She headed for the elevator. "I can hardly afford to make the house note and put groceries in the refrigerator, much less do everything else."

"I'm sorry things are so bad right now, honey, but if we were still married it would be the same way." He pushed the elevator button and stood as close to her as he thought she would allow. Her spicy perfume swept him with memories.

"Your excuses don't put food on the table, Jim Dorman." The elevator doors opened and she stepped on.

Jim bit his tongue to stop himself from saying something snide. If her boyfriend hadn't gone back to his wife, Pat would have married the man. "You got everything in the divorce. What more do you want?"

"Just for you to support your children." She crossed her arms and stared above the elevator door.

Jim put his hand on the wall and leaned over her, whispering into her ear so the other people on the elevator wouldn't overhear. "You know you're turning into a bitch, Pat. You really are."

"Like I'm worried about what you think." She sidestepped away from him.

He brushed her hair behind her ear. "No matter what you do to me, my feelings for you will never change."

Knocking his hand away, Pat said, "You're a fool, Jim Dorman. A stupid, loony fool." She shook her head. "Look, all I want is the money. You can come get the kids anytime. Visit night or day, but I need more money. I know you can get it if you really want to."

The elevator door opened on the first floor. As Jim traipsed behind Pat, he couldn't help but think again of how nice she looked from the rear. When he caught up with her, he said, "That's all you care about, isn't it, Pat? That's all you ever cared about. Money. Well, I loved you. I would have done anything for you."

"Let's not get into that."

"Ms. Reinhart." Deputy Wink called Pat from the direction of the elevators. "Hang on." She made short shrift of the distance between herself and Pat, her gleaming black leather holster bouncing up and down on her meaty hips. "Bitsy Wink. Need to talk to you a minute." She put her hand on Pat's shoulder, propelling her away from Jim.

Jim turned his back on them but eavesdropped on their conversation.

"I know how hard it is for you," Deputy Wink said. "I've got kids, too."

Patty said, "I can barely provide for two children on my teacher's salary."

Jim glanced over his shoulder and saw Wink lead Pat even farther away. He wanted to follow, but one glance from the bailiff kept him at a distance. Not only did she wear all the uniform regalia, but tiny handcuffs adorned each earlobe, and a small six-shooter replica tie clip held her tie together.

As the imposing woman waved a business card in Patty's face, Jim wondered what could be on it. She'd given one to that Mrs. Johnson as well.

Jim had other things to worry about, like getting a job in the next thirty days. The look in the judge's eyes made it clear she had no sympathy for him. He edged toward the rear courthouse door. He knew Patty could see him. He hoped she'd stop him, ask him to wait, but she didn't. As he started to leave, he saw her take the card from the bailiff, read it, and slip it into her purse. He had a bad feeling about it, something that he couldn't quite put his finger on. Seconds later, he realized that paranoia would get him nowhere. After all, the worst thing that could happen would be what, he'd go to jail? The judge had already threatened him with that.

TWO

After court, Jim ran some errands and stopped off at Tex's Tea and Coffee Clatch. When he opened the door, the yeasty aroma of baking bread assaulted his nose, accompanied by roasting coffee beans. Though Jim hadn't been in for weeks, Tex, a woman the size of Bitsy Wink but much more of a motherly figure in her flowered full-length apron and toothy smile, made him feel welcome.

"You're looking mighty fit," she said, pouring his coffee.

"Been working out." He didn't mention doing maintenance at his place in lieu of part of the rent kept him outside and physically active. "Great to see you." He paid for the coffee and moseyed across the room.

Ethan Hale sat at a corner table. He stared outside, as if reviewing a movie in his mind. His blue work shirt rolled up to the elbows and his brown tweed jacket hanging over the back of his chair, Ethan looked like he would be there all day.

"How's it going?" He shook Ethan's warm, soft hand.

"All right for the middle of a semester. Looking forward to summer. Sit down." Ethan sipped from his over-sized teacup.

No one knew why Tex allowed Ethan, and only Ethan, to keep his personal cup at the coffee house. But then, Ethan could be found there any afternoon from three to five and often on days he didn't drive into the city to the university. People knew that and gravitated to his table, pouring out their hearts or listening to him talk books. "What you been up to, Jimbo? Haven't seen you around here lately."

Jim sank into a chair. "Since I got laid off, I drink a lot more tap water than coffee."

"Still haven't found anything?" Ethan pulled on his right ear as Jim had seen him do many times. Both of Ethan's ears folded over like the flap of an envelope. Jim had found it quite distracting when they first met. He remembered wondering whether Ethan could hear well but apparently, he could.

"No, nada, nothing." Jim shook his head. "Now Patty's taken me to court for back child support. Just left there." He cringed inside at the memory. If he never went back to court, it would be too soon.

Ethan nodded and stroked his ear again. "Pretty bad scene?"

"The judge gave me a month to get a job." Jim gulped his coffee and set the cardboard container down so hard that it sloshed onto his fingers, the heat sending a tingling sensation along his hand. He grunted. "About the way my life's been going." Pulling some napkins from the dispenser, he wiped his hands and mopped the table.

"What're you going to do?" Ethan fixed his blue-gray eyes on Jim.

"The judge thinks I should get a job paying a lot more than my unemployment." Jim pulled out another napkin and continued drying his hands. "She even mentioned a fast-food place."

"At least you'd get your meals provided."

"Very funny. I'd lose my unemployment. As little as it is, I still think it's more than a hamburger joint would pay. I've been giving Patty twenty-five percent of my unemployment check and she's still not happy." He wadded up the napkin and tossed it down on the table. "The judge didn't seem to care that I'd at least been paying something." He sipped his coffee, savoring it.

Ethan nodded and fingered the newspaper folded in front of him.

"I already let everything go except food, utilities, rent, and gasoline. Even my cell phone," Jim said. "I've kept the Internet so I can look for jobs, but I may have to let that go. Then what am I going to do?"

"Whoa, calm down boy." Ethan signaled Tex who brought over a teapot and refilled his cup.

Jim waited until Tex left before continuing. "I just can't believe Patty is doing this to me. I told her I'd pay up as soon as I got a job. If we were still married, things wouldn't be any different."

"So, what's really bothering you? That you can't pay the support and have to report back to the judge or that you wish you and Patricia were still married?"

Jim grunted. How did one person get so wise? "Both. Damn, I think I love her even more now than I did before the divorce."

Ethan smiled. "Hate to be trite, but what do they say about absence and all that rot?"

Jim nodded. "She called me a fool."

"Patricia?"

"I know she cheated on me, but I can't help how I feel. Deep down I think she's sorry."

"Not that this would solve your immediate problem, Jimbo, but have you thought about trying to reconcile?"

"Yeah. I think about it all the time."

"Have you ever asked her?"

Jim kicked back in his chair and crossed his arms. "Nah. How can I ask her when I can't even pay my bills. Besides, she's the one who should ask me." He shrugged. "Anyway, whenever I get around her, I end up saying stupid stuff—baiting her. Like today I called her a bitch."

Ethan sipped from his cup and leaned forward, whispering, "I see. Have you thought about why you do that?"

"Are you going to charge me by the hour?"

Shaking his head, Ethan said, "See, that sort of thing. Why do you get flippant when someone is trying to help you?"

"Okay. Okay. I apologize. Sometimes I think that since everyone thinks I'm an asshole I might as well act like an asshole." He didn't add that he felt like an asshole after what he'd said to the judge.

Ethan shook his head. "Everyone doesn't think of you that way. I don't think of you that way."

"Good to know. Okay. So, your question about baiting her. Why do I do that?" Jim glanced at Ethan like a child seeking approval from a parent. "I wish to God I knew. Anger at her for getting a boyfriend and kicking me out? At not speaking except through lawyers for the first six months? At getting most everything we owned? Of separating me from my children?"

Ethan nodded. "Those could be some of the reasons."

"I got totally screwed by the system even though she was the one at fault."

"Because . . . "

"Okay, so I didn't want to put the sordid details in writing. So, I didn't want my kids to see someday what their mother had done if they read the court's file. I thought she'd be fair with me. Stupid me."

"So long as you realize that things could have been different if you'd acted differently."

"Yeah. I know. But it's like she keeps on screwing me every chance she gets."

"And you keep on taking it."

"One of these days I'm not going to." Jim drained his cup and tossed it into the wastebasket. "I gotta go. I only have thirty days to produce some results to keep her honor happy."

"You talking about the judge or Patricia?"

"Both."

"So, what are you going to do?"

"Keep trying to sell my books. And some essays and other nonfiction stuff. I've been thinking I'd widen my job search." All the things he could do started racing through his mind. He didn't want to be rude to Ethan, but Jim yearned to sprint for the door.

"And then—"

"Be nicer to her. I did tell her I loved her today."

"She probably thought you had an ulterior motive. Like staying out of jail."

"Probably. But I meant it. When I can pay my bills, I'll be able to say it with more conviction. I just know if I can get a job or sell a book or both, I'll be able to forgive her and get her back again." He drummed on the table, picked up the wad of napkins and threw them down again.

"And I say, if that's what you really want, then you should do whatever it takes."

"I'd better get at it, friend. See you." Jim stood.

"Just a minute," Ethan said. "I have a favor to ask of you."

"Anything, you know that." Jim hoped it had nothing to do with money.

"They need volunteers at the library. With budget cuts, they've lost employees by attrition. Now they're short staffed."

"Oh." Jim thought it would be something simple. He wondered how much time volunteering would involve. "What would I have to do?"

"Any number of things. Catalog books. Read to children."

"How many hours will it take?"

Ethan scrutinized Jim's face. "If you don't want to do it—"

"No. I'll do it. Just wondering, that's all." He hoped Ethan didn't think him ungrateful for his friendship. He could count on one hand the number of friends he had left.

"Go talk to Frieda Boggess. She can tell you what she needs."

"Okay, sure. I'll go this week." Jim continued to rein in his urge to run.

Ethan's smile was like a male Mona Lisa's, elusive, but when it came the recipient felt warm inside. "Fine. By the way, they have Internet access. If you have to give up your server, you can use the library's."

Jim laughed. "Thanks, Buddy. See you." As he loped out the door, Jim wondered what Ethan could be smiling about. Ethan had lost his wife years before and never had any children. Maybe something had happened in Ethan's life to the good. He'd have to ask next time he saw him.

At the post office, Jim picked up his unemployment check and headed for the farm-to-market road that would take him to the other side of the small town and into the country where he lived. Bluebonnets blanketed the roadsides. Interspersed between the bluebonnet patches, clusters of Indian paintbrushes splashed red up and down the hills. Near the edge of the pavement, pink-tinged buttercups waved in the light breeze. He loved the flowers blooming on the roadside every spring. Ladybird Johnson could take credit for the surge in popularity of wildflowers. She'd done a good thing. Jim would miss them if he had to take a job in a far-off big city.

21

On the other hand, he should be so lucky as to find a job at all.

Jim's parenting time, as family lawyers called it now, included Wednesday nights during the school year. He loved his children but had the feeling their mother had them ask him to buy them things. Patrick always needed another pair of tennis shoes. Jeanette just pointed to stuff she liked when they walked around on Main Street, never complaining if he didn't purchase them. Lucky his check had come. He could take them to McDonald's and, since night didn't fall as early, to the park. In the winter, he'd taken them to a movie every Wednesday night if a suitable one had come to town. It had left him flat broke.

Jim drove around the perimeter of the main house, eyeballing the doors and windows to make sure it remained secured. Then he drove the short distance to the tiny cabin, parking in the carport beside the place. Inside, a light blinked on the answering machine, but when he checked he found two hang-ups. Probably automatic computer marketing. Little did they know they were barking up the wrong tree. He laughed.

After resetting the machine, he gulped some water and went to change his clothes. He had a good deal going, cheap rent in exchange for looking after the main house. Upstairs, his place had one bedroom and bathroom, a kitchen dividing them from the living room, and downstairs next to the carport, a big utility closet with a furnished mini-washer and dryer. When he had the kids, he and Patrick slept on the sofa in the living room. Jeanette got the bed upstairs.

Sitting down at his computer, Jim had an idea for a new story, but a little voice in his head told him that he'd better revise his resume. Swallowing his pride, he changed the paragraph that stated he was in the market for an investigative reporter position to a statement that he would be interested in any position with their newspaper. As this point, he'd do anything but give advice to the lovelorn. And truth be told, he'd even do that if it would keep him out of jail.

The other thing he did was change the paragraph where he listed his experience. Instead of limiting it to the most important positions he'd held, he included every job he'd ever done, no matter how remote to publishing. He might as well show them that his experience was from the ground up. He might feel he was too good to do those jobs anymore, but he didn't want them to know that. He just wanted a job.

After printing his resume for newspaper jobs, Jim revised it for magazine jobs. He searched through his boxes until he found a list of newspapers and magazines within a five-hundred-mile radius. He'd made the list when he'd lost his job but had hoped he would never have to use it.

The phone rang at five-fifteen. "You coming to get us soon, Dad?" Patrick asked.

"You ready to go, son?"

"Yep. Jeanette's not, but I am. She was lying around reading a book, but I told her to go get ready before I punched her lights out."

"Hey, you know I don't like that kind of talk. We don't hit girls."

"I know. And we don't even joke about it, right?"

Jim smiled. "Right. Be sure to bring your soccer ball. We're going to the park after we get some hamburgers."

"Great. See you in a few minutes." The phone clicked and Jim went back to assembling his mailers.

After Jim stamped the envelopes and stacked them near the front door, he dashed to the shower and rinsed off, threw on a pair of jeans, and old Polo shirt, and laced up his running shoes. The shirt was one of Pat's favorites—a sea green color that she always said brought out the green in his hazel eyes.

Peering into the mirror, Jim rubbed his cheek. He could use a shave but had run out of time. He had to deposit his check and get some cash before the drive-in closed. He ran a brush through his thick, coffee-colored hair, shrugged his shoulders at his reflection, and bounded down the stairs.

PATRICK'S BICYCLE lay in the grass in front of the house when Jim pulled up. If someone stole it, neither parent could afford a replacement. Jim parked and when he pulled on the screen door, he noticed a hinge had come loose. Stepping back and taking a good look at the house for the first time in a while, Jim saw flaking paint and an overall appearance of fatigue. The next thing he could expect would be cracks and peeling pieces floating to the ground. The grass alongside the sidewalk needed edging. Other than those things, their house looked the same as ever. Somehow, it should look different since she'd taken him to court and gotten him threatened with jail. That court appearance changed things between them, as if they were becoming strangers. Jim didn't like that feeling. People could do things easier to strangers than to someone they knew. His years of investigative reporting had proved that.

Jim straightened his shirt, checking to make sure the collar turned down all the way around his neck, one of Pat's bugaboos, and rang the doorbell.

"Sorry I'm late," he said when she opened the door. "Long lines at the bank drive-in."

"It's okay. Jeanette's lagging behind as usual. Come on in." Her tan line ran all the way up her legs to the edge of the short-shorts she wore. She looked way better than good. Delicious. He would never stop wanting her.

"Don't you think you should be wearing a bra under that

shirt?" Jim called to her back as he followed her into the kitchen. He could see that she'd been drinking coffee and reading the newspaper at the counter. She wore no shoes, and her make-up had worn off over the course of the day, but the thought foremost in his mind was that he'd like to drag her into the bedroom and do lewd things to her.

"Why? You've seen it all before." She slipped onto a barstool, picked up the edge of the newspaper, and began reading.

"I'm still human, you know." He sat on the other stool, his covered leg resting just a hare's breath away from her naked one.

"Really? I hadn't noticed." Pat didn't look at him, but he could see the corners of her mouth turned up in a small smile. He wondered at what point in their lives she would admit her mistake. It had been well over a year. They were divorced. He'd lost his kids. Her. Did she blame him for her being unhappy? What else did she want to extract from him as punishment? Maybe she'd feel better if the judge would put him in jail for a while. Maybe that was what she wanted.

"I've got something for you." He reached into his back pocket for his wallet and extracted a check made out to her.

She took it from him, glanced at it, frowned almost imperceptibly, and set it on the counter. "Thank you."

"I thought you might need it today, that's why I'm giving it to you directly." He felt like a puppy putting his head up hoping for a hand to pat him.

"You know you're supposed to send them to the A.G.'s child support office."

"I trust you . . . you will notify them to give me credit, won't you?"

She raised her eyes to his. "Yes."

"You're very sexy."

"Don't talk to me like that. We're not married anymore."

"You're not dating someone else again, are you?"

"That's none of your business, Jim. What I do is my affair, not yours."

He didn't want to fight with her; he wanted to make up. Maybe someday she would explain why it happened. Maybe someday she would understand herself.

"Pat, would you be sorry if I got a job in another city?"

She looked up from the paper. "Why? Is that a possibility?"

"I mailed over two dozen resumes a few minutes ago."

Her forehead wrinkled up. "To whom?" She sounded like an English teacher, not a woman concerned that he might move away.

"To every newspaper and magazine I could think of within five hundred miles. I want you to know that I'm serious when I say that I'm not in this financial situation because I want to be."

She nodded and seemed to think that over.

"I'd hate to go so far away." He desperately wanted her to say that she didn't want him to go, would hate for him to be that far away.

Pat didn't say anything, but let go of the newspaper, which floated down to the counter.

"I'd miss the kids. I wouldn't be able to visit as often."

"That's true, but you know I'd work with you on your visitation. I always have. You know that."

"I'd miss you, too, Pat. Patty." He reached for her hand, but she pulled it back. He dropped his hands into his lap and felt like she'd just kicked him where it hurt most. Glancing over his shoulder, he said, "What's keeping the kids? Patrick." he called. "Jeanette."

Trying to catch her eye, Jim hoped for some signal that she hadn't totally shut him out. She looked everywhere but at him.

Perhaps she needed more time. He would keep trying if it took his whole life. As soon as he had some money, he could be more direct with her. Footsteps sounded in the hall. Jim turned in time to see Patrick swaggering up to him. Whom had the boy been watching on television or at the movies? An absent father missed so much. He pulled his son to him.

"Hey, Dad. Watch it." Patrick struggled.

"What do you mean, watch it? You'd better give me a hug, and I mean right now." Jim tousled Patrick's hair. "It's me, remember?" He got down from the barstool and hugged the boy. "Got the soccer ball?"

"Yep. I left it by the door. I thought we could practice kicking." Patrick grinned, that momentary aloofness that came from their not living together, gone.

"Great. Where's your sister?"

Jeanette ambled into the doorway with her nose buried in an open book. He took two steps and bent down before her. "Hi, Sugar Bear," he said, giving her shoulders a squeeze. Placing his finger on the opening of the book, Jim said, "Got a bookmark? Time to go."

She smiled up at him, her small eight-year-old face a mirror image of his own. "But it's so good. I've only got a few pages left."

"Later, Toots," he said, encircling her and kissing her temple. "Both of you kiss your mother goodbye."

The children lifted their faces to their mother. "I'll miss you," Pat said when she straightened up. Jim glanced at her and could have sworn she'd said that for his benefit but decided it was wishful thinking when she smiled in the children's direction. As she ushered them to the front of the house, Jim's eyes lingered on her until she closed the door, but she wouldn't look at him. Still, he could always hope.

THREE

Jim and the kids ate hamburgers at McDonald's. He let them hang out awhile on the slides and swings and tunnels before taking them to the town park where there were rows of trees, baseball fields, and ducks swimming in a pond. Jeanette brought her book and was content to read under a tree and watch her father and brother chase a soccer ball. When he was worn out, Jim retired to the grass beside his daughter. While Patrick continued playing with other children, Jim talked to Jeanette about her book. He asked her questions about the plot. They discussed some of the authors whose works she enjoyed reading. She expressed surprise that he had heard of them.

Jim liked to think that each of his children got some of their characteristics from him. Patrick, his love of sports, his friendly way with people. Jeanette's love of books he guessed she got from both parents. Many a long winter's night he and Pat had sat in front of the fire, each of them reading a novel, talking about it to the other every once in a while. After the children arrived, one parent always read to them at bedtime. Sitting under the tree with Jeanette now, Jim reached out and hugged his daughter. It made him feel good inside when she wrapped her arms around him.

At the end of the evening, Jim walked the children to the door and rang the doorbell even through Patrick had a key. Pat opened up after a second ring. She was wearing a too-familiar housecoat and some fuzzy slippers. The kids pushed past her.

"Don't even think about going to bed without a trip to the bathroom," she called after them. "Be sure to brush your teeth and wash your faces. I'm going to check after you get ready for bed."

"We went to the park," Jim said. "After Patrick ran me ragged, he found some kids to play with while Jeanette and I talked. Hey, I'm surprised at her reading level. She's reading authors that a lot of kids don't like until high school."

Pat frowned. "Yes, but I'm worried that she might become too much of a bookworm. Since her little friend, Becky, moved away, she's been doing nothing but moping around the house with her nose stuck between printed pages."

Jim stood one step down from the stoop and looked up at her. In the porch light, he could see that her face was shiny clean and devoid of make-up. She was a natural beauty. "That's too bad, but I wouldn't worry about it for a few more weeks. Give her some time. She'll find another friend."

Pat stared down at her house shoes and shrugged. "I hope it's before school lets out for the summer." She started edging the door closed on him. "It's getting late."

Bracing his arm across the door, Jim said, "I'm going. I just wanted to ask you something first."

"What is it?" He heard the fatigue in her voice. She spoke slowly and didn't enunciate well. Being a single parent was taking its toll on her.

"When we left court, I saw the bailiff give you something. It looked like a business card. I was wondering what it was."

"That's exactly what it was. She was just telling me about a women's support group. It's for women who are divorced and having trouble making it."

"Like a consciousness-raising group or group therapy?"

"More like informational, I think. You want to see the card?" She turned toward the inside of the house.

"No. No. I was just wondering. I saw her give one to that other woman. Ms. Johnson? I was just curious, that's all."

Pat smiled. "You're not missing out on anything, Jim. It's like those pamphlets the judge gave us at the time of the divorce—those guidelines for divorcing parents. But I don't mind finding the card and showing it to you if you want."

"No." He should go before he overstayed his welcome. "Are you going to go to a meeting?"

Pat shook her head. "I don't know what's gotten into you." She shoved his upper arm, trying to make room to close the door. "I'll let you know if I do. Now, goodnight."

"Goodnight." Jim let her close the door in his face. It must be his writer's mind, to think that something was wrong. His imagination was running away with him. It made perfect sense that anyone who had a women's support group for divorced and separated women would hand out information at the courthouse. Now that he thought about it, he remembered seeing some AA pamphlets and some Legal Aid booklets on a coffee table in the clerk's office. And there were bulletin boards inside and outside the courtroom with the child support rules, domestic relations stuff, and mediation information tacked on them.

As soon as he got home, Jim checked his answering machine. There were no messages. There weren't even any hang-ups. Turning on his computer, he began revising a short story. He did his best writing at night. He knew some people got up early in the morning, but his mind was sharper in the evenings. Always had been. The world seemed more at peace. He was able to relax. His thoughts flowed more easily.

He always re-read what he had already written before continuing. He worked until early in the morning. As soon as the story was ready for publication, Jim's plan was to call a magazine editor he knew who had published a couple of his stories in the past instead of just emailing it. The piece would fit right in with the kind of thing that magazine had published before.

The following morning, after Jim phoned the magazine and they agreed to look at his story, Jim emailed it before heading to the library to see what the volunteering thing was about. In all the years he'd known him, Ethan hadn't asked him to do anything without a reason. If the library needed help, they must be in very bad shape.

The library sat on the top of Mueller's Hill. It was so-called because almost one hundred-fifty years earlier the Mueller family built and lived in the mansion that now housed the library. Upon the death of the last surviving Mueller, Louise, a spinster, at age ninety-two, the house and hill were left to the citizens of Angeles with a large cash endowment for a library. Since one of Louise's favorite pastimes had been reading, she also left a vast collection of novels and nonfiction hardback books that she had purchased over the years. Until the day she died, no one ever saw Louise without a book in hand.

Halfway down the hill, town park, where he had taken the kids, was on one side of the street. A few years earlier, even with protests from some of the citizens, the town leaders had sold most of the opposite strip to Walmart to gain funds to develop the park. Wendy's hamburgers had the remainder. Jim and Pat had taken the children to the grand opening of both and before their divorce, they'd gone to the park as a family.

Jim entered the very familiar library and walked around to the front desk. When the woman finished with the people in front of him who were checking out books, Jim said, "I'm looking for Frieda Boggess. I believe she's the executive director?"

The woman, who had the slightly sagging neck of someone in her mid-fifties but had jet black hair and jet-black eyebrows, turned startling royal blue eyes on him. "I'm Mrs. Boggess."

He put out his hand. "Hi. I'm Jim Dorman."

She shook his hand firmly with her warm one. "What can I do for you, Mr. Dorman?" She wore a long, brown skirt and a long-sleeved flowered blouse with a button-up sweater over it. Glasses hung down from her neck on a beaded chain.

"I heard a rumor that the library needs volunteers. I wonder if you could point me to the Volunteer Coordinator?"

"You're looking at her."

Jim stepped back. "But I thought you were the Executive Director." He dropped his keys into his pocket.

She nodded and rolled her lips together. "I'm a bit of everything, I'm afraid." Walking over to the returned book bin, she picked out books and began stacking them on a cart. "We never had a large staff to begin with. Now we have even fewer employees. I'm in charge of just about everything: grant writing, fund raising, public speaking engagements, volunteers, and training. I'm also the head librarian, research librarian, and children's librarian. You name it; I'm it."

"Doesn't anyone else work here?" He glanced around but didn't see anyone who looked official.

She laughed. "Yes, of course. The city won't let me hire anyone to fill vacancies, but they didn't fire anyone, either. We have a maintenance man. He's also janitor and the security guard. Also, Merrie Fleiss is our adult section librarian. We've been using volunteers for everything else."

"Wow. And this place used to be a first-class library for a small town." He drummed his fingers on the counter and glanced around the premises.

"You don't mind if I sit down, do you?" She perched on a tall, wooden stool. "Money is tight all over. So," she looked him over, "you want to volunteer? What is it, court-ordered community service work?"

Jim chuckled. "Now, Mrs. Boggess, do I look like a criminal to you?" He leaned on the counter and stared at her.

"You never know these days. We had a community service worker here for a while. He wasn't half bad. He was on probation for driving while intoxicated. We used him to police the grounds and re-shelve the books."

"I hope you can find something better for me to do."

"What exactly is your motive?"

"What are you, a mystery reader?"

She smiled. "Yes. I have a suspicious mind."

"I have no motive. My friend Ethan Hale asked me if I could give you a few hours, being as how I'm unemployed right now."

"Well, I can't pay you."

"No, ma'am. I know that. I've already been paid in kind. I've been using this library for years."

"This library has been good to the people of Angeles. I don't know why they don't want to support it now."

"Times are tough all over. So, could you use me? I'm a writer by trade. I'll be over here anyway using the library's computers to access the Internet." He thought of the money he could save, not much, but at this point, every little bit mattered.

"At least we still have that," she said. "Tell you what my immediate needs are. Someone to supervise the Internet room. Also, come summer, someone to read to the young children."

"So how many hours are you talking about?"

She looked at him sideways. "You could use one of our computers to do your work and supervise the room at the same time. We have an extra. Got it on a grant."

"Are you evading the question, ma'am?" Jim grinned. There was something about her that drew him in, something warm and motherly in spite of the stark black hair that he guessed she had dyed.

She pursed her lips. "How many hours can you give me? Keeping in mind that the city reduced the hours we're open anyway. We're not open on Sundays at all. We close on Saturdays at six p.m. We also don't open Monday through Friday until ten a.m. and close at six p.m. except for Thursdays when we stay open until nine."

"I'm going to have to write that down."

"It's on the door. I'm not asking you to work all of that."

"I hate to admit I'm relieved, but I am."

"Thursday nights would be really helpful. That way there would be two of us here."

"And once school is out for the summer?"

"One morning a week? I can schedule the children's program around that."

"No problem. I'll do even more if time permits, but I have to warn you. I'm looking for a job. As soon as I can find one, I might not be available."

She stepped off the stool and extended her hand. "I understand. Thank you. I'm very grateful."

"What is Ethan to you?"

"My half brother. We had the same mother but different fathers."

"So, he's trying to take care of his little sis, huh?"

"Big sis." Her eyes twinkled. "I'm glad you decided to come in. Ethan told me you might."

Jim chuckled. "So, I'll start tonight in the Internet room?"

"That would be delightful," she said.

CHAPTER

FOUR

Several weeks passed. Jim didn't hear a thing about any of his manuscripts. He'd drawn up a schedule for himself. In the mornings, he'd warm up, run five miles, come home, shower, and eat breakfast. At least once a week he went to the unemployment office—more often if they told him to. He kept a record so he could show the judge. On Wednesday nights, he'd take the kids for a couple of hours. On Thursday nights, he worked at the library, supervising in the Internet room. He also taught newcomers how to make the best use of the computers and their time on the machines since if there were more people than machines, the library limited each person to an hour.

In the afternoons, Jim studied the markets until he found magazines that would make good homes for his pieces. If they didn't accept email submission, he'd spend hours printing copies, addressing envelopes, and taking them to the post office. After dinner, if it wasn't his turn to have the kids, he would re-read whatever he'd written the night before, correct it, and try to write at least ten new pages of serious stuff

Each day resembled every other day. Each day flew with there never being enough time to get everything accomplished. When he'd been working, there had always been enough money for him to occasionally hang out at The Shy Ann Inn with other writers and reporters. Now, he hadn't been there in over six months. He couldn't spare the money; and the time he'd waste would be better used writing. He did miss it though. Even Ethan, who was one of his best drinking buddies, had quit calling him to see where he was. Jim hoped that Ethan had understood from their conversation at Tex's that he couldn't afford to go out.

The phone rang, shaking Jim out of his reverie.

"Are you still carrying life insurance on yourself?" Pat asked.

Jim's stomach lurched. "I'm fine, Pat. How are you?" He leaned back in his chair and propped his feet on the wastebasket.

"Sorry, but are you?"

"Why do you want to know?"

"It was one of the requirements of the divorce decree. You're supposed to carry two-hundred-and-fifty thousand dollars worth of life insurance with the kids named as beneficiaries."

A shiver ran down Jim's spine. "Well, yes, I believe the policy is still in full force and effect."

"You believe?"

"Well, gee, Pat, I have been in financial difficulty lately." Jim picked a pencil out of the cup on his desk and twirled it between his fingers.

"So, you haven't paid the monthly premium, is that what you're saying?" Her voice grew high-pitched. "For how long?"

"What's going on?"

"You're in breach of our divorce decree. You agreed to carry the insurance, and the judge ordered it as part of the child support award."

"Okay. Okay. Jesus Christ. As soon as I get some money, I'll catch the premiums up. I just figured it wasn't as important as some other things that need to be paid—like child support."

"But suppose something were to happen to you, Jim?" Her voice was a bit softer.

Anger nipped at him. "God forbid, you're supposed to say."

Neither of them spoke for a moment.

"There's always Social Security, babe," Jim said sarcastically. "Like the judge told that Mister Johnson. I've been working since I was fourteen. I'm sure the children are entitled to Social Security benefits if something happens to me. At least until they are grown."

"I know. I've thought about it."

"Why did I know that you would say that?"

She sighed, long and hard. One of the things she did a lot of the last year of their marriage. "Okay. Okay. Can we discuss this rationally? When can you catch up the premiums?"

"Now that you've calmed down a little bit, you want to tell me what the hell is going on? What got you so hot and bothered about the topic of life insurance?" Jim's had to hold his shaking knee down.

"I went to a WiNGS meeting last night."

"What the hell is that, a wings meeting?"

"It stands for women not getting support."

"You're getting support. You get twenty-five percent of my unemployment check every time I get one."

"Yes, but that's a lot less than you were originally ordered to pay me."

"Is this that support group they gave you information about at the courthouse?"

"Why?"

"So how long have you been going to meetings? And why didn't you tell me about it?" Jim wanted to bang the receiver on the desk, hard.

"I don't have to tell you everything I do, Jimbo. We're divorced, remember?"

"You don't have to remind me. Have you been going to a lot of them? How often do they meet?" He pulled out a notepad and began making notes.

"They meet every Thursday night, but a lot of people just go when they can. It was my first meeting. I liked it. It was informative. I've needed moral support since the divorce."

Jim muttered, "They need to give me the name of one for men."

"What?"

"Nothing. So, what happened? Were they all picketing men? Are they all a bunch of man-haters? Are you going to end up hating men?"

"Don't be ridiculous. It was kind of like I always imagined an alcoholics anonymous meeting would be like. A woman stood up and introduced herself. She told how many years she'd been divorced. Then she talked about some of the problems she's still having."

"So, you all compare notes and talk about how much you hate your ex—husbands."

"There was a speaker. She was a woman lawyer, and she spoke on "Understanding the Terms of Your Divorce Decree.""

Jim breathed deeply and forced himself to relax. He knew he shouldn't let her get to him. He kicked back in his chair again and propped his feet on the trash can. "So, what did she do, point out all the parts of the decree that had to do with money?"

"Yes, she did. She went over a sample decree from beginning to end, then she took questions."

"And you just happened to have your copy of our decree in your back pocket so you could ask questions from it." Why was he getting an uncomfortable feeling in the pit of his stomach?

"You're not very funny."

"Sorry. I'm just trying to figure out why you needed a stranger to tell you all this. You had an attorney when we got divorced. You could have called him."

"Yeah, Jim, but first of all, this was free. Secondly, I always felt like Phil was your attorney, not mine, since we used the same one. I never felt comfortable with him."

"Why? Between him and me, we gave you almost everything."

"I just didn't. I felt better today with a woman. I can't explain it. I just trust her more."

"Okay, so she pointed out to you that I was supposed to keep up the life insurance for the benefit of the kids."

"Right. And if it will make you feel any better, when I called to find out about the meetings was when Bitsy told me to bring my divorce decree."

"That would be Deputy Bitsy Wink?" Jim liked that even less. "Okay. I'm sorry. I have to tell you though, Pat, I can't pay the premiums up—not totally, but I'll pay something on it."

"All right. Just so long as the policy doesn't lapse."

"It's not right now. It's whole life, so the cash value is being used to pay the premiums."

"I'd forgotten there was a cash value, but I did see it listed in the decree. It's not very much."

"No. That's why I was awarded it."

"Ha, ha. Well, I need to go now. I'm on my off-period, and there're just a few minutes left before my next class."

"Is there anything else I'm not doing that you think I should be doing?"

"Like what?"

"I don't know. Is there anything else they said at the meeting that I should know about?" The phone suddenly sounded like it had gone dead. "Pat? Are you still there?"

"Uh. Nothing worth mentioning right now, Jim. Listen, I really have to go now."

Jim couldn't help feeling that there was something she wasn't sharing with him, but it was no use trying to get it out of her over the phone. The next time he saw her, he would sit her down and make her go over with him in detail everything that happened at those meetings, from the invocation—if there was one—until the benediction. In fact, he thought he just might find out where they held those meetings and see if he could attend one himself. He'd have to miss a Thursday at the library, but it would be worth it.

After hanging up, he turned back to the computer. His greatest desire at that moment was to sell something big—sell a blockbuster novel. He wanted to get a huge advance. Cash money. And he knew what the first thing he would do was. He would go down to the courthouse and pay his child support in full with interest at the legal rate.

THE FOLLOWING WEEK, a check for an essay came. The check was enough to pay three months premiums on Jim's life insurance, catch up his rent which had fallen two weeks behind, buy a few canned goods, and give Pat a few extra dollars. He had a great desire to celebrate by going for a drink to the Shy Ann but was afraid he might be seen there like Mr. Johnson had been seen at the grocery store. He wasn't going to give Pat a chance to tell the judge he was spending his money on booze. But the day he sold his first novel, he was going to go out and buy drinks for everyone in the joint. In the meantime, he treated himself to a cappuccino at Tex's. It was nice to taste something that wasn't mixed by his own hand. He had hoped to see Ethan, but he wasn't there.

Jim was also tempted to find himself a woman. If Pat wasn't going to forgive him and take him back, he might have to start thinking about finding someone else. After all, he had needs. But he also still had hope—that Pat might change her mind one day. As long as he thought there was a chance that they'd get back together, Jim wasn't going to jeopardize it by sleeping with another woman. And, being realistic about the situation, who would want to go out with a man who couldn't even buy her dinner, drove an old broken down '67 Mustang, and couldn't get his wife out of his mind.

After he had run around making all the payments, Jim got out his book of market listings again. Maybe he was on a roll. If he could sell one essay, he could sell another. It was getting more and more difficult to sell fiction. The markets were drying up. Big publishing houses had been bought by large corporations and consolidated. Fewer midlist books were being published. A lot of magazines that once were a large fiction market had either gone under or just plain quit publishing short fiction.

At the same time, though, the market for nonfiction seemed to be growing. Jim thought he might try writing some magazine articles. He could send out some queries. It couldn't be that much different from newspaper reporting and essay writing. He could do some research while he was at the library.

His third option would be to learn about Internet publishing. He'd avoided it because it seemed so complicated. The time he would use learning all the ins and outs he could use writing actual marketable prose. But maybe now he'd better learn.

The next morning, when Jim got to the library, Frieda sat at a table behind the front desk. A new volunteer stood checking out books. Jim leaned over the counter, "Frieda, hi. Came to do some research."

"Hi, Jim. Would you mind rolling the cart up to that section for me? That way I don't have to go all the way up there."

"Not at all." He pushed through the side entrance behind the front desk. "How've you been doing?"

"Busy. Tired." The sides of her mouth turned down. "Nothing new. I'm writing a grant. If we get it, we can get some relief."

Jim put his briefcase on top of the cart and pushed it out and toward the elevator that had been installed in better times. He took it to the third floor where he let another volunteer relieve him of the cart and then found a place where he could spread out at a table. The magazines stood on racks facing the tables. To his recollection, there were fewer than in earlier times. He'd study what was there. Hope filled him. Perhaps he could write by assignment for a magazine. All he needed was a topic to write about. Research was his thing. If he came up with an idea, he could query a magazine with it and see if he could get an assignment. He started pulling magazines off the shelves, searching their tables of contents, hoping for something to jump off the page at him. He knew he couldn't write about the same topic that had already been published. A different angle, a different perspective, or a responsive article was what he was after. By the end of the afternoon, he had several ideas jotted down and one he was really interested in that just wouldn't quit. Deadbeat dads.

It was all in the news the last few years. Deadbeat dads and why they abandoned their families. Deadbeat dads and why they didn't pay their child support. Why they didn't visit. Why they didn't seem to care about their kids. The effect of nonsupport on the family. The poverty level of households run by single mothers. The effect not having a father figure had on the children. How much more detrimental it was to boys than girls not to have a father in their lives. How male juvenile delinquency was caused by absent fathers. What the government was doing to collect the money. The federal government. The states. Innovative ideas to get fathers to pay.

The only thing that Jim was not able to find, was an article on the father's perspective. Why fathers abandoned their families. No one had ever asked a father—except in a threatening way. How did fathers feel about all the bad press they had been receiving? What solutions did fathers have to the dilemmas in which the children found themselves? Jim thought he was on to something. All he had to do now was find someone who was interested in publishing an article from the fathers' viewpoint.

He made a list of magazines to contact. If he had thirty dollars in his pocket, he could go to the bookstore and buy a copy of the market book for nonfiction, but that would have to wait until he sold something big.

THE FOLLOWING FRIDAY, when it was his weekend to get the kids, Jim showed up at Pat's a few minutes early to question her about WiNGS. When she answered the door, she looked like she was in the middle of getting ready to go out. She wore a pair of jeans, a decorated t-shirt, and a pair of very white, leather walking shoes. Her hair, which she had had cut even shorter since the last time he'd seen her, was still wet, and her make-up was only half done. He was disappointed about her hair. He had always liked it long, the way it flowed around her face. He had thought it sexy when they were making love.

"You're early." She pulled the door wide and walked off.

Jim thought she seemed to have something on her mind.

He closed the door and followed her. "That a new shirt? The zebras are neat looking."

"I did it myself. Listen, I've got to go dry my hair. You want to wait for the kids in the living room? They're still packing their bags. Or you can help them if you like."

"Can I talk to you?"

She turned and squared off with him, her eyes sparkling like crystals caught by the sun. "I'm trying to get ready to go out."

Jealousy reared up in Jim. He wasn't used to that feeling but recognized it for what it was. The thought of some other man holding her in his arms made him sick to his stomach. Though he knew he had no right to her anymore, he couldn't help feeling a possessory interest. "You got a date?"

"Huh uh, a meeting. It starts in forty-five minutes, do you mind?"

Jim tried to hide his relief. "Can I talk to you while you're getting ready?"

She rolled her eyes. "Honestly, Jim. Can't it wait until another time? I have to do my hair and finish my make-up.

"It's not like I've never seen you do those things before."

"How're we going to talk over the blow dryer?"

"Yell."

She shook her head in exasperation. "Come on then."

He followed her into the bathroom. He put the toilet lid down and sat on it. The room smelled of a sweet perfume and other female chemical aromas. It brought back a rush of memories that he shoved to the side in his mind.

"By the way. Thanks for the extra check."

"You're welcome. Wish it could have been more. It was for an essay I took a chance on and sent out. But that's why I'm here, Pat. I've got a terrific idea for a magazine article." He picked up her hairbrush and stroked the tangled hairs.

"An article? You've never done that before." She flipped on the blow dryer.

"I know," Jim yelled. "But I've got to make some more money and I figured this might be the way to do it."

"So what's the idea?" She was fluffing her short hair with one hand, holding the blow dryer in the other, and staring into the mirror.

A rush of apprehensiveness, like the warm air blowing in the room, snuck up on him when faced with explaining what he wanted to do. He didn't want her to think he was trying to court sympathy. He'd given the article a lot of thought in the past few days and was quite serious about doing it. He'd already sent some query letters to several magazines. He caught her looking at him. His pits had become moist. The silence grew long. What if it made her angry? If he wrote any of it from his own viewpoint, especially how he felt when she took him to court, she might quit being as friendly as she had been recently.

She turned off the dryer. "Something the matter?"

"It's just that I don't want you to get angry." He searched her face for a hint of empathy.

Her eyebrows drew together. "I can't get mad if you don't tell me what it is."

"True. All right. Well, you know how the focus everywhere is on how fathers aren't paying their child support and all these single parent families headed by women are on welfare?"

"Yeah. I'm real familiar with that."

"Don't get sarcastic. This is serious. I thought I'd write an article or maybe a series of articles on how fathers feel."

"How fathers feel about their children being on welfare?"

"Pat. No. From different fathers' perspectives. For example, that Mr. Johnson who was ahead of me in court. I want to talk to him and find out why he got so far behind. Was it his fault or is he a victim of circumstances? How does he feel about having to go to court every few months for what may be the rest of his life? That sort of thing."

"My first inclination is to make an ugly remark like 'Who gives a shit?'" But you may have something there, Jim. I'm trying to be fair and unbiased about this. You might really have something."

Jim smiled and sat up a little straighter on the toilet. "I'd really like to develop it into a series. Not only because I'd make more money that way, but also because I could do some interesting research. A different slant on the statistics. Stuff like that."

She cut off the dryer again and fanned herself with her hand. "God, it's hot in here." Peering at herself closely in the mirror, she asked, "Why are you telling me all this?" She picked up a brush and began stroking powdered blush on her cheeks.

"Because I need your help, honey."

Pat cocked her head and pursed her lips and seemed to stare straight through him. Jim thought that was probably one of the skeptical looks she normally reserved for her students. "What do you want now?"

"Now don't be like that. It's nothing difficult. See, what I want to do is interview women like yourself that are on the receiving end of child support."

"Supposed to be on the receiving end, you mean."

"Right." He wasn't going to argue with her. "Okay, to be perfectly honest, I wondered if you would talk to some of the women in that WiNGS group and see if they'd give me an interview."

"You said this was going to be from the man's viewpoint."

"It is. But I want to interview maybe half a dozen of the women. Maybe more. Get their side. Find out what questions they sincerely would like their ex-husbands to answer. Get at what they're like and what they think the problems really are."

"And then get their husbands' sides, is that it?"

Jim nodded. "That would be, say the introductory article. A statement of the problem from several women's perspectives."

Grinning, she said, "You want to interview me?"

"I don't think so."

"Don't blame you." She closed one eye and lined it. Then the other.

"Don't you think this is a really good idea?"

"Yes, but Jim, I'm not sure some of the women would talk to you. They're very angry. Especially the ones whose ex-husbands have gotten out of jail on a technicality."

"Will you ask them?"

"Well, I guess. If it might mean you'll be able to pay your support, why not?" Her laugh was not all that pretty.

"Is that where you're going tonight? A WiNGS meeting?"

"Yep. But it's a board meeting."

"You've been elected to the board? That was quick."

"I volunteered to be secretary. The lady who held the job moved out of town suddenly." Shrugging, she said, "Anyway, I wanted something to keep me active. That's it." She dropped her mascara into her make-up bag and ran her fingers through her hair. "I'm ready."

Jim wondered if she felt anything for him. They were in the same exact setting as they'd been many times before. Did she feel nostalgic at all? He wanted to say something, but was afraid to. For a moment, he thought he saw something in her face, then it was gone. He stood. "So you'll ask some of them the next time you all have a regular meeting?" He followed her into the bedroom.

She stopped and turned to face him. "I'll do better than

that. I'll ask the board whether I can make a general announcement, okay?"

"Great. Say, Pat, is it a real board? I mean is WiNGS a not-for-profit corporation—a 501 (c) (3) nonprofit corporation?"

"I guess so, Jim. I'm not sure. Why?"

"Well, you'd better find out. You may be biting off more responsibility that you want. Who are the other officers?"

"Nobody special. Just women in the same situation as I am. There's a big variety. Some are really dirt poor, too. Not capable of earning anything other than minimum wage. Some are like me."

"Is Judge Lopez on the board?"

She shook her head. "No. As I understand it, there's an advisory board made up of people like her. Important people in the community. It's just for show, though. They have maybe one meeting a year and that's an appreciation luncheon. Mostly they lend their names."

"Do they have any handouts or anything like that?"

"Sure."

Pat went into the kitchen. He followed her, two steps behind like a small puppy.

"I put mine over here someplace." She dug around in a stack of mail and papers piled up on the telephone book on one end of the counter. "Kids," she shouted. "Your dad's here. Come on." She found what she was looking for and handed it to him.

Jim looked over the pamphlet. It was an eight-and-a-half by eleven piece of paper with printing on both sides, folded into thirds. The front third had the name of the organization and the acronym. The address was a church out in the country. "Whose phone number is this?"

"It's an answering machine except when someone is at the church."

Inside was a description of support services that were available to women. Referral to various agencies. Free legal advice. Referral to low rent housing. Jim looked over the back of it. It all appeared to be normal. He didn't know what he had expected. "Can I keep this?"

"Sure." She set her purse on the end of the counter and reached into the refrigerator for a soft drink.

The children came in, each of them carrying his or her child-sized suitcase. "Hi, kids," Jim said and bent over and kissed and hugged each of them. "Ready to go?"

Patrick hollered, "Yeah."

Jeanette nodded, silent. She handed her suitcase to her father. From the weight of it, Jim could tell that she had several books in it. He pulled out the handle and set it on the floor so she could haul it behind her.

"Well, I guess we'd better be running along." He herded them toward the door.

"Give Mom a kiss," Pat said as they started to leave.

Each child reached up and gave her a hug and a kiss before going out the door.

Jim held the screen open. "Hey, thanks for all your help, Pat. I have a feeling about this project. I think it's going to be a great success."

She raised her eyebrows and nodded. "I hope it works out. I just remembered, in case you're interested. Remember' the bailiff from Judge Lopez's court?"

"Yeah. How could I forget her? Bitsy Wink. She's an Amazon." Psycho Amazon warbitch from hell, he thought, but he'd never say that aloud to Pat.

"She's on the board of WiNGS. She's the president. You might want to interview her." Pat looked at Jim's expression and burst out laughing. She was still laughing when she pushed the door closed in his face.

CHAPTER

FIVE

T hey call them compliance hearings. Jim was scheduled for his first one. He'd phoned Mrs. Peterson of the district clerk's office to see if he could skip it since he'd been paying Pat twenty-five percent of his unemployment check and had paid her extra from his essay sale. Mrs. Peterson had replied that he was further behind than ever so he'd better come tell it to the judge. Jim wasn't anticipating a pleasant experience.

When he arrived, Jim realized that he recognized some of the faces from the previous time, both mothers and fathers. Some of them were visiting like old friends, the mothers with the mothers, the fathers with the fathers. Commiserating, he guessed. Taking his place on a bench, Jim decided not to get too friendly with anyone. There wasn't one person he'd seen that he'd like to invite to his home for dinner or even have a drink with.

Jim didn't see Pat anywhere. He wondered whether Judge Lopez would cancel his hearing if Pat didn't show up. If Pat wasn't around to testify, how could the judge do anything? No complaining witness. Wasn't it like a criminal case? He wasn't sure, but he could always hope.

As the time for the hearings drew near, the bailiff entered the courtroom from the hallway door. The room immediately grew quiet. The bailiff was still the same imposing woman who had been there before. Bitsy Wink. The same person Pat had said was president of the WiNGS group. She looked taller and meaner than ever. Jim didn't know a thing about her. He wondered whether she had ever been married, and if so, to what sort of man. She looked like a ball-breaker if he'd ever seen one.

While he waited for the judge to arrive, Jim reflected on his own situation. He was losing ground on his child support. Over the last thirty days, he'd sold the essay for a nice sum and then just recently, a short story for two-cents a word. Out of that money, he'd given Pat two large portions. He'd still been giving her the twenty-five percent of his unemployment as well. What was he supposed to do, starve?

He supposed he could go before the court and ask for a reduction in child support. After all, it was set pretty high, being based on his salary at the time of the divorce. Still, he couldn't afford to hire a lawyer to file the papers.

He could save up for a lawyer, for he doubted one would take him without the money being paid up front. But while he was saving, his unpaid child support would be mounting up.

Wouldn't it be better to pay what he could, when he could? What was a man to do? It was a Catch-22 situation. Besides, he could just hear the judge saying that if he could afford to hire an attorney, he could afford to pay his child support.

He remembered what he'd heard the judge say the last time he was in court, although she hadn't said it to him. Would his kids be better off if he was dead? He shuddered at the thought. Probably so. If he was dead, Pat would not only get his life insurance for the kids, but Social Security, too. But his kids needed him. And not just for money. Kids needed dads. There was no question about that.

Judge Lopez entered the courtroom, her black suit looking ominous. Jim wondered why she didn't wear a robe. The bailiff hollered out. Everyone stood. Everyone sat. Mrs. Peterson took a chair at a desk next to the judge's bench. She called out a case number and name. She handed the judge a green computer printout. A man and a woman stepped forward.

Jim could show the court that he'd been to the unemployment office on a regular basis. He had a card with dates stamped on it and initials next to the dates. Oh, yes, he'd been a regular customer. He'd stood in the lines until his feet hurt. Sheaves of papers had been shoved in his face. He'd filled them out. Probably more eloquently than most.

At the front of the line, a woman had taken his papers. Jim had thought she was looking down her nose at him. He had caught himself staring at the floor and thought if he ever joked again about the masses, about the great unwashed, he deserved to be horsewhipped. Another woman interviewed him. He was sent away. Nothing for him that day. Or the next. Or the one after that. But still he went back. He had to. It was required. He had to have the unemployment check.

He also checked on the Internet for jobs. They were posted almost daily. He'd gone to job search places online. Nothing for an unemployed reporter.

The word jail brought Jim back to the present. The judge had just threatened the man standing before her with jail. She asked him if he could afford a lawyer. She explained that if she intended to put him in jail for more than six months, she must appoint a lawyer if he appeared to be indigent.

Judge Lopez launched into an explanation that indigent for the purposes of getting a court appointed lawyer was different from indigent for the purposes of incarceration for civil nonsupport which is different from criminal nonsupport. She asked him about his financial status. Did he own a car? What year, make, and model? Is it paid for? Did it run? Did he own any real estate? A home? Acreage? Any cash in his pocket? A checking account? A savings account? Certificates of deposit? Cash values of any life insurance policies? What about boats? Motorcycles? Airplanes? Stocks? Bonds? Federal income tax refunds? Any other expectancies? Had anyone died recently and left him any money? She exhausted any possible income sources.

Jim lapsed into his daydreams again. He felt lucky. He had a job interview coming up. It was a result of his sending out scores of resumes to every newspaper and magazine around. It was finally his turn to have a bit of success. The interview was with a small newspaper in a small town fifty miles away. It wasn't an investigative reporter position. They could not afford an investigative reporter. It wasn't as a columnist, either. They didn't have a regular one of those. But it was a job. And it was with a newspaper. He would be doing a bit of every-thing. Everything but throwing the paper, though he had an inkling that if one of the carriers got sick, he might be doing that as well.

Assistant Editor. The title sounded good. The money was not substantially more than his unemployment, but enough to keep him out of jail. He hoped. Enough to enable him after a while to hire an attorney and go into court for a reduction. A permanent, full-time position. The money would not run out like his unemployment. The President would not have to grant any extensions.

He would still be close enough to visit his children in accor-dance with the possession guidelines the judge had approved in his divorce decree. He would be able to continue seeing them on weeknights as well as weekends. As long as his duties permitted it. Although as assistant editor, he might end up missing his weeknight visits. But he would still have the weekends. Most of the time.

The judge cleared her throat and everyone in the courtroom looked up as if expecting something dramatic. She continued talking to the man in front of her. Explaining the right to a jury trial, the judge sounded bored. She sounded like she was making every effort to cover all bases, to patiently answer all the man's questions, but to make sure he understood the seriousness of his situation.

The woman, the ex-wife, spoke in a whining voice. Cutting her eyes over at the woman, the judge explained that the only remedy she could give the woman for non-support was the jailing of her ex-husband. There was no other form of coercion available to her that was as effective. Jail was the ultimate remedy. If the woman was not willing to let the man go to jail, then the judge would dismiss the woman's Motion to Enforce Child Support by Contempt. What was it going to be?

Jim's mind wandered again. In addition to having proof that he had been a regular at the unemployment office, and that he had a job interview coming up, Jim had made a list of every job that he had applied for on his own. The list included every place that he had sent his resume. Also, every door he had knocked on. Every letter and email he had sent. Every ad that he had replied to. He had also made a list of every publishing house he had sent his novels to and every magazine he had sent his stories to. The judge would have to be impressed. Give him another chance. No court appointed attorney for him.

Jim glanced behind him. He saw Pat. She was on the back row across the aisle. She was writing notes back and forth with another woman. Most of the regulars knew to keep their mouths shut after the judge entered the courtroom. They'd all previously been victims of her or Bitsy Wink's wrath. Pat saw him out of the corner of her eye. She smiled and nodded and shifted her attention back to the woman sitting next to her.

The man that went ahead of Jim last time, Mr. Johnson, was not present. Jim's eyes swept the courtroom. Neither was the former Mrs. Johnson. Where could they be? Had they made an out-of-court agreement? Did the judge allow that? But, Jim recalled, Mr. Johnson owed fifteen thousand dollars. He hadn't looked like he could come up with fifteen dollars. On the previous occasion he had said he was broke.

Jim whispered to the warm body next to him. He hadn't looked earlier, but now it turned out to be the same man he had sat next to the last time he came to court. "Have you seen Mr. Johnson anywhere?" Jim asked. "He'd not here. Didn't the judge tell Mr. Johnson that he had to be back today also?"

"You don't have to come if you pay up," the man whispered. "By the way, I'm Richard Cook." He extended his hand.

Jim remembered his vow not to get too friendly with any of the other men. But what would it really hurt? Besides, maybe he could use him as a source. Jim shook the other man's—Richard Cook's hand. "How long have you been coming here?"

"Over the last ten years? A lot.

"Ten years?" Jim's life passed in front of him. Ten years of sitting in court. Ten years of humiliation. Degradation. Demeaning glances from courthouse people. Lawyers waiting for their cases to be called. And the judge. "How do you stand it?"

"You get used to it," he whispered. "Besides, I haven't been coming every month for ten years. Just occasionally. Depends on my circumstances."

"Circumstances?"

"I work construction. When I get laid off, she files on me.

Makes me come in. Says terrible things. Won't let me see my kids. Lies. The judge chews me out. I keep coming back until I get hired again. I pay up. I don't have to come anymore. Get it?"

Jim nodded, ever the wiser. If only he could pay up so he wouldn't have to come back. "You laid off now?"

Richard smiled. "No. Injury. On the job. I have a suit filed. I assigned the case to her, my ex-wife, but she wants me to come to court anyway. I gave the assignment to her the last time I was here and a copy to the judge for my file. They don't trust me or my lawyer to pay when it comes in."

"It's a lousy system."

Richard shrugged. "What else do I have to do? I can't work."

"You think Mr. Johnson paid up?"

"I don't know."

"How would he? Where would he have gotten the money?"

Richard shrugged again. "Maybe he won the lottery."

Laughing behind his hand, Jim whispered, "I would have read about it in the paper, if I could afford to buy one on a regular basis."

Smiling, Richard asked, "Why are you worried about Mr. Johnson?"

"I don't know." He shook his head. Whispering through his fingers, he said, "It's kind of like when you go to school and the teacher arranges you at desks in her classroom in alphabetical order. You get used to the same kid sitting in front of you every day. When they don't show up, they're sick or something, nothing seems right. There's an emptiness." He paused and looked at Richard. "Besides, if Mr. Johnson isn't here, it means that I have to go in front of the judge earlier. He was in front of me."

"You ever wonder how they decide what order we go in?"

"No. Is there some significance to it?"

"Don't know. Just all the times I been in here, I got to wondering."

"Ms. Johnson isn't here either, so that means she knows Mr. Johnson isn't going to be here."

"You've really got a bug up your—"

"Order." The judge pounded her gavel on the bench. "How am I supposed to conduct court with all this conversation going on? You want to talk to your neighbor, take it outside."

Jim slumped forward, his elbows resting on his thighs, and stared at the floor. He felt like a school kid again. This time like one who has been chastised to wait until recess to visit with his buddy. He absolutely refused to look at the judge. His knee started bobbing. He pushed it down. Didn't want Richard Cook to think he was nervous.

Richard leaned back and crossed his legs. He had a not-a-care-in-the-world attitude. Maybe after ten years, Jim would act and feel like that. He hoped not.

Judge Lopez called the next case. "Johnson versus Johnson." Silence enveloped the courtroom. The atmosphere was still. The air-conditioner stopped blowing the Texas flag. No one coughed or sniffed. The clock didn't tick. There was no movement.

The judge called the case again, louder, "Johnson versus Johnson."

Mrs. Peterson cleared her throat. She handed the file to the judge. Concealing her mouth, Mrs. Peterson said something to the judge. The judge opened the file. She again read the cause number and Mr. and Ms. Johnson's names and the children's names. Then, "Let the record reflect that Mr. Felix Ostermeier, the court appointed attorney for Mr. Johnson, filed a Suggestion of Death in this cause. Attached thereto is a certified copy of the death certificate signed by the county medical examiner.

The Motion for Enforcement by Contempt in this cause is hereby dismissed. Next case."

Jim watched while the judge matter-of-factly closed the file on Mr. Johnson and exchanged it with the clerk for another one. Jim felt dazed. Curious as to Johnson's demise. He felt an elbow in his ribs.

"Am I going to have to baby-sit you every time? The judge's calling your name again, fella." Richard looked like he was enjoying himself. Easy for him, Jim thought. He knew he'd get out of his jam the moment his attorney settled his injury case. Not so easy for some of the rest of them.

Pat tapped him on the shoulder and beckoned at him to follow her.

As he stood before the judge and listened to the litany of his offenses, Jim found that his hands had grown sweaty. He wiped them on the sides of his pants. He held a sheath of papers for the judge, his documentation of his efforts for her to see, to keep, to place in the file if she wanted to. His thoughts went to Mr. Johnson—worth more dead than alive. He wondered what had happened to the man. Heart attack? Stroke? Cancer? AIDS? Or—what? An accident? Something else? Jim's stomach flip-flopped. It was silly. It was stupid. The judge did not kill Mr. Johnson. She had merely suggested that he was worth more to his children dead than alive.

"Yes, ma'am, Your Honor, I brought my papers to show you that I've been looking for a job. May I hand you the unemployment office records?" Jim tried to appear as respectful as possible. He remembered his behavior at the last court hearing. He could cut out his tongue for having said what he did, for giving an impression of an attitude of levity. Now he knew how serious his situation was.

"Yes, Judge, I do have other evidence of my attempts to find a job. In fact, I have a job interview next week." Jim handed the judge the letter in which he was invited to interview at the newspaper. He was surprised to see that his hand shook. He tried to hold it still. The judge smiled as she took the letter from him. He watched her face, trying to gauge her temperament. He wondered if she enjoyed seeing men quiver before her. When her eyes lifted from the paper, he said, "I brought you a list of every place I've sent my books, stories, and essays as well as queries. In fact, if you'll look at my printout, Your Honor, you'll see that I gave Pat—Ms. Reinhart, some extra money. That was from two pieces that I sold."

"That's correct, Your Honor," Pat said. "It would have been easy for Jim—Mr. Dorman, to have hidden that money from me, but instead, he voluntarily gave me part of it."

Studying Pat's face, Jim thought he detected empathy for him. Did she still care? Might he be able to get his foot in the door again?

The judge didn't smile, but her face wrinkled in such a way that Jim thought he had piqued her interest. "Short stories?"

"Yes, ma'am. I'm still hoping to sell my book, but I also write stories. Or did you mean what I sold? One essay. One story."

The judge nodded. "What else do you write?

Shrugging, Jim wondered whether perhaps the judge didn't remember him from the last time. He said, "I've got another book coming along. And a couple I haven't been able to sell."

"Nothing your children could sink their teeth into, I guess." Judge Lopez grinned and leaned back in her chair.

Jim's heart sank as he realized that she'd been toying with him. She had remembered him all along.

Pat said, "He's going to write nonfiction, too, Your Honor. She gave him an impatient look. "Tell her, Jim."

Jim stared at Pat, hoping she'd be able to read his mind. He was trying to send her a message that this wasn't the time or the place.

"Jim, tell her." Pat's eyes bored into his. "I'll tell her, then. He's hoping to write a series of articles on fathers who don't pay child support."

"Do tell." The judge rolled a pen between her fingers.

"Yes, ma'am. He wants to ask you if you'll give him an interview." Pat nodded at him as if to say, "Go on. Ask."

Jim wished he could vaporize and escape through the cracks in the floor. His eyes met the judge's, and he nodded in response to the quizzical expression in hers.

"If that is correct, Mr. Dorman, then I don't mind granting you an interview. It will have to wait until I get through in here, though."

"Yes, ma'am." Jim frowned at Pat.

"All right. Your efforts are duly noted, Mr. Dorman. This cause is reset for one week so we can see the progress you have made. You may wait in my chambers for me if you like. It will be a few minutes before I'm finished with these hearings."

Jim took the paper with the next hearing information form Mrs. Peterson, turned on his heel, and escaped into the hall. On his way out, he couldn't help seeing Richard Cook's grim face. He wondered if every man would be angry with him. He wanted to explain. In fact, he wanted to get permission to tell Richard's side of the story as one of his five—he'd decided to use five families as examples of how situations got to be so bad.

"I thought you'd never ask her, Jim," Pat said. "See, she's really pretty nice."

"If you're not on the wrong side of the bench from her."

"Now don't be shy. Ask her everything you need to know." Pat patted him on the arm. "Everything will be okay."

"And if it's not, I suppose the bailiff will take care of me." He mopped the sweat from his forehead with his sleeve.

"Bitsy?"

"Yes, big Bitsy from inside the courtroom."

"Bitsy Wink. That's her name, remember?" Pat laughed. "She's okay, too, Jim. Stop being paranoid." She squeezed his forearm.

Jim felt her cool touch and wanted it to be more. Did she leave her hand on his arm just a bit too long? Was she hinting to him? Or was she perhaps seeing his article as a family project? After all, it would benefit all of them. He'd accept that as a beginning on the rebuilding of their relationship. "You going to be home later?"

"Sure. Come by and tell me how it went." Pat grinned. "Just remember to be yourself with the judge and don't let her intimidate you just because she could put you in jail. Don't be afraid to get all the information you can out of her."

Jim watched Patty go down the hall toward the bank of elevators. He didn't like this at all. The judge giving him a week. One week? What the hell could he do in a week? He might know about that job in a week, but that would be it. He wouldn't be anywhere with his article. Didn't the judge know how long it took to get stuff published? No, probably not. It would take a miracle to have accomplished anything else in a week.

Heading for the judge's chambers, Jim wondered what kind of reaction he'd get out of Judge Lopez about Mr. Johnson's death. Would she let him look at the file? It seemed weird to him that Mr. Johnson, who had been alive and well thirty days ago, would be dead today. The judge had said that his children would be better off if he was dead and now he was. Jim wondered what Judge Lopez would have to say about that.

CHAPTER
SIX

J im sat in the judge's office as he waited for his interview. He had introduced himself to the secretary and now she had her back to him as she worked at a computer. There were few choices in reading material, Texas Monthly, Ladies Home Journal, or Parent's Magazine. The office was painted mauve and had gray carpet. On the walls hung framed art posters and painted country scenes. The furniture, though, was obviously purchased from the low bidder. It was standard black and chrome metal. Ugly but cheap and practical. An ivy and a philodendron and some photographs humanized the area. A faint aroma of flowers hung in the air. Luckily not that overwhelming smell of roses from big Bitsy.

From where he sat, Jim could see into the judge's chambers. There were bookshelves filled with law books, a sofa, some personal photographs, but that was all he could see from his vantage point. A door from somewhere inside her chambers opened, and the judge called out, "I didn't get to send anyone to jail today, Clarice." Laughter echoed through the office as she walked past the doorway and another door closed. A few minutes later, he heard the door reopen and she emerged from her chambers. Jim could hear the toilet still filling. It was good to know that judges had the same bodily functions as the rest of the world.

Clarice said, "Maybe next week, Judge," and winked at Jim. "There's someone here waiting to see you."

Jim squirmed in his chair and put the magazine down. The judge obviously had seen him sitting there and didn't care. He didn't know whether Clarice knew he was one of the men from the courtroom or not. He hadn't explained. All he'd done was tell her that he was writing an article about fathers who didn't pay child support and that the judge had agreed to give him an interview. Clarice had pointed to a chair, told him he could wait, and that had been the gist of their communication. It had been interesting watching her for the last thirty minutes, but it hadn't gotten him anywhere.

"Come on in, Mr. uh-ah . . . "

Jim smiled when what he wanted was to grimace. "Dorman."

"Dorman."

How could she put people in jail when she couldn't even remember their names? He stepped into her office and waited for her to offer him a chair. She slid onto a sofa and lit a cigarette. "My one bad habit," she said. "But don't tell anybody. This building's supposed to be smoke free." Wrapping her long skirt around her legs, she propped her feet upon a coffee table and held an ashtray in her lap. Her yellow, catlike eyes seemed to laugh at him. He wished he could say that he was glad to see that she enjoyed her work so much.

"Sit down." She waved her hand across the room like the sun rising and setting in one swift motion. She was smaller in person than on the bench. Really quite small.

Jim loomed over her before taking a chair opposite the sofa. He pulled a wire bound pad from his soft briefcase. Placing his briefcase on his lap, he unclipped a pen from his breast pocket and wrote her name at the top of the page.

"Don't have anything to offer you. None of us are coffee lovers." She gestured toward a white box resting on a small table. "The refrigerator is empty. Don't even know why I keep it plugged in."

"That's all right." Jim glanced above her head, rather than stare into her face, and saw an autographed picture of the President of the United States on the wall. Had she chosen her seat intentionally to intimidate him? If so, it had worked. Not that he needed any more intimidation after being in the courtroom.

"So you're going to write an article about fathers who don't take care of their kids." It was a rhetorical question.

Jim nodded and held back a shudder. His hands were sweaty.

"For whom?"

"For whom?"

"Yes, Mr. Dorman. For whom? Who is going to publish it? What's the matter with you? I've never met a reporter who didn't hit the door running, so to speak. Are you normally this quiet or has your personal involvement caused you to be this reticent?" She leaned forward, staring at him as if to get a reading from his face.

"You're very perceptive, Your Honor."

"I should hope so." She dragged off her cigarette and stubbed it out. Getting up, she walked to her bookcase and put the ashtray high up on a shelf. "I'm supposed to have quit."

Jim didn't say anything. He'd never felt so uncomfortable in his life.

Judge Lopez glanced at her watch. "I usually go home at

five." She stood near him, expectantly. She was short. Probably not five feet tall without her shoes.

Jim felt himself begin to relax. The clock above the bookcase said it was nearly five. "I wasn't planning to interview you today," he said. "I was caught off guard when my wife told you about the article."

"Your ex-wife?"

"Yes, ma'am." He shrugged.

"Tell me what your plans are." She sat back down and hiked her feet up under her.

"To write from the man's perspective. I don't think that's been done."

She shook her head. "I haven't seen it, and I've read most articles on the subject."

"And then a series with perhaps the focus on five different families with five different problems."

"Sounds good. Are you experienced enough to carry it off?"

"Yes, ma'am. I used to make my living as an investigative reporter. I'm working on the introductory article now. I've already mailed some query letters with a proposal to several magazines. If they bite, I want to have the first article ready."

"So why do you want to interview a judge?"

"To get a feel for what you think about the whole child support thing."

Shaking her head, the judge said, "It's my job. My feelings don't enter into it."

Jim smiled out of one side of his mouth. "You don't have any personal feelings about non-support?"

"I'm not saying that, Mr. Dorman. But my feelings are my own and I keep them separate and apart from the job. That's not to say I don't get angry if someone is intentionally rude or disrespectful in the courtroom, but that has nothing to do with the law."

"Example."

"Okay. If someone says that I'm unfair, that I didn't give them a fair trial, that I favor the woman—the obligee. Yes, that would make me angry because if you come here often enough, you'll see that it is simply not true."

"I've already seen it."

"I've had to throw out cases where I would have loved to have put the contemnor in jail and have thrown away the key, but there was an error somewhere. Unlike some people, I follow the law."

Jim didn't know to whom she was referring, wasn't sure it was any of his business, and didn't respond to the 'some people' remark. "So you enjoy putting people like me in jail?"

Jim wrote as fast as he could.

"Not people like you, no. I used to feel badly about putting men in jail—when I first got appointed to this position. Now I concentrate on how the children must feel when they don't have enough food on the table or decent shoes or a respectable place to live. I think of those things when I pronounce sentence, and that way I am able to get it out of my mouth."

"I find that very interesting, Judge Lopez. I thought—from my perspective out in the courtroom—that you performed your job with relish."

She waved her hand in the air. "All show. If I act like that, try to intimidate them, don't you think they'll get a job and pay?"

"I know I'm working on it."

"Hah. Hah. Hah." Her laugh was loud and came from the belly. Surprisingly, Jim liked the sound of it.

She wiped her eyes and got herself under control. "Exactly. Don't you see, Mr. Dorman, I don't want you to go to jail? I want you to support your children."

"I'm not sure everyone sees it that way."

The judge smoothed the wrinkles out of her skirt. "Not my fault. Their perceptions are their problem. I don't answer to them. I only have to answer to the administrative judge who appointed me as his associate judge, and I don't worry about anybody else." She glanced at her watch. "So, what else would you like to know?"

"About Mr. Johnson, if it's okay for me to ask."

"Mr. Johnson?" Her face was a blank as a clean blackboard. "Who?"

"The Suggestion of Death you read into the record?"

"Oh. The man who died."

"Yes, ma'am. First of all, why was he allowed to get fifteen-thousand dollars in arrears?"

"As i recall, it mostly happened before I got this job, but I'd surmise that his ex-wife didn't complain until his arrears were almost that high. Dumb broad. If you're thinking I'm a cynic, you're most definitely correct, Mr. Dorman. Now what else? I'd really like to get out of here before the crowd."

"How did he die? Do you know? Was it listed in your file?"

Shaking her head, she said, "It was on the death certificate, I'm sure. The death certificate was attached to the Suggestion of Death. You're welcome to look at it. The file is a matter of public record." She studied his face. "But why do you want to know?"

Jim got up and put the chair back exactly where it had been before he sat in it. "Just curious." He didn't think he could bring himself to remind her of what she had said to Mr. Johnson three months earlier. Not only would it be rude, but she might deny it or get angry, and he didn't want to incur her wrath. "It just seemed weird that he died, that's all."

Judge Lopez shrugged and stood up. "Well, people die all the time around here. Lots of collisions on the highways between small towns. I guess because we get so many of them it doesn't seem odd to me." They shook hands and Judge Lopez walked him to the door. "You feel free to go downstairs and look for that file. Ask Mrs. Peterson. And if you need anything else, you come on back and see me. Next Friday, that is."

Jim thanked her and wandered down the stairs to the clerk's office to see Mrs. Peterson. He hoped the woman would give him the file and let him study it. He'd really wanted to ask Mr. Johnson how a person got fifteen-thousand dollars behind in child support, but now his interest was more than that. Jim had a bad feeling about Mr. Johnson's death. He didn't know why, but thinking about the man raised the hair on his arms.

Jim could see right off that Mrs. Peterson wasn't in. A young lady at the counter was one he recognized from the times she brought papers to the court through that side door to the judge's bench. "May I help you? Dorman, right? You want a copy of your printout?"

"No. I came to see Mrs. Peterson about something else. Is she in?"

"No, sir. She's left already. In fact, we close in one minute. You want to leave her a message? You can give it to me."

"No. I was wondering if—well, about Mr. Johnson."

"Mr. Johnson? Which one, sir?"

"I don't know. The one who died."

A young man sitting at the first desk said, "Albert Johnson, Liz. Remember his lawyer filed a Suggestion of Death?"

"What about him?" She looked at Jim and then back at the clock. Clearly, she wanted to leave.

"Does anyone know how he died?" Jim asked.

"I don't, sir. You'd have to look at the death certificate, and you have to talk to Mrs. Peterson to do that. Or you could call his lawyer. Now if there is nothing else."

"Could I get his ex-wife's address?"

"We're not allowed to give that out, sir."

"I'm writing an article, see, and I wanted to interview her."

"Sure. You could go ask the judge, but I suggest you wait until the next time she's in town. She's probably going home now like everyone else."

Two other women came from the back of the room. It was obvious they were all accustomed to leaving at five. They clutched their purses in their arms. It was useless to argue. He went out the door and ended up on the same elevator with the child support woman who was in a rush. "Ma'am, do you know if he paid any child support before he died?"

She wouldn't meet his eyes, and Jim saw that she began to blush. "I—I couldn't say. You'd have to ask the Attorney General's office." She glanced at some of the other people in the elevator and mouthed, Social Security.

A vague uneasiness rattled in the pit of his stomach. The young woman stared up at the elevator numbers. When the elevator opened, she rushed away.

The sun was still high at five o'clock in the Texas hill country. Still high. Still hot. Jim crossed the street to his car.

"Mr. Dorman—Mr. Dorman. Don't turn around."

The young man from the clerk's office, the one who'd given him Albert Johnson's name, strode past him. He looked about twenty, thin, taller than Jim, and had light brown hair. Could be a college student.

"Keep walking and don't look at me." The young man's long legs made short shrift of the distance between the curb and the other side of the street.

Jim passed his car and continued walking. He sped up so he could keep up with the guy. It was like something out of a movie. He wondered what was going on but decided to play along for a few more minutes.

"Follow me to the alley, go into it. I'll go around the block and meet you at the other end. I've got something for you."

"Look—"

"It's Ms. Johnson's address. You want it, don't you?"

Jim turned his head to glance back over his shoulder.

"Don't look back," the young man muttered. "I don't know what's involved. I think there's something funny going on. I'm going to hand-off the address to you in the alley."

"Fine, son."

"It's not illegal. You could have gotten it from their divorce file. The divorce file is a matter of public record, and the law requires them to file every change of address with the court if there are children involved. So, I'm not breaking any laws. I just thought I'd make it easier for you."

"I appreciate that." Jim had known that; he had just not gotten that far. The alley was only a few feet away and he had so many questions. "Can I call you? What's your name?" Slowing, Jim made the corner of the alley and stopped when he was concealed by a building.

"Wait there. I'll be right in." He continued to the end of the block.

The alley was mostly overgrown with weeds and a few wildflowers. Jim took a few steps toward the other end. Heat radiated off the brick of the two buildings. His watch said ten after five. A few people from the courthouse headed for a parking lot in the other direction. Moments later, the young man jogged into the other end of the alley, out of breath.

"What's going on? What's so mysterious?" Jim asked.

"I'll call you. I've got ready access to your name and phone number. But keep away from me and don't tell anyone about me." He handed a piece of paper to Jim and walked on.

Jim wiped his sweating forehead on his sleeve as he stood just inside the alley and watched the young man reach the other end and disappear around the corner. He looked at the piece of paper. It not only had the former Mrs. Albert Johnson's name, address, and phone number on it, it had four others. He stuffed it into his pocket, took a couple of steps back out onto the sidewalk, and dropped down to tie his shoe. As he glanced around, Jim didn't see anyone watching. He got up and strolled the next half block to his car, feeling like an idiot for acting like a participant in a spy movie.

THE JOB INTERVIEW on Friday at The Daily Sun went well. Jim thought that he would probably be offered the job. Mr. Carpenter, the editor and publisher, seemed a nice fellow, not too strait-laced, not too liberal. He had shown Jim around the paper and then taken him to lunch at what was apparently a hangout for local newspaper and local radio people. Jim had gotten along famously not only with Carpenter, but the other folks. He seemed to fit right in. The trouble was, the job was just not Jim's idea of the way to spend the rest of his life.

First of all, he would have to work odd hours. There was no guarantee that on any given Wednesday he would be able to get off to visit with his kids, much less on the weekends. As assistant editor, he would have to be like a jack-of-all-trades. He would have to be the proof department. If someone from layout called in sick, Jim would have to cover for them. If the manager from circulation was on vacation, Jim would be rotated through and have to do his time as circulation manager. On a small paper, that meant being up in the middle of the night getting the paper out onto the streets. Then there was the advertising department. Jim would be expected to sell some ads each month. Sell ads? That was one thing he'd never done in his entire life.

Worst of all, Jim would have to help cover the sports section. While that hadn't sounded so bad at first, when Mr. Carpenter had explained that it would entail covering innumerable children's sports, Jim thought he would feel betrayal. How would he explain to his son that he couldn't come to his soccer games because he had to cover another child's?

Jim went away wondering if he shouldn't wait and see if something else opened up. Maybe another job would come through. Maybe one of his novels would sell. Maybe a solid gold bar would fall out of the sky and knock some sense into him. He ought to talk it over with Patty. The money was not that good. It was about halfway between what he was getting in unemployment and what he used to make as an investigative reporter.

During the fifty-mile drive back to his house, Jim pulled the piece of paper with the names on it from his pocket. He had studied it the previous evening, wondering what it meant, verifying some of the addresses in the telephone book. The list was the complete name and address of five women. Under each was written a man's name.

Albert Johnson's was the fifth name. What did that mean? Who were the other men? Why were their names on the list? Were the women their ex-wives?

How long had the young man worked for the clerk's office? It was obviously long enough to make him curious—suspicious—of something. But what? What was he trying to tell Jim and why was he being so mysterious about it? Maybe Jim ought to wait until Monday and just go up to the courthouse and ask. Maybe he could catch him out in the hall or in the stairwell since the guy was so paranoid.

The incident had seriously piqued Jim's curiosity. As he hit town, he decided that as soon as he checked his messages, he would run to the library and do a little research on Albert Johnson. Maybe he would be able to find out something that would help him come up with a solution to whatever was going on. It was like putting together the pieces of a puzzle except that Jim neither had all the pieces nor did he know what the puzzle was supposed to look like.

CHAPTER

SEVEN

J im's answering machine blinked rapidly like a morse code message. It had been a number of days since he'd had any messages, and he was curious to find out who the people were who had phoned him. Two calls in one day were a record for him lately. Pressing the play button, Jim sat next to the machine while he listened.

"Jim Dorman, this is Edgar Buck, Editor with Dallas Downtown Magazine. We've narrowed the list to three names and yours is one of them. If you're still interested in a job with us, your interview will be on Monday at 10:30 a.m. Call me back and confirm please."

If Jim had been a little girl, he would have giggled with pleasure. The Dallas Downtown Magazine job sounded much more like what Jim wanted to do with the rest of his life. He pressed the stop button and searched for something on which to write the number. His hand shook as he scribbled the information on the back of a paper bag. A job with Dallas Downtown Magazine would be worth moving away for. The money would be right. The work would be in his field. The kids would only be a forty-five minute airplane ride away from him. He wouldn't be able to see them on weeknights, but on most weekends, he would be able to make it.

Writing down the information, Jim reached for the phone to return Buck's call. This was one interview he couldn't miss. A few minutes later, the interview confirmed, the thought occurred to Jim that he was so busted that he would have to borrow some bucks to get to Dallas. He had planned to discuss the job with Patty, but he felt as if asking her to finance his trip would be sinking to a new low. He didn't doubt that she would loan it to him if it meant that she'd be getting a big return on her money, but could her opinion of him get any worse?

Hitting play again, Jim heard, "This is Mrs. Ethel Peterson of the district clerk's office. I understand you're writing a book and would like to interview me. If you can come in next Tuesday, I can see you then. Please call and let me know."

Jim called the clerk's office to confirm. After leaving a message for Mrs. Peterson, he asked to speak to the young man whose name he didn't know but was told he wasn't in. After he hung up, he realized if the guy knew he'd called he'd probably be pissed.

Things were finally trending his way. Popping the top on a beer, Jim guzzled it like a man who had just crossed the desert on foot. It was a generic brand, the cheapest the grocery store carried, but to Jim it tasted like the finest import. After the first long swallow, he savored the remainder. He'd bought a six pack the last time he'd sold a story and saved them, meting them out to himself as rewards for each minor achievement: a story completed, a rewrite accomplished, a painful job interview for a position he knew he would not get because he was overqualified.

But today was different. He was celebrating. Not only had he successfully sailed through the interview with The Daily

Sun, but he had another—better—position possibly opening up. And he'd begun gathering information for his Deadbeat Dad piece. Plus, he was intrigued with the Johnson thing. Figuring out what happened to Mr. Johnson was enough to get his mind off a lot of other things.

All Jim needed now was to sell a novel. What if he could get a big contract? And national recognition? Fame and fortune would be at his feet. He might even get a Pulitzer. Pat would really have to take him back then. He laughed at himself. It was about as likely to happen as getting hit with that gold brick, but he enjoyed fantasizing.

Kicking off his shoes, Jim reached for the phone again and dialed Pat's number.

"Hi, Beautiful," he said when she answered.

"Who is this?"

"Very funny. I was wondering if I could come over. I have something important to discuss with you and I'd rather not do it over the phone."

"Jim, it's Friday night."

"I know."

"It's Friday."

"Yeah? So, what's that got to do with anything?"

"Some people go out on Friday nights."

Jim felt like he'd been flattened by an eighteen-wheeler. "You have a date?"

"Is that so impossible for you to believe?"

"No. I apologize. I didn't mean anything. I just—well, there's something important I need to discuss with you."

"So, you said."

"I wanted to do it in person."

There was a long silence. "I'm only going out to dinner. You want to come at nine-thirty?"

"Thanks." Jim breathed a sigh of relief. He wasn't sure he

could handle the thought of her sleeping with someone else. "By the way, where are the kids?"

"Spending the night with friends. I've been doing battle with them for weeks over it. But that's another story. I finally gave in. I know I have to trust other kids' parents, but it isn't easy, especially when Jeanette's friendship with her little girl-friend is so new."

"It's tough with everything that goes on." They'd had that discussion many times. Jim had always thought Pat was para-noid until one day Patrick came home talking about some awful battering that had gone on while he was at his friend's house. Later, Patrick's friend's mother had asked Patrick to be a witness for her in court, but had ended up reconciling with her husband, much to Pat's disgust.

"Well, we can talk later," Pat said. "'Bye."

The phone clicked in Jim's ear as he muttered, "Goodbye." His wife had a date with another man. It was hard to believe she'd do that to him, after all they'd been to each other, and all they'd be to each other again. He felt betrayed. He knew they were going to reconcile. It was just a matter of time.

Pat had to do two things. One, forgive herself for what she'd done. Two, forgive him for whatever she thought he'd done. Their reconciliation wouldn't happen until she worked through both those things. But it was going to happen. Perhaps the date was part of the punishment for what she thought she'd done. Or she was still making up her mind about them. Whatever, he only hoped she wouldn't have sex with another man. Her boyfriend—ex-boyfriend—had been bad enough. But that was history. Jim shuddered at the thought of another man putting his hands on Pat. It made him feel more than vaguely sick to his stomach.

Going upstairs, Jim drank the rest of his beer and tossed the can in the trash. He pulled off his shirt and threw it into a corner before digging through his closet for a fresh one. Better yet, he'd take a quick shower. Half a day of driving in his car with its half-assed air-conditioning system would make him smell offensive to the other people in the library. At least, if his memory served, that's the way Patty would have phrased it. He'd better hurry if he wanted to get there in time to do anything significant before closing.

Jim soaped up and rinsed quickly. The best shirt he could find had only a few wrinkles. He couldn't wait for the day when he could afford to pay to have his clothes pressed again. He pulled on a pair of jeans and fresh socks and his running shoes and tucked a pair of shorts into a bag. If it was still light later, after the library closed, he might run a couple of miles.

As he headed for the library, Jim thought about the best way to organize his research. The first thing he'd do would be a little background. All the way to the job interview and back, he had scrutinized the list of names and wondered about their significance. They could mean anything, and Jim didn't want to let his imagination run away with him. Maybe he'd find something in Mr. Johnson's obituary that would give him a clue.

Jim parked the car and hurried inside, blowing by Frieda with a wave of his hand. He had about an hour left before clos-ing. On Friday nights, Frieda didn't hold the door for anyone. She was exhausted by the end of the week.

Finding the microfilm for the Chronicle, Jim selected dates that included his first court hearing and inserted the reel. He searched the obituaries for each day, looking for Albert John-son's name. The machines were old and outdated. The print was blurry. After the first few pages, Jim's eyes felt cloudy and burned. He knew it was just fatigue at the end of a long day, coupled with the bad conditions. Next time, if there ever was a next time, he would come in the morning when he hadn't already spent the day reading.

The obituary was not long. Mr. Johnson was apparently not from a large family. The survivors were his four children and his mother. It came as no surprise that no cause of death had been written up. Jim turned back to the issue of the newspaper that preceded the one with the obituary. There it was, a small, but succinct, article.

Car Flips Off Hill

One man died in a single car accident Monday night off Highway 80, police said. Albert Johnson, 35, lost control of his vehicle at the top of a hill five miles north of town. The car went through the guard rail, flipped over several times, rolled down the hill, and burst into flames. There were no witnesses. An autopsy will be performed, but it appears the cause of death was from the fire. Police are speculating on whether Johnson suffered heart failure at the wheel. Johnson is survived by his mother and four minor children.

Jim stared at the blurry article. So, Albert Johnson had a traffic accident and died. So what? What did it all mean? Anything? And why was that kid from the courthouse so secretive? If he could find a way of broaching it, Jim had every intention of asking Patty if she knew Mrs. Johnson. Maybe she knew more than she was letting on. He made photocopies of the relevant articles and left the library, briefly waving at Frieda again on his way out.

There were a lot of small parks in Angeles, surrounded by hills, trees, and picnic benches, but only one large enough for joggers. Jim drove over to Dunlap Park and ran several miles. It had gone from ninety-five-degree heat at midday to eighty, a more bearable temperature. The run made him feel better. The fresh air filled his lungs. He enjoyed looking up at the clear, blue sky, not a rain cloud in sight, which wasn't particularly a good thing up in the hills which had long been suffering from a drought.

There were a number of runners, but not nearly as many as the fall or spring brought out. He only recognized a couple of them and nodded as he ran. Afterwards, Jim stopped at a deli and ate the spud and sandwich special and felt guilty about spending four ninety-five. Finally, he headed for Pat's house. It wasn't close to nine-thirty, but . . .

Jim parked his Mustang on the dark corner near the house and ducked down in the seat on the passenger side so he could get a clear view of the front door. He didn't want Pat to see him when she came home, but he just had to see her. Not so much her, but he had to see who she was with. Visions of oiled biceps danced in his head. And a scalp full of hair, no receding hairline. And money. The guy had to have money, otherwise why would Pat waste her time on him? One bum in her life was enough. Maybe she truly deserved better than him.

Pushing that thought aside, Jim tried to be patient as he stared out the window. Had they gone for seafood? Pat loved grilled shrimp. The best way to get in her pants was to take her to dinner and buy her a couple of glasses of blush wine, grilled shrimp, and she was a goner. He wondered if the guy knew that. He wondered if the guy knew that she was divorced a year and hadn't had a man in all that time. Would he think she was easy because she was a divorcee? Did guys still think like that? There were so many people divorced lately. He'd seen some statistics recently that said fifty percent of all marriages break up. Everyone was either from a dysfunctional family or a broken home. Kids never had a chance.

After a while, Jim glanced at his watch and saw that it was past nine-thirty. Jealousy reared its ego-wrecking head. Jim felt weak from his toenails to his gums. Was she in that guy's arms right now? Had she forgotten she was supposed to be home to meet him, Jim, her husband?

A soft rapping drew Jim's attention to the driver's side of the car. Startled, Jim shifted across the seat and rolled the window down.

Pat said, "Aren't you coming in?" She had on two of those undershirt things she wore around the house, layered, as if two of them hid any more breast than one.

Jim nodded and muttered, "Just getting my thoughts together," and rolled up the window.

She stepped away so he could open the door. He could see that she wore those cut off jeans that were slit up the thigh to her hip on one side. He could see the elastic of her panties. Why was she doing this to him?

It was a still evening, no wind and the temperature felt like it was still in the eighties. Perspiration glistened on Pat's cheeks. Her eyes seemed to hold a question. Jim was searching his brain for some explanation for his situation.

They walked together back to the house. Jim waited for her to blast him, to accuse him of spying on her, to scream bloody-murder and make him feel like an insect so low on the chain that he wasn't even worth stepping on, but she didn't say anything. He thought he detected a quirky smile skirting the corners of her mouth. No way was he going to mention how totally asinine he was being if she wasn't.

"So how was dinner?" he asked as he followed her into the house.

The house was like an inferno. No wonder perspiration shined on her face and body. No wonder tendrils of her hair stuck together like an artist's damp brush.

"Fine." She sat at the kitchen table where there were pencil and paper and a glass of iced tea. Crossing her legs, Pat turned in the chair and leaned against the wall. "What's the matter with you, Jim? Sit down."

Sliding into a chair, Jim felt as guilty as a Jewish daughter. He was going to ask for carfare to Dallas when it was apparent she couldn't pay the summer electric bill? Finding it difficult to meet her eyes, Jim stared at the paper that was laid out on the table without really reading it. He could see that it was letterhead. WiNGS letterhead. He averted his eyes when what he wanted to do was grab it and stick it in his pocket to peruse later. His attention needed to be focused on her now. That was part of the problem. He was incredibly turned on by her scantily clad, sweating body.

She was smiling and nodding. He knew she knew she was turning him on, but she'd never admit it. Waiting for him to make a move? He knew her. He knew she wanted him too, but she was too proud to forgive either of them just yet.

"Want some iced tea?"

Jim nodded and watched while she filled a tall, blue glass with ice cubes, tea, and then bent over the produce drawer in the refrigerator ostensibly to fetch a lemon. He had a clear view of her upper thighs and the bottom of her buttocks. Dammit, why did she feel it necessary to torture him? Feeling himself growing hard, he untucked his shirt and fanned his face with his hand. "Air conditioning broken?"

"Nuh-uh," she said placing the glass on the flowered placemat in front of him, together with a slice of lemon and an iced teaspoon. "Trying to save money when the kids aren't here. It's not so bad, is it?"

The scent of her perfume clung to her skin. Flowers. A summer day. Making out in a patch of clover. "Is money really that tight?" Jim kept his eyes glued to her face to get his mind off the other parts of her anatomy. They were within a few feet of each other. It would be so easy to reach out for her, to her. And get slapped down.

"I was hoping to stay home with the kids the second half of this summer. To spend some time with them. Maybe take a little trip. They're growing up so quickly."

"So, you're not teaching summer school again?" Jim scraped some sugar from the sugar bowl into his tea glass, squeezed the lemon, and stirred while he listened for the hostility in her voice. It didn't seem to be there—or at least not like it used to be. Could it be that they could hold a conversation like two normal, rational, thinking adults?

Shaking her head, she said, "Not planning on it if we can get by. Though it's not too late to get a position. Why? What did you want to talk to me about? Is your unemployment running out?"

"What would you think if I left town? Would you miss me?"

"Why are you talking like that? Are you going to take that little job with The Daily Sun?"

That little job. "You don't think I should?"

"You can do better."

"I'd be close by." He sipped his tea and stared over the rim of the glass at her. Having a conversation with her was not what was on his mind, but he was trying to concentrate so she didn't see him as the fool he knew he'd been all evening.

"You'd be miserable, and you know it. Did the interview turn out to be any better than the job sounded over the phone?"

"No. I'd have a drab little office at a drab little newspaper. But it's a job."

"I don't think that's what brought you over here."

"It's a little difficult to ask you for money as we sit here sweating to death."

"What do you need money for?"

He thought that sounded rather offensive, but he wasn't going to argue with her. He wanted her to be as enthusiastic about his interview as he was. He wanted to take her in his arms and kiss her and fondle her and tell her that he wanted to take this job in Dallas and get married again and move the family to North Texas and forget all the bad blood that was between them. But, instead, he said, "What would you think if I got offered a job as an investigative reporter for a big city rag?"

She sat up. "How big city?"

"Dallas. Good money. Job of my dreams."

"But . . .

"Pat, I can't even fill up my gas tank until next Wednesday's check."

"And the interview is—"

"Monday."

"You've got it."

"What?"

"Honey—I mean, Jimmy, if a few dollars is all that stands between you and a job in Dallas, Texas, you came to the right place." She reached under her chair for her purse.

Jim felt that when he'd passed through the entrance of the house, he had entered a world fraught with ambiguities. This highly sexual creature who he knew would rebuff any attempt on his part to engage in play was now offering to give him money so that he could go away to find a job. While she was speaking, she slipped and called him by a term of endearment. He didn't know which of them was more confused. Did she want him? Or want to get rid of him?

"Will a hundred dollars be enough?" Pat held her pen poised over her checkbook.

"That's more than generous of you, Patty." Jim couldn't

help wondering what she was thinking of him now. Did she despise him for being unable to provide for her and his children? Could she perhaps admire him the teeniest bit for being willing to take a position over two hundred miles away, where he'd be separated from her and his children, in order to be able to meet their financial needs? Was it possible that she still felt something for him in a romantic or even a sexual way? Watching her write out the check, Jim hoped against hope that any of the latter thoughts were true, that she did still have some feelings for him.

When she finished, she pushed the check at him in a very business-like way. It lay between them like a bridge as she recorded it in the register. She tucked the checkbook and pen back into her purse and glanced at Jim's face after she noticed the check still lying on the table. "What's the matter? Take it." She held it out to him by one long end.

Jim reached for the other end and saw the whole transaction in his writer's eye as something symbolizing a change, a metamorphosis in their relationship. Was she reaching out to him? Was this a peace offering? He took the check, folded it, and slipped it into his breast pocket. "Will you miss me if I have to move to Dallas?"

"They haven't offered you the job yet."

"I'd hate leaving you and the kids."

"You mean the kids."

"No. I mean you. The kids come second."

"Don't talk like that, Jimmy. It's not right. We're not married anymore." She wouldn't meet his eyes.

"You'll always be my wife as far as I'm concerned."

She had her arms crossed over her chest, and he reached out and took hold of her left wrist, pulling her to him. "Honey, you know I still love you." She came around the corner of the table and sat on his lap. Jim knew she'd be able to feel his hardness against the back of her thigh, but he didn't care. Suddenly he found himself gulping air as he covered her face with his mouth, kiss after kiss, not being able to get enough of her.

Pat had hold of the hair on the back of his head in one hand and the skin on his back through his shirt with the other. Jim knew she wanted him as much as he wanted her. He rose up out of his chair and pinned her against the kitchen table, pressing his hips against hers so hard he thought he would come out of his pants. Suddenly she pulled away from him. "No. No." She pushed him away and distanced herself across the kitchen. "We're divorced, and we're going to stay that way."

"But honey, I love you." Jim was pleading with all he had. "I want you and the kids to come to Dallas with me."

"No. I'm not going through all that again." She crossed her arms over her breasts. "Take the money and get out."

"But, Patty, please—"

"Get out, Jim. Go on before I say some things you don't want to hear."

Straightening up his shirt, Jim started to stay and argue, but the expression on her face reminded him of the one the day of their divorce: murderous. Instead, he brushed at his hair, checked himself in the hall mirror as she followed him to the front door, and let himself out. "Thanks for the money though, Pat. I'll let you know how it comes out." Jim was going to go home, take a long cold shower, and see if sexual frustration would make a better writer out of him.

EIGHT

Betty Lou Johnson startled Jim when she answered her door on Saturday morning. There was no question but that he had stereotyped her. He had expected some trashed-out, substandard, government-assisted housing complex. Instead, the apartment complex stood in an apparently middle-class neighborhood and was well taken care of. The thick, green grass had been edged, the shrubs manicured, the pool cleaned, and no trash littered the grounds or the area around the dumpster.

Betty Lou appeared to be a changed woman. Jim's recollection of her from the courtroom was not a pleasant one—a shrieking, complaining, shrew of a woman. Describing her as unkempt would have been a compliment.

The creature who answered the ring of the doorbell that Saturday morning barely resembled the other woman, causing Jim to wonder whether he had the right address. Giving her the once-over, he decided that she could have passed for a younger sister. Betty Lou was a small, round woman, no more than five feet two, with black, shoulder length hair, round, brown eyes, and an artfully made-up face. She wore a short-sleeved painted blouse and a long, flowered skirt, and toes, with nails long and painted a bright red, wiggled in sandals.

"Betty Lou Johnson?" Jim asked when she appeared behind the screen door.

"Yes." Jim could see several children lying on the carpet behind her. They were watching cartoons on a large console TV, rather dated, but still giving good color and clear audio.

"Jim Dorman. I'm a writer. I'm doing an article on dead-beat dads and wondered if I could interview you."

"How'd you get my name?"

"At the courthouse, ma'am." He wasn't about to tell her of the young man in the district clerk's office. "All divorce files are a matter of public record. I was able to find several that would fill the bill."

"What bill? I've paid up all my bills. Just a minute." Over her shoulder, she yelled, "Y'all turn that TV down like I told you or it's going off."

The children groaned and grumbled, then lowered the volume. Betty Lou shook her head and stared at him, waiting for an answer.

"Not really a bill. That's just an—I meant that I found several cases that I thought would be interesting to write about and yours was one of them. I'm writing a series of articles, like I said. I'd like to interview you."

"Uh-huh." Her eyes wandered over his face.

"If I could come in, I could explain it to you. I'm not going to hurt you or anything. I can show you my driver's license or maybe you could come out?"

"You know, I feel like I know you from somewheres."

"Yes, ma'am, the courthouse." Like a spotlight, the sun beamed right where he stood. Sweat sprouted under neck hair that needed a trim. "I sure would like to speak to you in the air-conditioning, ma'am."

"I seen you there? At the courthouse?"

"Yes, ma'am. On child support Wednesdays or Fridays. I was there several months ago when you were there."

"Ah-hah, so you picked me out of all them ladies?"

"Picked out five ladies all with different circumstances, to do a story on."

"What are them circumstances?"

"Ms. Johnson, your electric bill is going to be mighty big next month if you continue to hold that door open while we have this conversation. Now, why don't you let me come inside where I can interview you properly?"

Betty Lou looked over her shoulder as if seeing her children could help her decide whether or not Jim was a serial killer.

Jim held his hands up in a gesture of helplessness. "I'm not a mad rapist. I promise. I can give you my ex-wife's telephone number if you like and you can phone her."

She smiled, showing rows of overcrowded teeth. "You can't be too careful these days. Can I see that drivers license?"

Jim pulled out his wallet and flipped it open. Holding it up so she could peer at it through the cellophane, he said, "You want me to take it out and let you hold it 'till we get through?"

"Naw. That's okay." She beckoned to him. "Come in."

Jim stepped through the opening and banged the door closed behind him. "A woman living alone with children especially needs to be careful."

"Come on in here." She walked past four children, the oldest of whom appeared to be preteen. The smallest three kids barely gave Jim a glance, enthralled as they were with their cartoon show. The oldest, feet hiked up in a wooden rocker, had a telephone pressed up against one ear while she picked at her toenails and watched TV over the heads of the others. Her eyes flickered to him a moment, sizing him up, before shifting back to the television. As typical an American family as one would find on a Saturday morning. The only thing missing was the father.

"Sit yourself down there at the kitchen table, and I'll get you a glass of tea," Betty Lou said, wrapping an over-sized dish towel around her middle. "Loosen up that tie before you die. How you can go about with that thing up to your throat in this summer heat is beyond me."

Betty Lou appeared as harmless as they come, though he'd seen her when she was angry and remembered what that was like. He pulled on the knot at his neck and sat back in a kitchen chair. Although there was no microwave or dishwasher, which Jim thought was a dead giveaway that the apartments were public housing, the kitchen had Formica counters over faux wood cabinets. The stove and woodwork shined as did the floor. Fresh paint covered the walls. Clean dishes sat in a rack on a drainboard on the left side of the double sink. It might be barely large enough to turn around it, but the kitchen was well done.

"That's mighty nice of you, Ms. Johnson. I could wet my whistle about now."

"So, tell me, what exactly are you writing about?" She poured tea over some cracked ice in a tall glass and set it before Jim. Ambling back to the refrigerator as if she hadn't a care in the world, Betty Lou pulled out some lemons, sliced them into a milk-glass bowl and set it together with a sugar bowl, in front of Jim, too.

"Well, ma'am, I'm a writer by trade but to be perfectly honest with you, I'm also one of the men who can't pay his child support."

"Ah hah." She picked up her glass and came over to the

table, sitting down opposite Jim. "I'm willing to hear more, go on."

What that ah-hah meant, he didn't know. He talked as fast as he could since he detected a hint of impatience now that he'd made his confession. "I got this idea that most of the newspaper and magazine articles, and even the shows on TV like 60 Minutes and 48 Hours, always show the woman's view of the child support situation." He squeezed lemon into his tea instead of meeting her eyes.

"Let me get you a spoon" She eased up from the table and opened a drawer and handed him a white plastic iced-tea spoon.

"I thought I might be able to make a sale if I showed the man's viewpoint. He stirred and prayed that she heard the word 'sale' in his explanation. "Sell an article."

"Ah-hah," she said again and sat silent until he looked up. "And what is the man's view, Mr. Dorman?"

"I just meant how each man got in that situation. This tea's good, by the way."

"Now don't you go trying to butter me up. You know, I don't think you're going to be able to sell a story that is full of a man's excuses why he can't make sure his kids have food on the table."

She was beginning to sound like the woman he'd seen in court. Now he knew he had the right Ms. Johnson. "Ma'am, I didn't mean to upset you or make you angry. I'm just trying to make a living so I can pay child support." He grinned what he thought of as his most disarming grin.

She let loose with a loud sigh and leaned back in her chair. "Didn't mean to get so worked up. My husband just gave me such a hard time all them years. It was hard to raise children that-a-way."

"Looks like you're doing okay now, though. All those kids in the living room yours?"

She nodded. "We're doing fine now. He died, you know."

He maintained eye contact and a poker face. "Yes, ma'am, I do know. What happened to him, if you don't mind my asking?" Jim took a long swallow of his tea and studied her face at the same time.

"Accident. I had to go down to that morgue and identify the body 'cause his mama wouldn't go. She's old and half blind. Poor thing. Can't really blame her. But he was a mess, I tell you. Roasted like a side of beef on a spit. I wouldn't have wanted the kids to see him like that even if I did hate his guts."

Jim was glad it was mid-morning, and he wasn't about to eat. "How did you identify him then?"

"His ring. His wedding ring. Can't believe he hadn't hocked it but it was right there on his overcooked finger."

Jim flinched. "Had he been drinking?" Her description was a vision he hoped he'd soon forget.

"I think so, yeah. That was always his favorite pastime. He was a beeraholic. That's like a alcoholic except with beer. I tell you, he couldn't live without his beer, but when we was married if I so much as mentioned that he was a drunk or a alcoholic, he'd slap me upside my head." She sighed. "He was a mean man, Mr. Dorman. I can't say I'm sorry he's gone."

Nodding, Jim asked, "Mind if I take some notes?"

"No, you go ahead. Let me freshen up your tea." She got up from the table and kept silent while refilling his glass.

Jim kept his head down and wrote on his pad. When she sat back down, he made it a point to assume his reporter's persona, nonjudgmental. He asked her some questions about how they had met, when they had gotten married, and what each of them had done for a living back then. In a few minutes, he had enough background to discuss what happened after the divorce.

"At the time you divorced him, Ms. Johnson, what was your husband doing for a living?"

"Carpenter. It had fallen off a little. I wasn't sure whether if it was because he drank so much or 'cause everything was going bust, but he was working eighty percent of the time." She doodled a finger in sugar that had spilled on the table.

"How much child support did the judge order?"

"Well, my lawyer and his lawyer agreed on twenty-five dollars a week for each child. Today that wouldn't even feed a kid. Didn't do that much more then. Tommy was a baby not even out of diapers." Her face screwed up. "Hell, diapers 'bout cost that much."

"But you couldn't stay married to Tommy's father?"

"I tried. He wouldn't go to no counseling." Shrugging, she pulled on the corner of the dishtowel still tied around her, loosening some threads. "Said I was the one with the problem. Yeah, big problem, him hitting me was my problem. I got sick of it. So, I left and took my kids. He made better money than me by a long shot, but I couldn't risk him ever beating up on the kids."

"He didn't fight you for them?"

Shaking her head, she said, "He said some awful, threatening things, but he didn't really mean them. He couldn't raise them kids, he just wanted to scare the daylights out of me. But you know what?"

"What?"

"If he'd of tried to really take the kids away, I'd of killed him."

Jim felt like he'd just caught a hard thrown football with his stomach. "Really?"

"Really. Once I got myself together, I knew I was strong enough to take care of all of us. You gitting all this?"

Jim licked his lips as he wrote. She seemed to be the mother-animal-protects-her-cub type. He liked her, thought she probably was typical of the middle-class American mother, making out the best she could.

"So, you want to know when he first missed a child support payment?"

"Sure." Jim hoped everyone he wanted to interview would volunteer information so readily. It would make his job a lot easier. He suspected the women would, since women liked to tell people their problems. The men were going to be the problem. That was why he wanted to interview the women first. That way he could get the men's reactions to what the women said, like, you know your ex-wife said . . . what do you have to say to that? He flipped over a page in his notepad and waited.

Betty Lou snorted. "That son-of-a-bitch. When we was separated and he was supposed to pay temporary child support. He missed the very first payment. And the second. And the third. And the fourth. Until my lawyer had to take him to court even before the divorce and ask the judge to put him in jail."

Jim nodded. Thankfully not all men were like that. He was not like that. "So, what happened?"

"He got put in jail and then his lawyer asked the judge could he get out if he paid up and the judge said yes so he got out. But I had to pay my lawyer for that and filing fees, so he won anyway if his aim was to make me and the kids suffer."

Jim saw why the woman was so bitter in court. "And did he pay for a while after that?"

She pursed her lips. "For a while. And then he got to where he would always pay up on the day we went to court. That way

I was still out the cost of taking him back to court, but nothing happened to him."

Old Johnson was a son-of-a-bitch. But did he deserve to die? "Do you think it was because he was angry over you leaving him?"

"He could of stopped me. All he had to do was agree to go to marriage counseling and learn how to quit hitting me. He wouldn't do it." She shook her head. "I went by myself and found out he was what they call a first stage alcoholic. I got to believe lately that he was in the early third stage."

"How long ago was this divorce?" The chair was beginning to feel hard. He shifted to another position.

"Eight years ago. Tommy is nine now. They're all a year apart."

"Stairsteps."

"Yes, sir." She preened like a proud mama duck.

"So it took eight years to get fifteen thousand dollars behind?"

She showed him her crooked teeth again. "You remember that, do you?"

"Yes, ma'am. It made quite an impression."

"You know, Mr. Dorman, the last few years since I went up to court, I heard of men that owed more than that—some of them twenty-five, thirty-five thousand dollars. Now how could a man not never pay child support?"

"That's one of the reasons I'm doing this article. I hope to get to the bottom of it. What are they thinking? What are they feeling? Do they care about their children, or do they hate their ex-wives so much that they'd do anything to make them miserable—even let their children starve?" He hoped for a favorable response to his words.

Her head bobbled on her shoulders. "They know the children won't really starve," she said. "They know the mamas wouldn't let them kids starve."

"Actually, some do."

"No." She slapped the table. "I never knew that. How could their mamas let that happen. I'd do anything . . . "

"Some of them can't help it. They get welfare, but it's not enough."

"I know all about that. I was on welfare before."

"Before what?" Jim asked.

"Before he died. Now I'm in the community college learning to be a nurses' assistant. Things are a lot better now."

"How's that?"

"Mr. Dorman, I get Social Security for each child. That adds up to more than that bum ever thought of paying. My kids might even get to go to college. Can you figure that?" She reared back in her chair and chortled like she'd heard the best joke ever.

A shiver danced across Jim's back as he waited for her to quit laughing.

Her pupils pointed at him like arrows. "If it took him croaking to make it possible for any one of my kids to be the first in my family to get to go to college, it was worth it. They're better off with him dead than alive."

The hair on the nape of Jim's neck stood up. He shivered. That's what the judge had told Mr. Johnson a little over three months ago. Funny Betty Lou should use that phrase.

She smiled now as she spoke, her face lit up, happy he was dead.

Uneasiness, like teetering on the edge of a deep hole, made Jim feel out of balance. "How are your kids taking his death? Do they miss him?"

"Nah. He never come to see them anyhow."

"In court he said you never let him see them."

"He was lying. He was just trying to get Judge Lopez to feel sorry for him. If that bum called them on Christmas Day, they was lucky."

"I guess there's two sides to every story."

"Three," she said. "That's what the judge always says. Her side. His side. And the truth falls somewhere down the middle." She shrugged.

"Are you a member of that women's support group?"

"WiNGS?"

"Yes, ma'am."

"Sure. But only the last month or so. They've been a big help."

"Really?"

She nodded. "They have volunteer lawyers. There was one told me about the Social Security benefits for the kids. Plus, they buried him."

"WiNGS?"

"No, Social Security. Or maybe it was the veterans? I don't remember, one of them agencies. I didn't really have to do that, his mama did."

"What else did they tell you?"

"To go to the union and see if there was any benefits left to the kids."

"He was union?"

"Years ago, when it was active around here."

"You do that?"

"Uh-huh. There was a small policy. It helped."

"How many meetings have you been to?"

"Me? Six, I think. Next one's pretty soon, but I don't know if I'll go back except for maybe I could help some other lady who's got problems. At least listen to her story. They offer baby-sitting, you know. The ladies baby-sit for each other."

"No, I didn't. You ever seen Judge Lopez at any of those meetings?"

She shook her head. "The bailiff though. She's one of the officers. President? I'm not sure."

"So, the whole thing seems on the up and up?" Even if it was, it made him feel uneasy, like a fighter when the game was fixed against him.

"What do you mean?" She rested her chin on her fist. "You think they're doing something against the law?"

Jim sat back in his chair. He didn't want her going back and telling them he suspected them of doing something wrong. He didn't. He didn't know what they were up to, if anything. "Nah. I just wondered if you saw anything that you didn't think was right."

"Nope. They was real nice to me." She got up from the table and went and stood against the kitchen counter where she'd left the iced tea pitcher.

"Oh." Jim flipped back through his notebook to the list of names that the young man had given to him. He had copied all the information into his notebook. "Do you know a Ms. Elizabeth Clark?"

Betty Lou shrugged and shook her head. "Should I?"

"Not necessarily, no. What about a Ms. Rosie Melendez or a Ms. Theresa Madison?"

"No, sir, I sure don't. What'd they do?" She stared down into her iced tea glass, stirring it vigorously.

"Nothing. I just thought you might know them from going to court. Their husbands were behind on child support also.

Betty Lou added some sugar. "No sir, I do not. I'm not big on names. Maybe if I could see a picture?"

Jim thought her voice sounded somehow different, but he couldn't put his finger on it. "Well, that's all right. I don't have their photographs with me right now, Ms. Johnson. Listen, is there anything else you think I should know? Anything else that maybe I should put in the article?"

"Can't think of nothing." She began straightening up the kitchen, pushing her chair under the table and picking up the lemon and sugar and carrying them back across the room.

The interview clearly over, Jim got up and carried his glass to the sink. He pushed his notepad into his back pocket and then reached his hand out to her. "Can't thank you enough for all your help, Ms. Johnson." Her hand felt cold and damp even though the temperature in the kitchen was not unreasonably cool.

She walked him to the door. "Well, you're more than welcome. You come back any time. Will you let me know when the article comes out? I'd like to buy a copy of the magazine."

"Sure." Jim stepped out onto the sidewalk which was already hot from the morning sun. "Bye now," he called as he waved to her. He walked out to the street and as he was getting inside his car, he glanced back. The curtain at the window next to the door dropped back into place. An uneasiness settled over him that he could not shake for the remainder of the day.

CHAPTER
NINE

J ust after dark on Sunday, Jim pulled into a cheap motel on the outskirts of Dallas. He had contemplated sleeping in his car to save money, but he would still need a shower and a shave to be presentable for Monday's interview. He also thought he'd do better if he'd had a restful night. He sprang for a room, asking for one on the end so neighbors on each side would not keep him awake with any raucous goings on.

He ate dinner in a greasy spoon just down the road from the motel and then returned to watch television and fall asleep. As much as he wanted to find a bar, he deferred it, hoping for good news and a celebration to go with it at the end of the following day.

As he lay in bed, Jim's mind started running like a race for the finish line. Was Dallas, Texas too conservative for the likes of him? Sure, there were folks with liberal leanings sprinkled throughout the city, but what if the personnel at the magazine were incompatible with him? Would he be able to keep his mouth shut in order to keep a job that would feed his children?

He was left of middle on almost everything except crime. He used to be a big individual rights freak, but when the children came along, he found himself cast into the role of the protector. Protect the rights of children first, alleged perpetrators second.

At any rate, other than his attitudes about children's rights, Jim thought he was a liberal. He despised governmental intrusion into a person's sex life. He believed in gun control. Hating organized crime, he thought people ought to be able to possess what he considered harmless drugs for personal use, like marijuana, and that drugs should be decriminalized so that organized crime wouldn't profit from them. He was for the welfare system if it could be run right but thought the Welfare to Work system a complete failure. Once when he was very young, he had marched with the women for the Equal Rights Amendment. If he'd been a college student in the 1960's, Jim was sure he probably would have protested the Viet Nam War since he hated violence of any kind and especially wars.

As he lay in bed worrying about the following day's interview, Jim found himself hoping most of all that he would find a home on Dallas Downtown Magazine. Not only a job, but a place where he would fit in, where people thought like him, where principles counted for something again. Knowing he could have the small paper job made him feel secure, even though it wasn't what he was looking for. And he had appreciated Patty's comments about it, also. If it came down to having to tell it to the judge, he was sure Patty would speak up about the failings of the small newspaper position. The big city job was his goal—if only there was a fit. He fell asleep with fear gnawing at him like a rat in a garbage pail.

Turned out Edgar Buck was a classic, stereotypical newspaper man. It didn't matter that he was editor of a magazine. A stogy smoking, balding, loudmouthed, bear-shaped man with a grip like a Dallas Cowboy, Edgar seemed to like Jim from the moment they laid eyes on each other. "Glad you came, Jim," Edgar said, releasing Jim's hand. His slap on Jim's back almost sent Jim flying into the chair he offered.

Jim dropped into a chair across from Edgar's desk, a battered and bruised, paper-laden, wooden monstrosity about the size of a small army tank. Stackable trays of every color held books, magazines, and computer printouts. Cigar smoke hung in the air like the atmosphere over a chemical plant on a windless day. Jim wondered how Edgar got away with smoking with modern sentiment against him, but he wasn't about to ask.

Edgar's chair was an old wood swivel, the cushions pitted with holes, stuffing peeking out, gray-brown in color. The top layer of wood was worn smooth on the arms and was as shiny as the skin on a baby's bottom. If Edgar talked like he looked, Jim would know he'd come home.

"So, you've been out of work since the Angeles Evening Times shut down, what've you been doing?" He struck a match and put it to a cigar stub he'd fished from a chipped, yellow glass ashtray.

"Short stories, essays, finished my first novel and wrote another one. Collecting unemployment."

"And lately?"

Jim met Buck's eyes. He hoped the man could read sincerity in his own. "Trying to make some sales. Sold a couple of things this year. Hoping to hear from my agent any day that one of my books has sold."

"That happen and we've given you a job, you going to quit?"

Jim's stomach churned. "Hell, no. Investigative reporting is my life."

"But you've been working on fiction." Smoke covered Buck's head like fog.

"I've got a proposal out for a series of nonfiction articles," Jim said. He was only fudging a little bit.

"On?" He puffed and coughed, turning his head toward the corner of his office where his suit jacket clung from a wooden coat rack. "On what?"

"Child support."

"That's been done to death."

"Not from the father's perspective."

Edgar shook his head. "Never make a sale. I wouldn't buy it."

"Why not?" Jim gripped the chair arms, disappointed. But felt that Edgar was wrong. Almost half the people in the country were men.

"Your readers are women. They'd hate it."

"I want them to be more sympathetic." Jim leaned toward Edgar Buck. "To see the men's side of it."

"That'll never happen." He tapped his cigar on the side of a huge green glass ashtray.

"I think it will. Even if you hire me, I'm going to keep working on it. There are some interesting things happening down in the hill country."

Edgar glanced at the yellowed windows as though reading a message on them. "Jim, I like a man who won't back down. I'm not telling you not to do it, but it would have to be really catchy to be published. Now, you bring anything to show me?"

Taking that as encouragement, Jim whipped out a portfolio of the best of his previous work. He'd assembled it himself, so it wasn't the most beautifully arranged but he'd done a pretty good job.

Edgar stood at the side of his desk and thumbed through the plastic-encased pages. "Yeah. I remember this one. You did a good job. Should have won an award that year." Edgar fingered an article Jim had done on the removal of a state appellate court judge from office. "Good work. I hadn't remembered that was yours." He nodded. "Educated the public, entertained them, in fact, with information that could have been quite boring."

Jim's stomach settled down. It had felt like a viper nest for two days.

When he was through, Edgar closed the leather cover on the book. "I like your work, Jim." He eased back into his chair. "Do you blog?"

Jim shook his head. "Never have."

"Didn't think so. Couldn't find one. If you get this job, you'll have to. That a problem?"

"Nope." Jim kept his hands in his lap where Edgar couldn't see them shake.

"Tell me about your background. Give me stuff that's not in your resume."

His hands felt sweaty. Nut crunching time. Would it matter that he'd never gone further than his bachelor's degree? "I don't have my master's. Never got around to completing my thesis. I wouldn't mind finishing it if it was a requirement for this job, but personally it's not important to me."

"Oh, hell, degrees look fine on the wall behind a desk, but they don't make a good reporter. I don't give a damn about that. What about your family?"

"Two kids, a boy and a girl." Jim hated to discuss his personal business. He wondered if Edgar already knew about Pat and him and was just trying to see how he'd react. Damn, he didn't know what people wanted these days. He shook his head and blurted out, "I'm divorced. I still love my wife. I can't pay my child support. And I really need this job to stay out of jail." A hard knot formed in Jim's stomach. He couldn't believe his mouth had just regurgitated his thoughts like that.

Edgar stroked his chin. "I suspected your interest in child support was not just a passing fancy."

"The judge is really leaning on me. I've given Pat as much as I can. I thought if people could see the way it is sometimes, they'd be more sympathetic. Also, I was searching for something that hadn't been done."

"Still think you're going to have a hard time selling it."

"I have another angle, too. I think something funny is going on in town. I can't quite put my finger on it, but I'm starting to investigate some people on the QT."

"What are you talking about?"

"I don't really want to say, but it's tied to the support issue. I don't want to look like a fool. I'll certainly let you in on it if it pans out."

"All right. I don't want to put you on the spot, Jim." Edgar's eyes flickered back and forth, searching Jim's face. "How soon could you wrap all this up if you had to? In terms of days or weeks."

Jim licked his lips. They were as dry as if he'd just walked across the desert on them. "I really should give a month's notice on my rent house, but—"

Edgar shifted the cigar from one hand to the other and stood. "Let me introduce you to some of the other people in the office and then we'll go upstairs. Later, I'll take you to one of my favorite little joints for lunch."

Jim rose from his chair and reached for his portfolio, zipping it up. He felt good about the interview. Really good. There weren't many like Edgar anymore where what you wrote was more important than how many degrees you could hang on the wall over your head. He appreciated Buck putting his mind to rest on the issue of the master's degree.

Edgar led him into the large outer office and introduced him to the staff who appeared to be equally proportioned between men and women, old and young, seasoned and fresh out of school, all different colors. Jim conversed with some of them. Hoped they liked him. Hoped they thought he'd fit in. Tried to figure out which ones might give him a thumbs down if they were put to a vote.

Afterward, Edgar drove him several blocks away to a locally owned restaurant in a strip mall. On the outside, the place looked plain and shopworn, but inside, the atmosphere was cozy and close. The corned beef on rye that Edgar recommended came with thick slices of sweet onions. The beer, locally brewed, had just the right amount of kick. And the owner/bartender treated Jim, and everyone else, like a long-lost close relation.

Jim thought he and Edgar hit it off famously. It was a feeling that he'd found a fit, a home, a place where he could be comfortable with the people and with himself. Edgar didn't offer the job, saying that he had several interviews lined up, but there was a sense of mutuality of purpose between them. At least from Jim's viewpoint. Over the miles and miles of flat Texas highway and well after he reached the rolling hills, Jim hoped and prayed that Edgar and his staff had felt the same. He knew the next few days would pass slowly as he agonized over the interview, the conversations with the employees, the lunch. As much as he knew his friend Ethan would tell him to stay in the present moment, he wouldn't be able to do that. He'd feel nothing but worry and angst as he waited for a phone call informing him that he'd been hired. Or not.

CHAPTER
TEN

Pulling into town at almost eleven o'clock that night, Jim was still so wired over the interview he knew he wouldn't be able to sleep unless he told someone about it. And he wanted that someone to be Pat. When he arrived, the house was dark, locked up for the night. He parked across the street.

The air was still hot, dry heat, as was the norm for the Texas hill country in the spring, summer, and early fall. Breathing was easier after it got dark, but a sweat would still break until the air grew cool in the wee hours of the morning.

A glow came from her bedroom window in the back of the house, reflecting off the leaves of the magnolia tree they had planted in the corner of the side yard. Jim hopped the white picket fence and tiptoed around to the back of the house, scratching on the window screen, next to the bed.

The crickets, locusts, cicadas, and all the other insomniac insects were warming up the orchestra. The smell of the honey-suckle that blanketed the back fence filled the air. Their backyard had always been a peaceful haven. He used to enjoy sitting out back late at night with Pat. They might share a beer at the picnic table. Cuddle against one another on the bench. Share their day.

Jim scratched on the screen a little longer and tapped on it with his fingernail. He hoped he wasn't scaring her. He told himself that he would have called, but he didn't have a cell phone. The truth be told, he just plain and simply wanted to see his wife.

Pat's face appeared and, a moment later, she raised the wooden sill. "You are lucky I don't shoot your ass off. What are you doing here?"

"You don't have a gun. May I come in? I need to talk to you."

"Jim, honestly, I'm tired. Can't it wait until morning?"

"Aw, honey, I won't be long. I just really need to share this with you. Good news. You'll be happy once you hear it."

"God, I hate it when you whine like that." Her head wagged in a familiar, exaggerated, disgusted manner. "Come around to the back door, but be quiet."

Jim waited outside the back door. By the moonlight, he could see the door to his old tool shed hanging open. He knew that Patrick used it to keep some of his large toys in and as a clubhouse when he had his friends over. Even in the dark, he could see the grass needed cutting. He should offer to come over to do that and perhaps a few other minor things that needing mending. If only she'd let him. He knew he should have tended to his chores a little more when he lived there instead of worrying about them now that it was too late. He pushed those thoughts from his mind when he heard the back door latch turn.

Opening the screen, Jim slipped inside when Pat unlocked the back door. Her hair awry, she stood in her nightgown with one arm hanging down by her side. Clutched in her fingers was a small revolver.

"You could have shot my ass off," he whispered as he held the door handle and eased the door closed behind himself. "When did you get that thing and where do you keep it so that the kids don't kill each other?"

"In my purse." She let the gun dangle from her hand.

"Damn, Patty." He could barely make out her face. A porch light in the distance illuminated the room so he could see only a bit more than shadows.

"Is that what you came over here for, to cuss me out?" She stared up at him, her face very close to his.

"You could at least put that thing away." He draped his arm around her shoulders and wondered at her not immediately shrugging his arm off.

"Maybe I should use it on you." She waved the gun around. "Say you were a prowler."

Had she been drinking? He didn't smell alcohol. Maybe vodka? "Not funny, Pat. Could you put it away?"

"Let me go put it back in my purse. It's next to the bed."

She padded back to her room in her bare feet. Jim followed. It seemed to him that she kept bringing him in there —was she sending him a message? Was he right that she really wanted him back? He really wanted her, but that was nothing new.

After she put the revolver in its small holster and snapped her purse shut, Pat turned and almost bumped into Jim. He was standing near the foot of the bed. "What are you doing in here?"

Jim held up his hands. "I thought you meant for me to follow you. You want to talk in the kitchen? The kids might wake up."

"I guess it's all right. You sit over there on my vanity stool," she said, pointing halfway across the room. She turned on the bedside lamp.

Jim wondered if she felt that she wasn't safe with him. Maybe she felt an attraction to him and putting him halfway across the room made her feel that she could resist him. Their sex life had, after all, always been very good. Maybe she was remembering that. Maybe—

"Now what is it that you want, Jim?" She sat on the side of the bed, pulled her knees up under her chin, and covered them with the folds of the long, familiar nightgown.

"First, I want you to promise you'll lock that gun away."

"I will. I'll lock it in my jewelry box. Okay?" She scratched her head and pushed her hair behind her ears and yawned. "Now tell me why you're here."

"I went on that interview today, to Dallas."

"Yes, I know." She turned her head to the side, regarding him with a wide-eyed look.

"It sounds good, Patty." Patty had always been his favorite name for her. He wondered whether she would notice. "Real good."

"Don't call me that."

He crossed the room and knelt on the floor at her feet. "Honey, I think they're going to make me an offer. I fit in like the missing piece of a puzzle. Edgar Buck and I hit it off from the very start. He's a classic, like—like—well, I can't think of like what right now, but trust me when I say that. The staff liked me. We talked and talked, Edgar and I, for hours. We have the same philosophy about reporting, the same ethics. That's so rare these days. You know that. Especially with the Internet and print publishing in so much trouble."

"So, you would move to Dallas?" Her hair fell over her eyes and she brushed it back again.

"In a millisecond." The faint flowery aroma of her perfume

filled the air. Jim tried not to think about sex with her. Her toes were about level with his chin. He looked up from where he knelt and studied her face. He would always love her whether there was sex or not. He wanted her, the whole person. He had never fully appreciated her until he lost her. Did she feel the same?

He wanted some indication that she would be sorry to see him go—that she wanted to go with him. He held her eyes in his. She was without make-up. He hadn't noticed before, but small lines had appeared at the corners of her eyes. Jim wanted to run to a mirror and check his own reflection. He had always planned on their growing old together and here she was doing it on her own. "Would you miss me?"

She sighed and rubbed her eyes. "Oh, Jimmy—"

"Patty, come with me." The words rushed out before he got a chance to formulate exactly what he wanted to say. He grabbed her hand, kissed the back of it, and held it up to his cheek. "Patty, you've got to forgive me for neglecting you. Take me back and let's be a family again. I love you."

She jerked her hand away and got up and rushed to the opposite side of the room. "I can't think." She put her palms out toward him, as if to stop him from coming close to her. Shaking her head, she said, "I just don't know."

"How long are you going to punish me—punish both of us?" Jim stayed where he was, on the floor next to the bed. He didn't want to get in her space, make her feel threatened. He hoped she would come to him, not retreat from him.

Her eyes wore a stricken look. Had he said too much before he'd even begun saying everything he wanted to say? "I know I was a bad husband—that I put my work first—that I hurt you. But you've got to see how you're destroying both of us with your anger. And the children."

"I . . . still feel confused inside," she said and clutched her middle. "Like I ate a bunch of stuff that didn't go together." She backed up against the closet door, leaning over with her knees bent, her nightgown caught up with her hands between her legs, as if she were in pain.

"I'm so sorry," Jim whispered. "I didn't realize what I was doing. I just got caught up in my job, the stories, and totally lost sight of what was important—you and the kids. Then when you started up with that man—I was just so shocked. So angry. I know I got unreasonable."

He watched her face as he spoke. The lines softened around her eyes, her mouth. She chewed on her bottom lip and her eyes shifted from his to the floor and back again. Hope filled Jim like helium in a balloon. This was the closest she'd let him get to her in a long, long time. He wondered if he reached out would she come into his arms.

"All I can do is apologize and say that it'll never happen again and ask for your forgiveness." He was watching her eyes; afraid to look anywhere else for fear she would realize what they were saying and throw him out.

She looked like a trapped animal. He hoped she didn't feel that way. He thought he had her fixed in place with his eyes and he felt the same, transfixed. "I love you and want you, Pat, more than I ever have before. I want you to love me, too. I want you to come away with me, take our little family to Dallas, Texas, and make a new start. I can only promise you that things will be different."

She let out a deep breath and visibly relaxed. "I just don't know." She sank down on the carpet, her back still against the wall. "I don't know what I would do if you abandoned us there. I have friends here. A life."

Jim reached out, wanting to cover her mouth with his hand, but he was too far away. "I would never do that." He inched closer to her.

"But if you did, I think I would die, Jimbo. Don't you understand? I'm not tough. I'm weak. I need someone to support us —I don't mean in a financial sense—in a family sense. To want to come home and be a family. If you left us again—emotionally or any other way, I couldn't take it. It would kill me."

"Honey, I guarantee—"

"You can't do that. Suppose you were sent out on assignment to some foreign land. To the Far East. To the Middle East—"

"I don't think Dallas Downtown Mag—"

"Suppose they asked you to go there for a month then two months then three months—suppose they asked you to take a permanent assignment there?"

"Pat. Come on."

"No, really, that could happen. You can't tell me you'd turn that down. You'd jump at the chance to be a famous reporter, win awards, never thinking of your family—"

"What are you talking about? Have those women at the WiNGS meetings been messing with your head? Where did you get ideas like that? When did you start talking like that?"

"You would, wouldn't you?"

"Would what? Dallas Downtown Magazine is an urban magazine, not Newsweek or Time.

"Well, it could lead to a job with one of those."

"No. I'd never consider a position we—you and I—didn't agree on. I can promise you that."

"I don't believe you. You never asked me before. You just took off to wherever." She'd begun to pout and looked like an agitated child.

Jim sat cross-legged on the floor. "I've learned so much from our separation."

"You didn't answer my question."

"I'm confused. What's the question? About taking assignments? No, I wouldn't go off to the middle east without your blessing. I wouldn't go anywhere unless we agreed upon it. Okay?"

"I don't know. Can I trust you? Could you really have changed?"

Jim had to bite his lip to keep from smiling. He couldn't tell if she was deliberately goading him so they'd have a fight and she could get out of the situation, or if she wanted him as much as he wanted her and was hoping all this talk would serve as a prelude to foreplay.

Pat lay down on her stomach and propped her head on the heel of her hand. She pulled at the carpet. "You think we could —could talk more about it? Is that what you want?"

"Yes. I think we could talk more about it. I think we should talk more about it. And what I really want is you."

"I know you do." She reached out with one hand and stroked his hair. "I just hope that I'm not making a mistake." Her fingers slid down to his cheek and caressed it.

"You're not. Marry me, Pat?"

"I'll marry you, James. But this will be the last time."

"And I'll make you happy, I promise."

"And I promise that if you don't, you'll be sorry." Her eyes flashed and she chuckled gleefully. Then she slipped her hand around to the back of his head and pulled herself to him, kissing him lightly on the lips.

Jim reached his arms out and pulled her on top of him, enclosing her in a bear hug. It felt so good to be able to touch her again that he caressed her all over, her cheeks with the back of his fingers and her arms and the sides of her legs. He wanted to make sure that he was not imagining things. This was really her. His wife. His Patty. And she was allowing him to be with her again. His hands went to her breasts and as she nipped and kissed him on the neck and ears and lips, he stroked her nipples and felt them grow hard under his touch. And he kissed her, too. All over her face. His need to feel her whole body and assure himself that he was not dreaming was almost greater than his need to be inside of her. He had thought of this moment so many times over the last year and a half. In his heart, he never believed that it would ever happen. He had hoped, but he had never assumed that he would be able to touch Patty again.

After a few minutes, Jim got to his knees and scooped Patty up in his arms, carrying her to the bed. Their bed. Locking the bedroom door, he began unbuttoning his shirt on the way back to the bed.

"No, let me do that," she whispered. "It's been so long." She sat up on the bed and began slowly slipping the buttons through the holes and caressing his chest, his chest hair, and his nipples lightly each time she succeeded in unbuttoning one.

Jim clutched her to him. Her soft skin and the smell of her hair as he pressed his face into it brought back memories of long past intimacies. He tugged at her nightgown and managed to slip it away from her body, not even really knowing when or how but only that its removal revealed the glistening, naked body of the woman who had more control over him than in his youthful dreams he ever thought it possible that a woman would have. Her body was essentially unchanged from his memories. If anything, it was more svelte. He reached down and stroked her breasts, holding them one in each hand, enjoying the renewed pleasure of her body.

Pat tugged his shirt away. Beginning with his belt buckle, she slipped three of her fingers down behind the button and caressed the soft fur of his abdomen with the backs of them. The fingers of her other hand fumbled with the leather tongue of the belt and finally pulled the belt from its loops. Then suddenly she had tossed it aside, pulled his remaining clothes down, and held him tightly as her tongue ran up his torso to his mouth.

Oh, God. He struggled to maintain control. He ran his hand down from her breasts to her soft pubic hair and knew then that she really did want him as much as he wanted her. He glanced at the lamp on the bedside table, the only source of light in the room, gave fleeting thought to turning it off, then cast that thought aside. He wanted to see everything he had been missing out on for the past eighteen months, twelve days, and six hours of his life.

CHAPTER

ELEVEN

J im awoke and felt Pat's bare bottom pressed up against his thigh, her back to him. Her breath came evenly. Glancing past her, he saw that it was six a.m. In a few hours, he had to meet with Mrs. Peterson of the district clerk's office. In the meantime, he wanted nothing more than to lie next to the woman he loved and enjoy the memories of the night before. Maybe he'd even get lucky again if she awoke before the kids. He could go again, if she was interested. If not, there would be other nights. He was sure of that. The months of wooing her had finally paid off.

All he needed was to get that call from Edgar. Would it come this week? Next week? The administration and staff had done everything but offer him the job. He just knew they were going to do that, too. The timing was perfect. The children's school wouldn't start for another month. He'd have time to find them a house. Correction. They'd have time to find a house. He'd have to start thinking in plurals again.

Pat turned over and pulled his arm around her shoulders. "What are you thinking about?"

Warmth enveloping him, Jim drew in a slow, deep breath and released it as though putting himself into relaxation for yoga. "Everything."

"You know, Jimmy, we might have trouble selling this house. It's still a buyer's market."

The word we pleased him. "We'll rent it out. We'll move from the bourgeoisie to the upper class."

"I didn't know we were in the bourgeoisie. I've felt pretty poor lately."

"Me, too. But just think, Patty, with our combined incomes, we'll do a lot better again."

"You're counting pretty heavily on being offered that job in Dallas, aren't you? You could take that other one, and then we could keep this house, and the kids wouldn't have to leave their friends, and I'd keep my teaching position at Smith—"

"Is that what you really want?"

"Maybe you'll sell your novel."

"My agent thinks so." He turned and faced her. "But the other position is not what I want out of life."

"If you sell your book, you could stay home and write full-time."

"Do you really want to stay here that badly?" He kissed the tip of her nose and pulled back from her so that he could see her whole face. Sleep had gathered in the corners of her eyes, mascara rings lined her lower lids, and her hair had sprung up behind the back of her head like turkey feathers. She was the most beautiful sight he had ever seen.

"I don't know whether I want to leave or not." She ran her fingertips over his stubbled chin.

"I want that Dallas job so bad I can taste it."

"They haven't offered it yet." She kept looking from his mouth to his eyes, her own eyes dancing.

"They will. They will. I can feel it. Haven't you ever wanted something so much that you'd do anything, anything to achieve it?"

She nodded.

"That's how this is, Patty." He pulled her closer to him. "But if you don't want to go, if you really don't want to move away, I won't take it. I'd rather stay here and be with you than go to Dallas without you."

"Oh, honey." Pat slipped her fingers behind his neck and brought his face down to hers. "Would you really give it up for me?"

He nipped at her ear. "I'd give up my life for you."

Giggling, Pat nuzzled him and caressed him until he got to the point where he couldn't stand it anymore. He grabbed her and they went under the covers until the kids began banging on the bedroom door thirty minutes later.

Pat suddenly lost her sense of humor. "Quiet," she whispered.

"It's just the kids," he said in his normal tone.

"Mama, why is the door locked?" Jeanette asked in a small, plaintive voice.

"Be still, Jim." Pat pushed him away. "I don't want them to know." She called loudly, "I'm fixing to take a shower, kids. Go ahead and get some breakfast."

"Why not?" Jim rose on one elbow and stared at her back as she slid out of bed. It was a nice back. Smooth. Freckled around the shoulders. Two moles on one shoulder blade. "They'll know soon enough anyway."

"It's too soon." She was still whispering. "They won't understand."

"They'll have to." He found he was whispering, too, but didn't have the courage to go against her wishes when things were still being put right. Jim felt like a coward in the face of battle but was reserving his energy for later when he would make himself be more assertive with her.

She had gone into the bathroom, so he followed her. "I couldn't hear you."

"Not right now, Jim." She stepped behind the shower curtain almost shyly. "Isn't there some way you could let me break it to them gently?"

"Break it to them gently?" He was having to raise his voice to talk over the shower and shower curtain. Ludicrous, knowing the children were in the hall wondering why their mother wouldn't come out of the bedroom. It was reminiscent of many an earlier discussion between them.

Jim liked to shower with Pat, but if she was shaving her legs, it got crowded when she bent over and she fussed at him about not waiting until she was through. He wanted to get in with her now. He wouldn't mind her bending over, shaving her legs, with him in the bathtub with her, but he wasn't going to press his luck. "What do you mean, Patty? The kids would be delighted to have me back here. Why don't we get dressed and let them in?"

Her head, full of bubbly shampoo, popped around the curtain. "Please let me do it my way. I'd just like to sit down and explain things, that's all."

"I don't see what's to explain. We're going to get married again, aren't we? What's the big deal?"

"I don't want to shock them. I also don't want them to think that it's okay for people to sleep in the same room when they're not married." She gave him an exasperated look and disappeared around the curtain again.

"Much less in the same bed," Jim muttered, anger nipping at him.

"What?"

"Nothing." He sat down on the toilet and stared at the shower curtain. "So, when do you plan to tell them?"

"Give me a few days." she called. "To the end of the week, maybe?"

"That's four days."

"No, I meant until next Sunday."

Jim wandered back into the bedroom while he waited for his turn in the shower. Did that mean that he couldn't come back until Sunday? Why did she want to wait? Was there someone else she had to tell besides the kids? Were there some arrangements she had to make? Women. He'd never understand them. They didn't think logically. They might have a reason for doing something, but it wreaked havoc on a man's mind trying to figure it out.

Picking up his clothes, Jim made a nice, neat pile of them on the bed. He smoothed the wrinkles in his shirt, in hopes that they wouldn't show up too badly. Glancing over his shoulder, he decided to get a look at Patty's gun and reached for her purse. She had pushed the gun to the bottom. Jim emptied the contents out onto the bed. The gun was in a small holster. It was a shiny, chrome-plated revolver. At close range, it would have no trouble doing the job. He flipped open the cylinder. It was loaded. What in the hell did she need that for? Well, the most he could do would be to take it up with her at some later date and pray that the kids didn't get hurt before then.

After dropping it back into her purse, Jim reached for the other things that he'd dumped out. Keys, billfold, lipstick, tissues. He came across two pieces of typing paper stapled together and folded in half. Even though it wasn't his intention, even though Jim wouldn't never have considered himself a snoop, he opened it. It was a list of women's names and addresses and across from them, men's names and addresses.

Several of the men's names were crossed over so many

times that they were almost eradicated. Jim tried to read through the marks. He recognized Johnson. On the second page, he found Pat's name and then his name. There was a hand drawn asterisk or X next to it and several others. He didn't have time to wonder what it meant. Pat called his name.

Jim replaced the pages and the rest of the contents in her purse and put it back on the floor where he had found it. He'd have to try to make sense of the whole thing later. He hurried back into the bathroom.

"You coming in?"

"Yes, don't turn the water off."

Her leg came out, followed by a shiny, wet body. She grabbed a clean towel from the rack and held it to her chest. Though he was temporarily incapacitated, he enjoyed admiring her. She was a properly proportioned size eight, nothing spectacular, but the way she was put together had the right effect on him. As he glided past her, she stood on her tiptoes and gave him a peck on the lips.

"And how am I supposed to get out of here without their knowing I was here? My car is parked out in front of the house." Jim put his face under the warm water, then immersed his whole body.

Now it was her turn to raise her voice. Jim could hear her but with his head in the water, her voice came in muted tones.

"Out my bedroom window, then you can come around the front as if you just drove up and are having breakfast with us."

Jim moaned. He didn't think his kids were dumb enough to fall for that old trick and there were the prying eyes of the neighbors to consider. But if that would make her happy.

"Okay? I'm going out to get dressed now."

She didn't even wait for his answer, she was so sure of him. She knew that she had him by the balls and she knew he knew she knew. Hell, she was worth it. He shampooed his hair, soaped up and rinsed, and was in the bedroom fully dressed and crawling out of the window in under ten minutes. Bending at the knees, he came just below the high windows of the house, swung around to the front, stepped up onto the porch, and knocked.

After a few moments, Pat came to the door. "Oh, it's you." She winked. "Come on in." She scooted away as he attempted to swipe her on the rear end.

Giddiness threatened to overcome him. He breathed deeply, swallowed, and pasted a wan smile on his face as he followed her into the kitchen. The children were scooping cereal into their mouths and trying to watch the television in the next room at the same time.

"Hi, Daddy," Jeanette said. She put her thumb up to her mouth and began chewing on the side of it.

"Hi, Dad," Patrick echoed.

Jim thought they were both looking at him curiously but considered the fact that it might be his imagination. He kissed each child on the cheek in turn.

"What are you doing here, Dad?" Patrick asked. "Is something wrong?"

Jim felt like a trespasser. Did something have to be wrong for him to be there at times other than the court-ordered possession schedule? Yes. He grimaced over their heads at Pat. "Your mother invited me for breakfast."

Pat was digging around in the refrigerator. "I've got yogurt and granola."

"I'm trying to quit," Jim said.

"Toast and an egg that's as old as the hills is the other option unless you want cold cereal like the kids."

"Make that toast and egg with coffee and you've got a winning deal."

"And I suppose you want me to cook it."

124

"Your house. Your rules." Turning to the kids, he said, "So, what have you two monsters been doing with yourselves this week?"

"Dad, the week just started yesterday," Patrick said. He stared from his father to his mother. "Is something going on here? Did somebody die or something?"

"No, dear," Pat said. "Why do you ask?"

"Because you're being so nice to Dad. Is something wrong?"

Jeanette's eyes followed the two of them.

"Nothing's wrong. Now eat your breakfast. Jim, I'm going to scramble this egg unless you advise me otherwise." Pat turned on the fire under the frying pan, adjusted it, and cracked the egg over a bowl. She poured some milk in with the egg, beat it, and splashed it into the pan, all the while not meeting Jim's eyes.

Jim forced a grim look onto his face, afraid to look at her, afraid if their eyes met she'd burst out laughing or, worse, afraid she'd have a screaming, angry fit—realizing what they'd done—and throw him out. He poured himself a cup of coffee. It would have been better if he'd left. Was she having second thoughts? He leaned against the counter and watched the kids watching them. Their children were anything but stupid. He decided it would come as no revelation to them when Pat finally sat them down and told them.

Pat buttered a slice of toast, scraped the scrambled egg onto a bread plate, and handed it to him. "Thank you, ma'am," he said as he made himself comfortable in his old place at the table. It was a familiar, nostalgic feeling to see his family as they had once been and shortly would be again. Did any of them feel what he was feeling?

Pat poured herself some coffee and sat next to Jim for the few minutes it took him to gulp his food down. He wanted to reach out and take her hand right there in front of the children but didn't for fear of weakening their newly formed bond. He could wait 'til Sunday if he had to. But he didn't have to like it.

"So, can I drop anyone anywhere on my way downtown?" Jim glanced at their faces when he got up. Rinsing his plate, fork, and cup, he placed them in the dishwasher just the way he knew Pat liked and dried his hands on a dishtowel.

Knowing that he still had to run home and change clothes, Jim fervently hoped no one would take him up on his offer, but he was willing to go out of his way to keep his cover of just coming over for breakfast. He hoped Pat appreciated it. "Patrick? You going anywhere today? Jeanette?"

"That's okay, Dad," Patrick said. "Mom is going to take me to Michael's later."

"Okay, then . . . see you when I see you." Jim kissed each child on the head, smiled at Pat who he thought was acting as stilted as a boy meeting his girlfriend's parents for the first time, and let himself out. As he started up the Mustang and headed toward his house, he could hardly wait until she broke the ice and told the kids. It was just too uncomfortable.

Jim ran by his place to change his clothes and check his answering machine. When he approached the door, something didn't feel right. He stopped short of entering. Everything seemed to be in place. The door sat firmly closed. His eyes swept the landscape. No one there. A vehicle would have been obvious. The house and cabin weren't near the public road. Shaking off the feeling, he went inside.

There were two calls and three hang-ups. The first call was from the editor of The Daily Sun. Knowing what he wanted— an answer—Jim didn't return the call. He could afford to wait a few days, knowing he'd take the job as a last resort, but he wanted to give Edgar a few days to get back with him. It was a calculated risk, but one worth taking.

The second call was from his agent. Jim crossed his fingers as he punched in the long-ago memorized number. He ordinarily wasn't superstitious, didn't believe in astrology and things like that, but it seemed to him that his planets must be lining up in the same house or whatever they did that was good. He just knew that his agent was going to tell him that his first novel sold.

Luck, for once, ran his way. His life seemed to be coming back together. His wife was going to remarry him. He was going to be offered the job he wanted. And his novel was going to be published. What else could he hope for? A two-book contract? A three?

But his agent wasn't in. And no one seemed to know anything about his book. Jim hung up, disappointed. Checking his watch, he saw that he was running late for his appointment with Mrs. Peterson, so he quickly changed his clothes and drove across town to the courthouse.

Late morning in the middle of summer could be brutal. A jailhouse crew of three inmates policed the courthouse grounds, picking up trash, blowing leaves off sidewalks, trimming hedges. Sweat glistening on their bodies. Large dark rings encircled their underarms and the waistbands on the olive drab cotton jumpsuits they all wore. Their distinct body odor wafted across the courtyard. He casually wondered what the three of them had done. Obviously, they were not serious felons; they were without handcuffs or leg irons. Were any of them were non-payers of child support? And would he smell like that if the judge put him in jail?

Jim nodded at one of the men who stepped aside and stopped sweeping the wheelchair ramp while Jim walked up it. Better be friendly in case he joined them some day. The thought crossed his mind that it could be as early as the upcoming Friday, and an uneasiness quivered in his stomach.

The cool interior of the first floor of the courthouse was a relief. The worst thing he smelled was the cleaning solution the janitorial service must have used on the floor the night before.

Jim got in line to pass through the metal detector. When it was his turn, he emptied his pockets into the plastic bowl placed on the counter before the walk-through. He could still remember when their county courthouse had no security system. Now, after the country had witnessed episode after episode of violence in courts across the country, the county fathers had sprung for a system on the first floor only.

There had been a lot of grumbling, but Jim was not amongst those who felt they were inconvenienced by the slow-moving, unnecessary lines. As far as Jim was concerned, he liked knowing he was safe when he went to court. He didn't want to tangle with any nuts.

Everyone seemed to get off the elevator prior to the floor where the district clerk was located, so Jim rode up alone. The courthouse corridor was almost empty. It was quiet, even subdued for the middle of a morning. Jim pushed the door open and came face-to-face with a woman who had a small girl in tow. Backing up, Jim let them go past. There was something about the woman that seemed familiar, but he didn't know what it was. She looked over her shoulder as she and the little girl rounded the corner toward the elevator.

Jim bellied up to the counter. "Mrs. Peterson in?" he asked the young woman who had waited on him the last time.

"She stepped across the hall," the girl said. "Would you like to have a seat?"

Jim nodded and said, "I have an appointment with her."

"You're Mr. Dorman."

"Correct."

SUGGESTION OF DEATH

"She said to tell you to wait. She had to see our boss about something, but she'll be with you as soon as she can."

"Okay." Jim looked around for a place to sit and saw only a plastic chair that didn't look like it would hold him. The plastic was cracked above one leg. Feeling rather awkward, he leaned against the counter.

The girl stared at him in-between her computer input. She typed something in, looked up at him and smiled, and typed something in again.

She answered the phone and stared at him while she talked. She slit open some mail and glanced up at him from time-to-time as if to reassure herself that he was still there. She typed something on her computer keyboard and glanced alternately at the screen and then at Jim again.

Jim wished Mrs. Peterson would show up. After a while, he cleared his throat and said, "Are you the only one working today?"

The young woman shook her head. "One lady is in court, and one is coping stuff across the hall. Why?"

"Just curious about the guy who was sitting at that desk the last time I was here." Jim pointed to a black metal desk opposite hers. "He off today?"

"Noel? He doesn't work here anymore."

"Oh." How odd. He'd been hoping to hear from Noel again. He'd thought the guy was going to contact him again. Jim wanted an explanation for the list. "When'd he quit?"

The girl came to the counter. She was young, probably not over twenty. Long strawberry-blonde hair hung over her shoulders. Her cheeks looked like shiny ripe apples. "You know, he just didn't show up for work this week. It was the weirdest thing. Noel just went home on Friday and never came back. Didn't turn in his notice or anything. No one answers his phone, 'cause I called him. Don't you think it's weird for someone to just quit like that with no notice?" She glanced through the glass behind Jim and straightened her blouse.

Jim could see the outline of her nipples through her gauzy blouse. She stood taller when she saw him looking. "I mean you need to give notice so you can get a reference for your next job, right? I thought it was weird, but Mrs. Peterson says that it's happened a number of times around here." The girl shook her head and licked her lips, rubbing them together. "I never heard that before. No one ever told me that. But I'm sure that if Mrs. Peterson says it happened, it happened. She's been around a long, long time." She leaned toward Jim, over the counter, and whispered, "Don't you think it's strange that he's never called in or anything, Mr. Dorman? And I owe him ten dollars, too."

TWELVE

S omeone behind him coughed, and the girl winced like she'd been injured. Turning around, he found Mrs. Peterson. Her gaze at the girl was icy at best.

"Good afternoon, Mr. Dorman. If you would like to follow me back to my office?" She walked around him and through the swinging door. Jim followed her. The girl he'd been talking with found something to do back at her desk and retreated. She wouldn't lift her eyes from her computer keyboard as he walked past. He felt sorry for her, but he hadn't made her stand up at the counter and talk to him. Clearly, she wanted to tell someone what she thought.

At Mrs. Peterson's invitation, he sat down in another, more stable-looking, plastic chair. Perhaps the one at the front was so positioned to discourage people from hanging around the office. He glanced back at the girl to whom he'd been talking. She seemed to be intent on her work. He didn't know whether she would be able to hear their conversation since they were in the back of a large office behind a glass enclosure, but he didn't intend to close the door unless Mrs. Peterson asked. He hoped that if the girl was disgruntled enough, he might be able to turn her into an ally. He sure would like to find out more about Noel.

Mrs. Peterson hung her jacket on a large wooden coat rack in the shape of the state of Texas. It had bluebonnets painted on a background of red, white, and blue. It was the kind of thing sold at fairs and flea markets. Jim knew that because Pat had dragged him to many of them in the past.

Mrs. Peterson's smile reminded Jim of a toothpaste commercial. Gone was the tough taskmaster that he'd observed a few moments earlier. She was all sweetness and light. She sat in a worn secretarial chair and stacked computer printouts one on top of another until she'd cleared the area between them.

She was not unattractive for a woman in her mid to late fifties. She had bony shoulders, deep crow's feet, and well-pronounced smile wrinkles. Her blue eyes were the shade of the sky immediately preceding a thunderstorm. She had a pug nose and weak chin. Her brown hair was cut short and feathered around her face. Large, gold-colored, plastic earrings matched her dress and jacket. "I understand you're doing a magazine article on errant fathers." She picked up a ballpoint pen and began twisting it in her fingers.

"Yes, ma'am." Jim watched her hands. They never stopped moving. "Actually, it's about the reasons why they get behind —from their viewpoint. What they are doing about it. What they think they can do about it. How they feel about it."

"Well, I've heard every excuse in the book, I guess you could say. I'm not unsympathetic to them, it's just not my job to do anything for them."

"What do you think are the most common reasons an obligor, I think you would call him, does not pay his or her support?" He'd pulled out his wire bound notepad, written her name at the top of a page, and the words 'Common Reasons.'

"I see you're catching on to the lingo." Her lips spread wide, showing a lot of yellowed teeth. "Let me see. The most common reason is they got laid off or otherwise lost their jobs. It's probably not fair, but in order for them to get a reduction in child support if they lose their jobs, they have to file a motion to modify which means they have to hire a lawyer—unless they're smart enough to do it themselves, which most of them aren't." She began doodling on a yellow Post-it note pad. "You aren't the typical child support contemnor."

"Thank you. But I intend to catch up on all my back child support as soon as I get a new job." He wanted to tell her about his and Pat's plans for getting back together but didn't.

"That's what they all say, but rarely do any of them catch up. That's what gets them into trouble. But I'm getting ahead of myself. It's a shame, but we don't have the funding to do anything for fathers." She waved her hands over the paperwork on her desk. "I don't mean to sound sexist, but mostly it is fathers that get into this situation, though we do have some mothers."

"What do you mean?"

"Well, we no longer file the paperwork here, the attorney general's office does. But I wish we had some funding to help the fathers. I mean, people who need a reduction have to hire their own lawyers. People who need enforcement have the state attorney general. Doesn't seem fair. But what can you do?" She folded her hands on her desk in front of her like a banker turning down a loan application. "It's really not fair, Mr. Dorman, but the obligor must hire a lawyer. If they had the money to hire a lawyer, they would be better off paying it to the mother of their children. If they do hire a lawyer, not only the judge, but everyone looks down on them for not paying the money instead. So . . . "

"It's a Catch-22 situation. Damned if they do, damned if they don't." Jim glanced down at his notepad and flipped the page, writing as fast as he could.

"Just about. I tell them to file the motion no matter what the feelings or consequences if they know they are not going back to work soon or if they know they will not be making the same kind of money. Otherwise, they will never get their account back up to par." She hesitated and glanced at Jim's face. "But I've been instructed to only tell them if they ask. And I can't help them file it."

"So, if you tell them that, why don't they?" Jim had heard the implication but decided to skip discussing what she'd been told to do. At least for the moment. It really wasn't the emphasis of his story. Anyway, he wouldn't soon forget that the system favored mothers—or rather the people who had custody of the children—over all others. He knew that very well.

"Other than not being able to hire a lawyer? They don't know how to do it themselves. No one thinks they'll really get that far behind, or they'll really go to jail." She stacked up more papers, making a pyramid between herself and Jim. "Part of the problem in the past was that we had a judge who would hardly ever put a man in jail for nonsupport. That's not true anymore. Judge Lopez now handles all child support cases. I thought the word had gotten out about Judge Lopez, but sometimes I'm amazed at the men who go to court and take their chances." She chuckled. "They get the most surprised looks on their faces when she orders them to jail."

"Don't mean to sound lame, but ha ha ha."

"I guess you'd have to be there. It's usually the ones that

are real smart asses to her or to their ex in front of the judge that go to jail."

"Oh. She doesn't make a real practice of it?"

She jabbed her finger at him. "Don't get the wrong idea—she regularly puts them in, but it's slowed down considerably since she first was appointed. Back then I lost count."

"Tell me briefly, if you can, exactly what Judge Lopez's status is. I've figured out that she's not the elected judge, that she is appointed, but how does that work?"

"Humph." She looked grim. "Okay. This is how I've figured it out. There's this administrative judge. He was a real judge in another county, but he also has the job of kind of watching over other judges in a region of the state. I think the governor appoints the administrative judges."

"I didn't know that. I thought in Texas we elected all of our judges."

"Me, too, until we got Judge Lopez. I had heard of this judge who came down to meet with people, but I'm just a peon. No reason for me to know."

"So, he appointed her?" Jim asked.

"Yes, best I can tell. She goes to different counties on different days and hears nothing but child support cases." She sat back in her chair, apparently satisfied with her explanation.

"How does the elected judge feel about that?"

"About Judge Lopez? He likes not having to hear the child support cases, but I heard that he didn't like having someone else appoint the associate judge without even talking to him about who it would be."

"Can't blame him since the people of this county elected him."

"Oh, but Mr. Dorman, I hope you won't mention this to Judge Lopez." She scratched her nose. "I don't want to cause any trouble."

"No, ma'am." Jim tapped his pen on his leg. Interesting courthouse politics, but probably not relevant to his article. Still, he would file those notes away in case he wanted to do something on it in the future. He'd bet most people in Texas didn't know that non-elected judges were hearing thousands of cases. The voters in Texas revered their right to elect their judges.

Jim chewed on his thumbnail as he wrote, making a note in the margin to talk to Edgar Buck. Buck might be interested in such a story. "Okay, back to the guys who aren't paying. So, we've got men who think they'll be able to catch up and don't hire a lawyer and then can't catch up and end up in deep . . . trouble."

"Right. That's probably what we have the most of. Then we have those who don't pay because they hate that—excuse my French—bitch and ain't going to give her a damn thing no matter what no judge tells them."

Her accurate imitation of some of the men Jim had seen in the courtroom brought a snort from Jim. "You get a lot of those, do you?"

"A fair share. And a good deal of them will go to jail, too. They don't care. Some of them eventually start paying, but some of them are a lifetime struggle for all of us. If they'd just put their children first and their anger at their ex-wives behind them, we'd all be better off." She nodded curtly for emphasis.

"What percentage would you say that is?"

"Um—twenty, I guess. I'm not really sure. Maybe less, but they're so much trouble that it seems like more."

"Is there any solution to that?"

"Besides lining them up against a wall and shooting them?"

Jim did a double-take. It wasn't clear to him whether she is joking or not.

"Excuse me if I'm rather cynical, Mr. Dorman. I've been in this business for over twenty years."

Jim wanted to say something snide about burnout, but he thought better of it.

"Do you know of a solution to that problem? I mean, for the good of the children?"

"Judge Lopez says that we should send them to mediation. She says that they've never gotten a chance to and I quote 'vent their spleens' and once they got all of those awful feelings out in the open and cleared the air, things would be a lot better between them and for the children.

"What do you say?"

"It couldn't hurt. But we don't have money for a mediation program so, as the lawyers would say, it's a moot point."

"Okay, what else?"

"Well, the ones who think that if they leave town, they don't have to pay. There are a lot of them, too, but the attorney general's office will track them down."

"You don't get any?"

"An occasional one with a private attorney. They're usually a good deal of money behind and they've been found and have a real possibility of paying. Like maybe they are a banker or lawyer or doctor in Oregon or someplace."

Nodding, Jim was getting the idea. There were probably as many reasons as there were men—obligors—who had to pay support. "Any others?"

"Sure." She smiled again. "There are those who need a new set of tires for their truck and intend to catch up the next time. The trouble is, the next time it's something else, so she is lucky if he ever pays what he's supposed to.

"It starts out like this: First, he's just a bit short so instead of paying say two hundred, he pays one-seventy-five. The next time he maybe pays the full two hundred. The next time he may be short and only pay one hundred. Then the next time two-twenty-five. Then something else happens. He goes on vacation or something and he misses a whole payment. You see how it is, pretty soon he's hundreds, if not thousands, behind."

"They go on vacation instead of paying their child support?"

"Every day. And don't forget the interest."

"Interest? I guess I didn't realize either of those things."

Her eyes wavered on his face, but she didn't say anything, as if to say there was a lot he didn't realize.

"So, there are a lot of reasons they get behind. You've been a great help, Mrs. Peterson."

"Oh, is that it?"

He ducked his head, surprised. "There's more?"

"Well, everyone has their wages garnished these days. But some don't pay during the interim period between court and the time the wage order goes into effect. There are those who remarry one or more times and have more children with no consideration for the ones they already have."

"Could they come to court and get a reduction for that?"

"Yes, but it's frowned upon. They're supposed to think before they make more babies—but, of course, they don't." She began doodling again. "We have some cases where the men have fathered three or more sets of kids. The pie can only be divided into so many slices, Mr. Dorman."

"Is that it?"

"I forgot the job-related injuries or even the non-job-related injuries. If it's job related or if there is some insurance to cover the injured party, now that Judge Lopez is here, the obligee usually gets all her money eventually. It comes from the lawsuit."

"They didn't before?"

"Well, if you leave it up to the obligor, he'll only give her what he wants out of the proceeds. It was the same with one of the judges who used to handle these cases, though I never understood why. Let's say the man is ten thousand behind and his personal injury case is finally settled for twenty thousand. The previous judge would probably have told him to pay five of that twenty on the back child support."

"That makes no sense," Jim said.

"I know. Go figure. It's all in how people think. Judge Lopez, on the other hand, makes them sign an assignment so that the back child support gets paid before the proceeds are given to the obligor. Then she causes the assignment to be sent to the attorney for the obligor who is handling the lawsuit and to the insurance company."

"She doesn't trust the obligor's attorney?"

She shook her head. "There's a reason for that. One of her first cases involved a lawyer who lied about the proceeds of the lawsuit."

Jim cringed. "I'd hate to be that lawyer."

"She's not practicing anymore."

"That sounds about right for Judge Lopez."

Mrs. Peterson played with one of her hoop earrings, running her finger around and around in it. "Listen, she's strictly by the book. Honest. Straight forward. Gives no favors. Accepts none."

"What kind of lawyer was she?"

"Same way. Her word was good. The others trusted her. There aren't many of those left, unfortunately."

Jim could see that he wasn't going to get anything helpful about the judge from Mrs. Peterson. If there was anything to be gotten. "What about her bailiff? Isn't it unusual to have a female bailiff?"

"Yes, but Bitsy was a deputy sheriff first and applied for the job when the last bailiff quit."

"A deputy sheriff? Well, what's her story?"

"Her story? I don't know what you're getting at." She sat up stiffly in her chair.

"Does she have a personal stake in these cases? For that matter, do you?"

"Just a minute, Mr. Dorman. What exactly are you implying?"

"Look, I don't want to offend you, Mrs. Peterson, but both you and Bitsy uh—"

"'Wink,' she finished.

"Wink, seem to relish your positions."

"What're you talking about?" Her neck was growing red.

"That club you are in. The way you recruit members for it. Your attitude about lining men up against the wall and shooting them."

Shaking her head, Mrs. Peterson sputtered, "You're wrong. That last statement was a joke—a bad joke, I agree, but I haven't done anything wrong in my job and you can't say I have. I've been dedicated to helping people with their child support problems for over twenty years and now you come forward and imply that I've done something I shouldn't." Her eyes welled up. She pulled a tissue from a box on the corner of her cluttered desk.

Jim thought it was a good act. He felt like he'd caught her with her hand in the cookie jar and she didn't know what to do so she was resorting to tears like most women. Well, it wasn't going to work on him. He sat and stared at her as she blew her nose and patted her eyes.

"How would it look, Mrs. Peterson, if I put in my article that you thought all men who didn't pay their child support ought to be lined up against the wall and shot?"

She bit her lip as she glared at him. "Why are you doing this to me? Don't you realize what that kind of thing would do to me and what it would do to my boss? She's an elected official. It could really hurt her in the next election."

"I'll make a deal with you. You cooperate with me and I won't print what you said."

Mrs. Peterson got up and closed the door to her office. "What is it that you want me to cooperate about? I've been telling you everything I know about child support. I don't understand."

Though she appeared to be confused, Jim was convinced that it was an act. "WiNGS."

"The WiNGS support group, you mean?"

"Yes, exactly"

"I can only tell you what I've heard, Mr. Dorman. I don't belong. I've never even been to a meeting except for one time when I was a speaker and told them about how to file through our office if they had a lawyer."

"You weren't one of the founding members?"

"Whatever gave you that idea?"

Jim adjusted his glasses. "Okay, so you're not a member. What can you tell me about it?"

"It's a women's support group. Oh, I suppose men could go if they wanted. It's really for people not getting child support, to tell them what their alternatives are. To support them in their struggles as single parents. To explore possibilities with them, resources, that sort of thing. I still don't understand what you are getting at."

"Shouldn't you be a member?"

"What for? I'm not getting child support."

"You work here."

"So, what has that got to do with anything?"

Jim was confused. Didn't she feel the same about men as

the rest of them? Wasn't she out to get them? How could he ask her that without sounding like he was accusing her? "Okay. Okay. Let me ask you this. Do you have any affiliation with that group?"

Shaking her head, she said, "Other than being available as a speaker, no. My husband thought that I shouldn't even be on the advisory board because it could be a potential conflict of interest, but since the judge is on it, I agreed to serve also."

"Your husband?"

"He's a Justice of the Peace and an attorney."

"I thought—"

"I know what you thought, Mr. Dorman. That I'm a man hater. That I was probably done wrong by a man and that's why I have this job. Etcetera etcetera. Correct?"

Jim sure was getting tired of hearing his name. Her use of it was almost comical. Did he make her that uncomfortable that she had to rely on formalities to conduct a conversation? "I apologize, Mrs. Peterson. I somehow got that impression, yes."

"It's your own sexist attitude—"

"I'm not—"

"Yes, you are. You don't even realize it. Now is there anything else I can help you with?"

"You're still willing to talk to me?"

"I said I was. What else do you need to know, Mr. Dorman?

"Who was the founder of WiNGS?"

"Hmm, let's see, couple of women lawyers who don't even live here anymore and the bailiff, Bitsy Wink. If it's information on WiNGS you want, you should ask Bitsy. As one of the first members, she'd have everything you need. I understand that currently she's the board president."

Jim let that go by. "But you are on the advisory board? How often do you meet?"

"Supposed to meet twice a year. It's a formality, that's all.

They use us on their letterhead, my boss and I, and others, like the judge. They apply for funding through the United Way and grants. They pay expenses for speakers if they have any from out of town. They have a small office with a part-time secretary they have to pay for and office supplies. The office is in the church where they have their meetings."

"And you say that you've only gone to meetings when you have been the speaker."

"Correct, one meeting, except for the advisory board."

"So, have you never been to an executive board meeting?"

"I wouldn't even know if they have them. You can ask Bitsy that."

"Do you remember Mr. Johnson? The man who died not too long ago? Wasn't his wife a member?"

"I wouldn't know, Mr. Dorman. "What are you getting at?"

"I understand that Ms. Johnson is now receiving Social Security for each of her four children."

"I don't know off the top of my head, but that wouldn't be unusual. I believe that if a spouse has ever paid Social Security, his children are eligible for an entitlement until they turn eighteen. It used to be until they graduated from college. I don't know why that would be any different for Ms. Johnson's children."

"And you don't think it's unusual for her to be better off now that Mr. Johnson is dead?"

"What are you after?"

"You would agree that she is better off now that he's dead."

"I suppose so, Mr. Dorman. He was not a good payer."

"Well, let me ask you this, Mrs. Peterson, have there been any other cases that you know of where the woman wasn't receiving child support and perhaps was living off welfare and then the payer, the ex-husband or ex-boyfriend, died and she was better off?"

"In the twenty years that I have been here, I'm sure there have been one or two obligors each year that have died. Are you implying that in Ms. Johnson's case something unusual happened to cause Mr. Johnson's demise? I understood that it was a traffic fatality."

Jim was trying to get an impression from her demeanor, but he couldn't get any kind of reading—not surprise, not fear, not a sense of threat or dread. Could she really be so dim as not to understand what he was getting at? Not that he, himself, was sure what he was getting at. Perhaps he was just imagining things. Did he just want something corrupt to be happening? Did he just want the story of the century? "You don't see any connection between any of them—the obligors who have died?"

"What?"

Her voice was quite loud, and she glanced in the direction of the window to see if anyone heard. The girl Jim had been talking to and one other woman glanced back in their direction. Peterson hunkered down over the desk.

"I'm sorry, Mr. Dorman, I may be slow on the uptake, but you can't possibly think that poor Ms. Johnson had something to do with her husband's death."

"I'm not sure if there is a connection or not, ma'am. That's one of the things I'm investigating."

"Have you gone to the police?"

"No, ma'am. I don't really have anything yet. And I would appreciate it if you would keep this all to yourself."

She wet her lips. "That's no problem. I should feel like a fool if I mentioned this to anyone. I suggest to you that you are way off base."

"Then how do you explain Noel—that was his name, wasn't it?"

She nodded.

"How do you explain his giving me Ms. Johnson's name and address? He gave me a list of other names, too."

She frowned. "Noel Wannamaker gave you a list of names? Whose names?"

"I'm not clear on that yet."

Shaking her head, she said, "Noel had a very active imagination. I assure you that there has been no suggestion of wrongdoing on the part of Ms. Johnson, and I have no idea what the other names are."

"How do you explain Noel's disappearance?"

"Noel's disappeared?" She seemed genuinely surprised.

"Hasn't he?"

"I don't think so."

"He's never showed up for work this week."

"He quit with no notice. Just called up and left a message on the office answering machine. Said he was leaving town and wouldn't be coming back."

Jim was beginning to feel foolish for his vague suspicions. "You don't think something's wrong with that?"

"You know how young people are. Very impetuous."

"Would you mind giving me his home address?"

"No, I don't mind. I think you'll find he's moved, though. At least that's what he said." She pulled a Rolodex forward and copied an address off a card. Handing Jim the piece of paper, she stood up. "It's about lunch time, Mr. Dorman. Now, if there isn't anything else."

Jim stood and reached out, offering his hand for her to shake. She laid her hand in his and let it be shaken, then let it drop to her side. Her hand was cool to the touch and damp and Jim thought that it was lucky that her boss was the politician, rather than she. People would not want to touch a person who had no personality in their handshake.

"I'm sorry if I upset you, Mrs. Peterson. It wasn't my inten-

145

tion. Thank you very much for all your help," he said. "I know the way out."

Jim left her door open and worked his way to the front of the office. "Bye, now," he said to the girl he'd been talking to earlier. He glanced at her desk in search of a nameplate. Donna. "Bye, Donna," he said. She nodded to him. He stepped into the hall and glanced back through the glass doors into the office. Mrs. Peterson waved. Jim waved.

Jim walked to the end of the hallway and got a drink of water. As he walked to the bank of elevators on his way back past the family section of the district clerk's office, he glanced into Peterson's section. The door to her office was closed, but through the glass Jim could see that she was talking on the phone and gesturing madly in the air.

THIRTEEN

J im hoped that Noel Wannamaker had left town, he really did. Though his having gone wouldn't do Jim any good. It wouldn't give him any more information for his article series. It wouldn't tell him what the other names on the list meant. It wouldn't cut down on the legwork that Jim would now have to do for himself. In addition, Jim wouldn't have an ally he had hoped he would have.

Noel's place was out in the country. It was a singles apartment complex located on the bank of the river. It was a high-priced neighborhood. How could Noel afford to live there?

The grounds looked manicured with scissors. The riverbank was set up with tables, umbrellas, a diving board and a slide—a swimming partier's paradise. The river was up. The partiers were out. Booze flowed faster than the water. Bikini clad girls squealed and splashed as boys threw them into the cool depths. There were too many young adults to count, but Noel wasn't among them.

After locating Noel's apartment and banging for a good five minutes, Jim looked for a way inside. The door was locked and the curtains drawn over the windows. Several editions of *The Wall Street Journal* made a pile to the side of the door. No sound came from within.

He tried the apartment next door. After a few moments, a brunette who appeared to be in her early twenties came to the door. She wore a beer t-shirt and cut-off jeans. Her perfume? Eau of cigarette smoke.

"I'm Jim Dorman." Jim shook the girl's limp hand. What was it with girls and weak handshakes? "Seen your neighbor, Noel Wannamaker?"

She stepped out onto the stoop. "What's he done?"

"Just need to talk to him and he doesn't answer his phone or door."

Shaking her head, she said, "It's been days. But he always kept to himself anyway during the week. Like he had something to do in the evenings—study maybe?"

"What about the weekends?"

She tugged at a cuticle. "We'd see him sometimes. We have this residents' group and sometimes he'll come to the parties for a little while. You think something's wrong with him?"

"I don't know. Did he have a roommate?"

"Not that I know of. He had a girl live with him for a few weeks once, but it didn't work out."

"Did he get many visitors?"

"No more than anyone else. Why? He dealing drugs or something?"

Jim laughed. "Nah. Just wondering. So, there wasn't anything weird or unusual going on with him?"

"No. Sorry. You might check with the office."

"Would you have noticed if he'd moved out in the last week or so?"

Shrugging, she said, "I don't know why not. I'm usually here."

"And you didn't?"

"Nope."

"Okay. So, where's the office?"

"On the other side of the complex in the corner. You won't have a problem finding it. There are signs everywhere."

Maybe she never had a problem finding it, but there were no signs and Jim felt like he was walking around in circles after about ten minutes. No thanks to a number of young people who couldn't be bothered when he attempted to stop them for directions, Jim finally found the management office after he'd broken a sweat. He was pretty angry with himself for not getting his car out and driving around. The trees that shaded the place couldn't do enough to keep the summer heat out.

The office was in an apartment in the corner of the complex facing the road, no view at all, farthest from any activity centers. Gargantua, with the face of a gargoyle, staffed it. He looked like he'd spent too many football seasons in the middle of the pileup.

His nose had scars that could only be from it being rearranged several times. There were scars where other people had regular skin. His eyebrows had white spaces between the hairs. His lips had a few fat, white lines running vertically down them. But there was something about his build that said football player, not thug.

Gargantua's greatest asset was his youth and his biceps, but it didn't hurt that he had a couple of college-aged girls hanging off each arm. The guy wore a muscle shirt and a pair of walking shorts. Somehow Jim didn't think a thug would be running an apartment complex for college kids with rich parents, because clearly that's what they were. Austin, San Antonio, Kerrville, and San Marcos were all within driving distance of Angeles. Each town had at least one college or university. Jim's recollection was that kids these days lived off-campus first chance they got.

He turned out not to be the most incredibly intelligent person Jim had ever met, which explained why he wasn't working for Dell during his summers off. He was nice enough. Jim introduced himself once more, but he didn't even think about offering his hand. Gargantua was a bone crusher if he'd ever seen one. "I'm looking for a guy named Noel Wannamaker."

"What'd he do?" Gargantua dropped into his official chair behind his official desk and began shuffling papers. The two girls just sort of hung around his shoulders like trained pigeons.

"Nothing. Does he have to have done something for me to be able to talk to him?"

"Nah." The big G smiled, but his teeth didn't look quite right. Like maybe they weren't all the ones God gave him at age six.

"Does he still live here?"

"He lived here?"

"You don't know?"

He shook his head. "Should I?"

"Would you check?" Jim wondered if he even had the correct address. It seemed conceivable Mrs. Peterson had written it down wrong. It was still inconceivable to Jim that Noel made enough money at the courthouse to pay the rent on an apartment that overlooked the Colorado River. Then the thought occurred to Jim that perhaps Noel's parents subsidized him, as well. Unless someone else . . .

The big G turned to a computer and monitor that were strategically placed on a credenza behind his desk and with his pointer finger, hit a key on the keyboard. Then another one. Then he turned back to Jim. "What did you say his name was?"

"Wannamaker. Noel Wannamaker."

"How do you spell that?"

"W-a-n-n-a-m-a-k-e-r."

"Slow down." He tapped on the keys with his pointer, but he had to find them first. "Okay. Go on."

"Maker. M-A-K-E-R."

Gargantua finished tapping it out and focused all his attention on the screen for a few moments. "Apartment two-fourteen."

Jim cleared his throat. "Yes."

He turned back to Jim. "So, what did you want?"

"Does he still live here?"

Glancing at the screen, he ran his finger over the words until he spotted something. "Computer says yes. His lease runs out September first."

"So, he hasn't given his notice."

"Nah. It would say so right here." He spun around in his chair and ran his finger across the screen. "Nah. It doesn't say so."

"Could he have left without telling anyone?"

"You mean like in the middle of the night?"

"Precisely."

"Yup, I guess so. But like, why would he want to do that?"

Jim shrugged. "I don't know. But he hasn't been seen lately."

"Who says?"

"Girl who lives next door. Does your record show what kind of car he drives?"

Gargantua checked his computer screen again. "Yup. Toyota."

"Could we check his parking space and see if it's there?"

Gargantua stood up and came around the desk. "You think something funny is going on with this fella, huh? Like, who are you anyway?" He towered over Jim. The thought crossed Jim's mind that he could probably crush Jim between his palms like biscuit dough.

Jim didn't see any reason not to be honest with the big lug. He probably wouldn't get it straight if he had to repeat it anyway. "A reporter. I'm doing a story and Noel was helping me. Then suddenly he quit his job and supposedly left town."

"Like on TV, huh?"

"Yep," Jim said. "Like on TV. Hey, if we're going to go looking for his car, you want to look at his apartment, too?"

Gargantua gave Jim a sideways look.

"I mean since I've been told he left town and all, you probably ought to see if he cleaned out his apartment and stiffed you for the rest of the rent."

"Yeah, right." He went over to a closet door and pulled it open. There were hooks for spare keys for every apartment on the inside of the door and on the inside of the three walls of the closet. Plus, there was a portable key maker on a platform in the middle of the walk-in closet. A convenient operation. Jim wondered how much they charged for making new keys. Probably ten or twenty bucks a pop.

Gargantua's pointer followed the numbers until it came to two-fourteen. Then he grabbed the key, slammed the door, and beckoned at Jim and the girls to follow him. As they left the office, he locked the door and turned the sign over, changing the clock until it said, 'Back at 3:00.'

"So, you play football, son?" Jim asked as they walked side-by-side. The two girls hung back behind them, talking and giggling between themselves.

"Used to, for Texas."

"What happened?"

"Flunked out last fall. After the season. Going back this fall."

"That why you work here?"

"Yeah. Had to do something. Going to junior college. Work here. They have a weight room. Stay in shape."

"Good idea. Junior college got your grades up?"

"Yup. Even made two Bs." He grinned, his teeth an unnatural white. He stopped and held out his hand. "My name's Howard."

Jim stopped and grinned back at the big boy. "Jim Dorman." He started to shake Howard's hand, but said, "Promise not to hurt me?"

Howard flashed a smile again. "I promise."

Jim shook his hand, and they started walking again. Howard slapped Jim on the back causing him to quickly take a couple of steps forward. What was it with large men and slaps on the back. Apparently as common as women's wimpy handshakes.

"So, you're a reporter for who?"

"Used to be for the Angeles Evening Times until they folded last year. Now I free-lance." Jim wanted to tell him about his job prospects, but knew the giant was just making an effort to be polite.

"Free-lance. That's what?"

"Where you try to sell articles to all different kinds of places."

Howard nodded as if he understood.

"So, what was this guy Noel helping you with?"

"Child support story.

"Hey." He clapped Jim on the back again. "My daddy used to pay child support." Howard sounded like he thought that deserved a medal.

"So, you know what I'm talking about."

"Yeah. My daddy used to send my mama fifteen dollars each and every week. 'Like clockwork', she said."

Jim swallowed a snort. He wasn't about to say anything to dispel the image in this moron's mind that his father was some kind of hero for paying regularly. "What I'm writing about is why some men don't pay their support."

"Nah. I saw something about that on TV."

"Well, that's what I'm writing about." Enough explanation. It probably wouldn't do any good to explain any further. They were near Noel's apartment. "You see Wannamaker's car anywhere?"

Howard stepped off the curb and began examining parking space numbers. It was not apparent exactly how they were arranged so Jim just followed Howard until he came to a Toyota. The space number was not two-fourteen, but it was a Toyota.

"This is it."

"How do you know?" Jim looked up and down the rows. There were several Toyotas.

"We have a system so the public don't know which car belongs to what apartment. You're the public, so I can't tell you, but this is Noel Wannamaker's car."

"Okay." So, why was it there if Noel wasn't? Jim's gut told him something was wrong. He stared at the blue Camry. Nice car. He circled it. No unusual dents or anything of a suspicious nature. Nothing resting on the seats. No newspapers, no magazines, no sunglasses.

Was the odor Jim thought he smelled coming from the car or the dumpster sitting two spaces away. He looked at Howard, but Howard apparently didn't notice anything unusual. Maybe football had cost him his sense of smell. "So, you think we should open his apartment since his car is here, Howard?"

Howard nodded his bowling-ball head. "You think something is wrong with him, don't you?"

"I'm starting to get that feeling. Maybe we ought to call the police."

"Let's open the apartment first, Jim." Howard pressed his lips together. "The police'll just get pissed if there's no body in the apartment."

"Okay. But, remember, it was your idea."

"Huh? That's okay. I'm the apartment manager. I'll tell the cops that, too. My decision." With that, he started for Noel's apartment. Jim and the two girls formed a parade after him.

Howard shoved the key in and threw the door open. The air-conditioning was on full blast, but all the curtains were drawn so the apartment was cold and dim. It smelled like the inside of an almost empty refrigerator. They stepped inside, closed the door behind them, and turned on the light.

Someone had tossed the apartment in the worst way. Except for the blinds and the curtains, it was a shambles, torn to pieces. They had pulled the stuffing out of the cushions and turned the sofa upside down. The liner hung over the side. Coffee table drawers had been emptied out or else were hanging open with their contents scattered.

Jim and Howard looked around for moment. The girls squealed. "Now, we'll call the police?" Jim glanced up at Howard to see if there was a meeting of the minds.

When Howard nodded, Jim said, "Don't touch anything." He went next door to use the phone. The brown-haired woman let him in and left the door open. Smoke circled in the air like buzzards. Dirty ashtrays overflowed. But Jim appreciated the loan of the phone and wished all the more that he had his cell phone back. Soon, he told himself. Just as soon as he got a job.

Remembering the slight odor coming from the car or the dumpster, he told the police dispatcher he thought someone should be sent out who could open a trunk. Thanking the brunette, he went back to Noel's apartment.

Howard stood on the sidewalk with the girls, telling them that they had to go on to the river without him. They were practically begging to wait and see what was going to happen next. He was resisting but not doing a very good job. For just a moment, Jim wondered what it would have been like to be a guy like Howard but pushed that thought away. Brains over brawn.

He went into the apartment and looked into each room more thoroughly. He knew that even his shoes could contaminate the scene, but the investigative reporter in him wouldn't allow him to stand on the sidelines when he had the opportunity to examine the premises. The mess was of equal proportions.

It was a two-bedroom. The smaller of the two was set up as an office. Without touching anything, Jim could see that Noel must have been a college student and attended at night. Textbooks lay on the floor; the bookshelves having been emptied by the searcher. Sheets of notebook paper had settled on the carpet like large snowflakes. Again, drawers stood open. Whatever they were looking for, Jim wondered if they had found it.

The laptop computer was on, the screensaver photographs stopping for a couple of seconds before moving on, pictures of people, hills, Texas flowers, and the river. Jim couldn't resist tapping on the spacebar to bring the screen up, but he used a pen so he wouldn't smudge any fingerprints or leave any of his own. The screen that came up was blank, a new document page.

Jim quickly clicked on the open file icon so that he could see a list of files. Noel had worked in Word; so did Jim. Nothing came up. No USB in the side slot. Whoever had been there knew something about computers. Quickly glancing around, Jim could see nothing indicating he'd backed up his computer either.

After giving the remainder of the apartment the once over, Jim went outside to wait for the police. The Angeles Police Department's finest arrived sans sirens about a quarter of an hour later. The girls had finally succumbed to Howard's orders and left. Howard and Jim sat on the concrete parking space barrier for the space right in front of Noel's apartment. In spite of the fact the sun was on the downward side, it was still midafternoon in the Texas hill country and that meant the weather was still searingly hot. He didn't know who gave off worse body odor, he or Howard. Sweat ran in rivulets down Howard's face. The only time Jim had seen that kind of sweat was in a reporter friend of his who was an avid beer drinker. Howard must be one, too. Jim was no slouch in the sweat department; it just flowed a lot more slowly.

Howard didn't say anything about the few minutes Jim had spent in Noel's apartment. Neither did he seem to want to go inside himself. As dumb as Howard appeared, he seemed to know that the police wouldn't want him stepping all over Noel's stuff or sitting on his furniture. So, there they were. Jim didn't tell Howard of his suspicions about the trunk. The police pulled up. Both Howard and Jim identified themselves. They were separated for interrogation after the cops did a walk-through of the apartment.

A Sergeant Ivan Denholt interviewed Jim. He was a thin, balding, bespectacled white fellow who was almost as tall as Howard. A short, stocky, black fellow who seemed to recognize Howard from the football rosters took Howard aside. Jim didn't catch his name, but thought that the man seemed almost pleased to be able to spend some time with Howard.

Denholt took Jim over to his police car, which he had left running, and took the basic information from inside where it was cool.

"Who called this in?" Denholt was a detective, Jim concluded, because he wore regular clothes: a coat and tie.

"Me. Howard had a couple of friends with him but I told them not to touch anything."

"How is it that you know the guy that lives in this apartment?"

"From the courthouse. Met him at the district clerk's office."

"So, what are you doing out here?"

"Looking to talk to him."

"About?"

"A story about child support."

Denholt scratched his ear. "For?"

"I free-lance. I've got several feelers out."

"This don't add up.'

"Sure it does." Jim didn't want to have to tell Denholt anything he suspected. After all, he didn't have any evidence of wrongdoing by anyone connected to the courthouse. All he had was a dead Mr. Johnson—from a traffic accident—and a list of names from Noel, which he didn't know what were, except for Mr. Johnson's. There just wasn't any more than that. To tell Denholt anything would be to bring a lot of problems onto himself. Maybe when he had more to tell he could get back with Denholt.

"You're writing an article for some unknown rag, you come out to interview this kid, he's not there, and his apartment has been ransacked. Tell me how that adds up."

"I went to see his boss—well, his supervisor to interview her. I just happened to mention him to this girl who works the counter, Donna-something, and she told me that he hadn't shown up for work since I was in court last week. Then I asked his supervisor, and she said he quit. So, since I'm doing this article from a man's point of view, I thought I'd get a man's point of view on the man's point of view. I already got his female supervisor's and the female judge's points of view on it."

"So, you couldn't call him."

"Didn't think of it." Jim tried to think of some way to tell Denholt his suspicions about Noel's car. "Didn't have his number."

"Are you sure you aren't working on anything else?"

"Like what?"

"I'm asking the questions."

"Look, Sergeant, I'm just trying to make a living."

"There's something I don't like about all this. You say this girl says he hasn't been seen since when?"

"Last week? Thursday, I believe, or maybe, Friday. Her supervisor said he called in and quit, I think it was on Monday."

"If he'd left town, he would have taken his stuff with him. His suitcases, his papers."

Jim grimaced and said, "His car."

Denholt rolled his eyes. "Yeah, right. Did you tell the dispatcher something about a trunk?"

"Sergeant, maybe it's just me, but I think there is something in Noel Wannamaker's trunk that ought to be checked out."

"Next you'll be telling me that you think it's Noel Wanna-maker." Denholt glared at Jim and heaved a deep sigh. He dropped his notebook into his jacket pocket and reached for his cruiser's door handle before looking at Jim. "I don't believe it."

Jim raised his eyebrows. "I don't want to believe it."

"You stick around." He pointed his forefinger at Jim's chest.

Jim nodded and remained in the back seat waiting for the sergeant. He didn't have to be there when the trunk was flung open. He didn't have to have the horrific odor of rotting flesh slap him in the face. The last decomposing body Jim had seen made him throw up and gave him night sweats for months afterward. There was a reason Jim hadn't gone into the medical field. He didn't have the stomach for it.

Nope. Jim would wait and get the word from the sergeant. It was cool in the cop's car and there was no reason he couldn't wait there for confirmation. He could think of other things. Listen to calls that came over the radio. Think about Patty and their future. Wonder whether Patty had caught hint of any wrongdoing in the WiNGS group. Jim couldn't help it. It came back to them. No matter what else came up, there was just something about that group.

It didn't take long for Denholt to return for further questioning. Noel Wannamaker wouldn't be making a statement.

FOURTEEN

"Okay, Dorman," Sergeant Denholt said in a voice that sounded weary of his routine. "You might as well get comfortable." After shedding his jacket and loosening his tie, the sergeant plopped at a worn gunmetal gray desk and faced an outdated computer screen. Files sat in stacks. His in-box overflowed. He rifled the center desk drawer and came up with a password and tapped on the keyboard.

Jim perched on an adjacent chair and leaned on his elbow. Desks were jammed up against other desks. Computer terminals rested on the corners of each. Few people occupied the room. The cool air smelled stale but was a vast improvement from the days when every cop smoked and thick air reeked from it.

"Want some coffee?" Denholt asked after he'd typed in Jim's name and address. "I'm not too fast with this thing so we might as well."

"Sure," Jim said, glancing around the room. Nothing else much had changed since he had the police beat years earlier.

Denholt walked to the back and returned with two Styrofoam cups with stir-sticks poking out. "I didn't know what you took so I brought some sugar. Okay?"

"Fine," Jim shook out the packet and stirred his coffee. Bitter even with the sugar, the hot substance was still welcome after a long afternoon. He sat back in the beat-up chair and crossed one ankle over the other knee, ready to deflect all questions.

Denholt slurped his coffee and placed it on a cardboard coaster bearing a beer emblem, the kind they put out in bars. "Okay. Got your name and address. And you used to be a reporter. I do remember your face from snooping around here." He smirked. "Let me put the vic's name here." He typed a bit. "And the address and the time. Okay."

Jim didn't say anything. He didn't trust anyone. Until he had something more than an uneasiness, some concrete evidence to show the police, he was keeping his suspicions—which he had not quite articulated anyway—to himself.

"So, you said you're writing a piece about child support. Why?"

Same old annoying question, like a mosquito around the bed in the middle of the night. No one had sympathy for people who had problems paying their support. No one. He met the sergeant's eyes. "Trying to make a few bucks so I can pay my own. Since the paper closed, I've been living off unemployment and it's about to run out."

"So, you've got kids?"

"Two. Obviously, they live with my ex-wife." That sounded kind of snide, even to Jim's ears. He shrugged and glanced around the room to see if anyone was in hearing distance.

"Obviously. If you're the one paying support. I pay, myself. Well, the Attorney General takes it out of my check every week."

"Used to come out of mine. Now I just wish I had a paycheck for it to come out of."

"Okay. So, you got some kind of hare-brained idea of writing about child support, and you said you already talked to the judge and a woman who works up at the district clerk's office at the courthouse."

"Right. And this young man, the dead guy, Noel Wannamaker, used to be the only male who worked in that office. I had seen him when I went in there occasionally."

Denholt scratched at his cowlick. "And you said you're writing this article from the man's side, right? And you wanted a man's view of a man's side?"

"That's right. I've never seen the man's viewpoint anywhere. Or, I should say the person who pays the support. But usually the man, right? Even though these days more men have their children live with them than they used to."

"Okay. You're confusing the issue." He sipped from his cup again. "Let's stick to the facts." He pulled his tie looser and unbuttoned the top two buttons of his dress shirt even though the air-conditioning was on in the building.

"Sorry. Don't want to confuse you."

"Uh-huh. So, you go to the district clerk's office, and some girl tells you—"

"Donna."

"Donna tells you that Noel quit. So, it don't make sense that you go out to his apartment."

"Mrs. Peterson said—"

"That's the supervisor?"

"Yes. She said he called in and quit. I thought I could catch him before he moved out of town."

"She said he called in and said he was moving out of town?"

"Right. So, I thought I'd try to talk to him at his apartment where he'd be more comfortable talking about the issue of child support anyway."

"And you got the address and went out there and talked that football player into letting you inside Wannamaker's apartment" Denholt had accusing eyes.

"Well, after the girl next door said she hadn't seen him recently. I thought they'd know in the office if he'd already moved. But he hadn't given notice. So, I suggested we go look at his apartment."

Denholt smiled, but it wasn't a pretty sight. "You suggested—it was that important to you."

Jim edged his Styrofoam cup with his thumbnail. "Well, I guess I've got a nose for something that isn't quite right."

"Wouldn't surprise me. So, when the door was opened, you could see that something wasn't quite right."

"Yes, sir, Sergeant Denholt, and at that point I suggested we call the police and went next door and did so."

"And the car? How was it you were sniffing around the trunk of Wannamaker's car?"

Jim realized then that Denholt might not be as slow on the uptake as he thought. He finished off his coffee and looked at the man, trying to decide whether he should say anything about the WiNGS group and what he thought they were doing. God, it sounded so far-fetched when he even thought about it. A bunch of housewives involved in questionable activities.

He couldn't tell Sergeant Denholt definitively what he suspected. It all didn't add up. Yet. He looked him over. He looked like a decent sort. Classic cop. Just doing his job. "I just thought I'd ask Howard if Noel Wannamaker's car was in the lot. Howard looked up the space and when we walked over to the apartment, there it was."

"Uh-huh." Denbolt stared at Jim as he sipped his coffee.

Jim's knee started bouncing up and down as it seemed to

do more frequently, lately. He put one hand on it as if to hold it down. "God's honest truth, Sergeant."

"So, you expect me to believe that you don't know anything else about this guy's obvious murder—since people don't often crawl into their trunks to die except when writers put them there—other than what you've told me?"

Jim's stomach felt like acid dripped into from a leaky faucet. "If I knew who killed him, Sergeant, believe me, I would tell you."

Denholt got up from his computer, crossed the room to a printer, and returned with a paper. "Sign here at the bottom after reading over your statement." He spoke in a monotone as he stood over Jim. His perspiration smell hadn't quite reached sweat sock level.

Jim read over it, signed it, and handed it back. "Can I get a copy?"

"What for? It'll be on file here."

"Sergeant—"

"Okay. Just a minute." He walked back to a copier and returned with a copy of the whole report. "Want to be able to keep straight what you told me, right?"

Jim stood. They were about the same height, but Jim didn't weigh nearly the same. "Am I a suspect? Is there some reason that you think I'm trying to hide something from you, Sergeant Denholt?"

"Oh, no, of course not, Mr. Dorman. No reason to suspect you of anything. Just take your copy and get out of here. Okay?"

"Okay," Jim said, parroting the sergeant. "Thanks for the coffee."

It was after six by the time he got out of there. The summer sun still cooked everything under it. The country grasses were brown. No flowers bloomed by the side of the road. The drought caused even the bull nettle to shrivel up to a fraction of the size of its pesky self.

Jim drove back to his own place and removed his tie. He settled onto a bar stool with one of his generic beers. Someday soon he hoped he'd be able to buy a name brand. He hoped he'd even be able to have a liquor cabinet with bottles of bourbon, rum, and scotch. He wondered if regular poor people—those who grew up really poor—thought about stuff like that. Television exposed them what they were missing out on.

Then he got to wondering whether a person with a TV was really a poor person. What did it take in America to be considered poor? No car. No telephone. Utilities cut off. Empty refrigerator. That line of thought would get him nowhere. He draped his tie and jacket over the back of a chair and guzzled the beer.

Finally, like a punctuation mark, he reached for the answering machine and punched a button, both anticipating and dreading the news the flashing red light might bring.

"Jim Dorman, Edgar Buck. You know who I'm with. Call me back if you get in before five-thirty."

An adrenaline thrill rushed through him. The call he'd been waiting for. Just his luck he wasn't home to answer it. The time was well past five-thirty. The next twelve hours would drag like a slow-motion movie. His hands quivered as he reached for his beer. A swallow for courage. To buck up.

But it had to be good news. No one ever said call back if it was bad news, right? Edgar would have had someone else call him and tell him he didn't get the job. Or he would have received a letter in the mail. Or nothing at all—people weren't very polite lately, they might not let him know at all. His chest inflated with a combination of glee and fear. But nothing he could do about it except wait until the morning.

"Jimmy, there's something I need to wa—talk to you

about. Please call me before you go to bed." Pat's voice. Something didn't sound right.

Jim pressed the stop button on the recorder and replayed the tape. He heard Edgar Buck, then Patty again. Her voice was high-pitched. Not screeching, but it seemed to him that she sounded stressed. He let the machine continue playing. He'd return the call in a few minutes.

"James, this is Caulfield Marshall. Your agent in case you forgot. Just like you forgot to call me today. I've got something that needs discussing as soon as you can get back to me."

Jim winced and gritted his teeth. What a day to be out.

"Mr. Dorman, you're going to have to pay your rent by this Friday or I'm starting eviction proceedings. The owner said he can't give you more time."

"End of messages." There was a click and his machine stopped. He called Pat.

"Hello." It was Patrick.

"Hi, son. Is Mom home?"

"She's at a meeting that came up all of a sudden, Dad."

He didn't like the sound of that. "Uh, well, did she say what time she'd be back? She didn't leave you kids home alone, did she?"

"Nah. We've got a babysitter. Don't you think I'm too old for a babysitter?"

Jim didn't want to upset Patrick, but with all the crap that went on in the world, he didn't think any child was too old for a sitter.

"You may be, son, but your sister certainly still needs one. Bear with Mommy. She's just trying to do what she thinks is best."

Patrick sighed. "Yeah, but I don't like some girl telling me what to do."

"I know." Just wait until you get married. "Did she say what time she'd be coming home?"

"Naw. She didn't say anything. She just got off the telephone and said she had to go someplace. Then she called Angie to come stay with us. She acted like she was mad but said she wasn't."

Jim really wanted to have a talk with her. Did she know Noel Wannamaker? What he really wondered was whether she was involved in something wrong. He hated to even think about it. His stomach roiled at the thought. He started to hang up and then remembered Patrick was on the other end of the line.

"So, did you have a nice day, son?"

"Dad, what's going on? I know you and Mom are cooking something up. I just don't know what it is. Are you going to tell us?"

"I don't want to lie to you, Patrick. I promised Mommy I'd let her tell you in her own way. It'll be soon, I can tell you that."

"Aw, Dad. Why can't you tell me?"

"You know why."

"Yeah. We don't break our promises. Our word is our bond."

"Good boy. Got to go now, son. Kiss your sister for me." Jim knew that would get a reaction out of him.

"Yuk. Kiss my sister?"

Jim laughed. "See you soon. Goodbye." He hung up and took another slug of his beer. It was going to be a totally boring evening. He would be left alone with his thoughts, a state which he wasn't sure he wanted. What he wanted was company. There had been too much time alone over the last eighteen months. Too many hours with no wife, no kids, and no job, and lately not even any friends.

He picked up the phone and called Ethan Hale, letting the

phone ring over ten times. Not even an answering machine picked up, much less voice mail. He put the phone down and went around the bar into the kitchen. If he whipped up some dinner and ate it in front of the TV, he could probably use up an hour. The rest of the evening he could spend writing. Even if he only wrote two pages a night his next book would eventually get written. The other thing he could do was go to bed early. Anything to avoid looking the facts of the child support thing in the face. Avoid the building distrust of Pat that he felt in his gut. Avoid finding out what the names Noel had given him meant.

Jim pulled the now wadded piece of paper from his pocket. Unfolding it, he stared at the names for probably the hundredth time. Who were those people and what did they have to do with WINGS and Mr. Johnson?

It was simple enough to call them and find out. His hand shook again as he got out the telephone book to look up the first name. He berated himself, told himself that he was a coward, that he had to follow up on this thing. Studying the telephone book, he decided that since the county was comprised of many small towns, he'd go through each town alphabetically.

The third name on the list he found in the first little town in the phone book. There was a listing in the man's name. Jim sat down on the bar stool again and reached for the phone. It rang three times before it was answered.

"Madison residence," a female voice said.

"Is Mr. Madison there?"

There was an abnormally long pause.

"Hello?" Jim said.

"Uh, he's not here," the voice said.

"Well, what about Mrs. Madison?"

"She's not here either."

"When will Mr. Madison be home?"

"Can I ask who this is?"

"Jim Dorman. I'm a writer and I wanted to talk to Mr. Madison about the possibility of interviewing him for an article I'm doing. Are you the housekeeper or babysitter or something?"

"Oh—no. I'm his—their daughter. My mother is at a meeting."

"It's really your father I want," Jim said.

The girl didn't say anything again for a few moments.

"Hello," Jim said.

The girl sniffed into the phone. "Well you can't talk to him because he's dead."

Jim's body tensed and he bent over like he'd been kicked in the stomach. Just what he'd thought and didn't want to face. His tone softened. "I'm very sorry to hear that. When did it happen?"

"Last March," she said in a very quiet voice.

"Do you mind if I ask you some questions?" Call him calloused, but he had to get to the bottom of what was going on.

"What kind of questions?"

"About your father. About you and your mother."

"What for?"

"Like I said, I'm writing this magazine article. I wouldn't have to use your name if you didn't want me to. What is your name by the way?"

"Olivia."

"Olivia," Jim repeated. "That's a nice name. How old are you, Olivia?"

"Sixteen tomorrow."

"Well, happy birthday, sweet sixteen. I have a daughter, but she's only eight."

Olivia didn't say anything.

"Would you mind answering some questions, Olivia?" Jim asked again.

"Depends on what they are."

"That's fair. I wasn't going to ask you about your love life or anything like that."

Olivia snickered. Jim thought it had a tinkling sound, like crystal.

"Okay. Here goes. How long had your parents been married when your father passed away?"

"Um. They weren't. They got divorced when I was little. Two, I think."

"But they were living together as if they were husband and wife?"

"No, sir." She whispered, "My mother hated my father."

"Is someone there with you?"

"No, sir."

"Okay, so how come when I called your father's number, you answered?"

"My dad willed it to me. This house. My mother is what they call my guardian of my estate."

"Oh. So, you and your mother are living there now?"

"Since about a month after he died. I don't like it here. I want my mother to move, but she won't. I want to go back to school with my friends again."

"Did you say that your mother is at a meeting?"

"Yeah. A WiNGS thing. Do you know about that?"

Jim couldn't get his breath for just a moment. His chest constricted. "Yeah, I've heard of it. Do you know when she'll be home?"

"No, sir. It's not a regular meeting. She left in a hurry and didn't say when she'd be back. Want me to write down your name and phone number for her?"

Shaking his head as if the girl could see him, Jim said, "I'll get back with her, Olivia. Listen, can I ask you one more thing?"

"Depends."

Jim smiled at the phone. "Okay. If you wouldn't mind—I mean, I realize that it's probably hard for you to talk about, but just how did your father die?"

"Car wreck off the side of a hill." She sighed. "They say it rolled—and then blew up before he could get out."

Jim opened his mouth to reply but his voice didn't cooperate. After a moment, he cleared his throat. "I'm very sorry, Olivia. I know this has been difficult for you."

"It's okay. I really didn't know my father that well."

"Well, I appreciate you talking to me."

"That's all right. I've got to go now, Mr. Dorman," the girl said and hung up.

Jim didn't feel good about things in general—the child support thing specifically. He fetched another beer from the refrigerator and began searching the telephone book for one of the other names. He found another of the men's and dialed it.

"Hello." A woman's voice.

"Mr. Wink, please," Jim said.

"Who's calling?" A monotone.

"My name's Dorman." Jim hesitated to say that he was a reporter. "I'm a writer."

The telephone clicked and he got a dial tone. Jim looked at the phone and redialed. He'd give her the benefit of the doubt. Surely it was an accident.

"This is Jim Dorman," he said when the voice answered. "We got disconnected."

The phone clicked and he got a dial tone again.

Jim took another swig of his beer. He wanted to get drunk. Checking off the two names, Jim began searching for the other two and hoping he wouldn't find them. But he did. He dialed the phone a third time. It was answered almost immediately.

"Yes, hello." Another woman's voice. "May I speak to Mr. Clark please?"

"This is Mrs. Clark. May I help you?"

"You mean the ex or the former Mrs. Clark?"

"No. Elizabeth Clark. I was the current Mrs. Clark, if it's any of your business. Who is this anyway?"

"Jim Dorman. I'm a journalist and I wanted to interview your husband for a series of articles I'm doing."

"Oh. I thought maybe you were a salesman or a lawyer. I'm sick and tired of them calling me."

"No. I'm a writer."

"I think they call everyone whose husband's or wife's name appears in the obituaries. It makes me so mad. They think they can make money off of me, but it ain't gonna happen. I tell them to call his ex. She's the one with all the loot."

Jim found himself feeling not the least bit surprised by the revelation of Mr. Clark's demise. This was obviously what Noel had wanted him to know. "Yes, ma'am. You mean they are soliciting your business?" He felt sick at the thought.

"Yes. The crumbs. They ought to be put out of business."

"And I guess you didn't get anything under his will?"

"Will? What a joke. We didn't have nothing to say grace over. His life insurance had to go to them kids—his divorce papers say so."

"Did the two of you have children, Mrs. Clark?"

"Nah. I didn't feel like it was right when he couldn't hardly pay his child support. I got a boy by my first husband, but he never paid no support either."

"You must be having a difficult time getting by."

"Yeah. I have a cashier's job at the cafeteria down on Pinemont. You ever eat there, Mister?"

"I have. Maybe I'll see you there sometime."

"Yeah. Well, I have to go. I got to get up early in the morning."

Jim hung up and glanced at his list. There was one name left. Then he realized that he really hadn't gotten any details of Mr. Clark's demise. He thought about calling the widow back but decided against it. He was going to do research on the others anyhow. He'd just go through the microfilm at the library and look at the newspapers for Clark also.

Spending the next ten minutes poring over the phone book, he discovered Roberto Melendez's listing in Berryville. It was the tiniest town in the county, a whistle and a blink and anyone driving through would miss it altogether. It didn't have much more than an antique store and a gas pump on the public access road. He punched in Melendez's number. A recording came on. "We're sorry but the number you have dialed is no longer in service. Please check your directory and try again." Jim hung up. Why was he not surprised?

So, he'd struck out on two and hit runs on the other two.

Counting Johnson, there were three deaths. Two from traffic accidents, one unknown. Also, one disconnect—for which Jim could only surmise the cause—and one hang up. Wink. He wondered what that was all about. The name sounded familiar, but offhand, he couldn't place it.

Perhaps Noel had made a mistake on Wink. It was unlikely, but possible. Glancing at his watch, Jim saw that it was too late to get to the library that evening. He could check on the details the following day.

Rubbing his eyes, Jim felt weary and only wanted to shower and fall into bed. As he started to fold up the list Noel had given him again, his eyes came to focus on it as a whole. He'd made large Xs over each man's name when he'd discovered he was dead. There were two left. One, the phone was disconnected. The other, the hang-up. He recalled the list he'd found in Pat's purse. There were small Xs or asterisks next to several names. There were cross-outs over others. Was it just his imagination or had they crossed out the same ones? And just why had there been a small x next to his? Jim got up to go to bed. But he didn't think he was going to get much sleep that night.

CHAPTER

FIFTEEN

J im awoke from a nightmare that five seconds later he couldn't remember. All he knew was there seemed to be something terrifyingly close to home about it. When he became focused, he realized the sun had been up for quite a while. The bogey man hadn't caught him. Time to get up. Get moving. Find out the good and bad news that he couldn't get the previous night.

Before falling off the night before, Jim had decided to go back to the library and do more research. He had to be there on Thursday night but didn't think he could wait that long. Besides, if got stymied, Frieda might have some ideas. He was optimistic about the calls, but pessimistic about what he expected to find in the obituaries. It had to be done. There was no way he could go off and ignore what he now felt was going on. He might move to Dallas, but he would be haunted forever by his suspicions about those men's deaths. He had to get to the truth. It wasn't in his nature to have a suspicion and not do something about it.

His stomach gnawed at him like a rat when he thought

about Patty being involved in something from which she couldn't extricate herself. Rolling toward the bedside table, he punched her number into the phone and lay back and listened as the purr of its ring went unanswered. After twenty rings, he replaced the receiver and began to study the ceiling tiles in the morning light as he had done in the darkness of the night before.

He was not a police officer. His job was not to catch anyone before, during, or after a crime. His job was not to turn anyone in. His job was to report. His job was to be unbiased, to gather facts, to write the truth.

But what if the truth was that his wife was—was what? Guilty of some sort of complicity? Involved with some unscrupulous women? Could she be implicated in the demise of any of those men whose names appeared on the list? That was a nice way of putting it, but Jim wasn't ready to say the 'M' word aloud or even admit his real suspicions.

He reassured himself with the thought that she hadn't even been a member of WiNGS the previous March. She couldn't have been involved in anything having to do with Mr. Madison. But what of Quincy Clark and the others—Melendez and Wink? What about Albert Johnson who had died after the first time Jim had gone to court? And Noel Wannamaker who seemed to have just worked in the wrong place? Could Pat have been involved somehow? It was inconceivable to him, but could they have enticed her into their fold, these women? Could they have gotten her help in their deadly business? In their conspiracy? And what was her ongoing involvement with those people?

Jim stumbled out of bed and down the stairs to the kitchen. Filling the coffee-maker, he tried to busy himself with fixing breakfast to get his mind off Pat. It wasn't working well. Tuning his radio to a news station, he tried to pay attention to what the newscaster said, but it became background noise to the wanderings of his mind. What had Patty started to say on the answering machine the evening before? Why had her voice sounded strident? And where was she this morning at—he glanced at the clock on the stove—nine-thirty? She wasn't teaching summer school. God, how had he slept so long?

When the coffee carafe was filled, he poured himself a cup and chewed on a slice of toast with a smear of marmalade on it. Although his stomach was queasy, Jim knew he needed to put something in it. He might as well have been eating cardboard; he couldn't taste anything.

He was weak—literally weak—sick with fear for Pat. Where was she and what she was up to? And was she really capable of what he suspected her of doing? He tried not to think past that. He wasn't sure if his psyche had prepared him adequately to face other complications of her involvement— other possibilities, perhaps even—no, he wouldn't even think it.

Jim tried to keep his mind on his double career as a writer and investigative reporter as he showered, shaved, and dressed before calling Edgar Buck and Caulfield Marshall. Those preparations were a ritual he'd gotten into after he'd lost his job. He always got up and dressed just like he was actually going off to work, except his clothes no longer came out of dry cleaners' bags. He would settle in front of his computer or at the telephone as if he were in a real office. Somehow it kept his spirits up. Made him feel more professional. Somehow, he couldn't see himself returning Edgar Buck's phone call while standing next to his telephone in his jockey shorts. Besides there was a delicious taste of anticipation in his heart that Buck was going to offer the job. He wanted to enjoy the anticipation a little while longer.

"Congratulations, Jim-Boy," Buck said in a hearty voice

when he came on the line. "We're prepared to offer you the job at the salary we discussed, plus moving expenses."

Pleasure flowed through his body like the warmth from a strong alcoholic drink. His knees weakened. He' sank to the easy chair. "I'm really pleased, Mr. Buck. I was hoping that's what you called for. When do you want me to start?"

"You name it. We could use you today if we had you. How about August first?"

"Can I let you know in a few days? I mean, exactly when I'll arrive?" And whether he'd be taking Pat and the kids with him.

"Sure—by Friday?"

"I definitely want the job, Mr. Buck, but there are some other considerations.

"Call me Edgar, Son. And I understood that. Just talk it over with whomever you need to and let me know. Oh, and Jimbo—we can also go the expenses for a trip up here to look for a house, maybe even a couple of trips. How does that sound?"

"Great. I'll call you back as soon as I can and let you know a good start date." Jim hung up. He had mixed emotions. Elated at his success in snaring the job, his excitement was overshadowed by his fear of Pat's involvement in that WiNGS thing. A dark cloud floated over his head, overshadowing his joy, ready to burst any moment.

If he could just grab Pat and the kids and get out of town, everything would be fine. They could buy a nice house in a Dallas suburb. Enroll the kids in a private school. Pat wouldn't have to worry about finding a teaching job.

The more he thought about it, the more absurd it was that Pat could be involved in anything sinister. She was a schoolteacher for heaven's sake. Sure, she was on the board of WiNGS, but no one in their right mind would let someone waltz in and become wise to their criminal activity after just a few weeks, if in fact there was criminal activity. In the light of day, it all seemed rather absurd. Jim laughed at himself.

No. He realized that it was just the dark of the night that made him so suspicious of Pat. That and the bad dream. Jim chuckled at the ridiculousness of his thoughts. What he needed was a celebration. And who he needed to celebrate with was his wife. He picked up the phone and called her again. There was still no answer.

The phone rang before he'd let go of it good, startling him. He needed to quit being so jumpy. He drew a long breath and picked up the telephone with a shaking hand.

"Hello." His voice sounded as weak and worried as he felt.

"Where the heck have you been, James?" Caulfield Marshall shouted into the phone.

Jim had been impressed with Caulfield as an agent from the start, except for one thing. Caulfield seemed to believe that no one could hear him unless he shouted. At least that was the impression Jim got from the telephone conversations they'd had. Jim hadn't met him in person. He had, however, been involved in long distance discussions with Caulfield where he'd had to hold the phone away from his ear to understand what the man was saying. And he'd heard Marshall shout to people in his office when he was on the phone with Jim. So, Jim believed, the man was either deaf or an eccentric. Jim suspected a little of both.

"Hi. Caulfield. What's up?" Jim's voice trembled. He hoped Marshall couldn't tell how nervous he felt. "Sorry I didn't call you back yesterday, but I didn't get in until late. I don't have but the one number on you. I've been applying for jobs down here and working on a magazine article so I'm out a lot

"Hey, chill, Pal. I have a contract on your book if you want to shut up long enough for me to tell you about it."

Heart palpitations and shortness of breath kept Jim from

responding with more than just a grunted, "Go ahead." Weird how things happened in clusters. Go for weeks, months feeling like a piece of dog turd and then all the hard work paid off at the same time. He felt just the way he thought he would. Way far from dog turd. Now. Beyond belief. Jim listened to what Marshall said but later could not recall half the conversation. What it amounted to was that a highly reputable publisher had made an offer. The advance was not as high as Marshall had wanted but wasn't bad, way more that Jim had thought he'd get for a first novel. It was in what Marshall called the medium range. The contract, though, was for two books and, of course, Caulfield said, options on the third. If the hard cover did well, they reserved the right to handle the soft cover deal. And of course, the hard cover included e-book publication. Something Caulfield said they'd have to scrutinize with a magnifying glass to be sure Jim wasn't being screwed.

Jim wanted to hang up and call Pat again. He wished Caulfield Marshall would shut up. The man rambled about the possibilities for a big publishing future, making references to trips Jim would have to make to New York, and generally raving about what a wonderful agent he was. They were mostly words Jim would have killed to hear a few days ago, but right then he had other things on his mind. He knew, though, that there was a certain amount of pomposity for which he'd have to give forbearance. It was Caulfield's personality. Harmless, though trying and time consuming. Ordinarily, Jim wouldn't mind. Now, he wished for an end to Caulfield's blustering pretentiousness. He found his mind wandering as he murmured uh huhs to Caulfield's monologue.

As soon as he could break loose, Jim dialed Pat's number again. There was still no answer. Should he go by the house? Could something be wrong? He could kick himself for not knowing what Pat and the kids did every summer morning if she wasn't teaching. Were the kids in day camp? He couldn't remember.

Jim gathered a notepad and pen and headed for the library. Again, Frieda stood behind the check out counter. Jim veered over toward her.

"Doing more research?" she asked. She wore a light blue short-sleeved blouse tucked into a gathered skirt. Almost prim looking, Jim thought. Her apparel didn't reveal the heart of the person inside.

"Yes. Wish I could tell you what it's about." Jim waited until the last person in line was gone. "Frieda, I got the job."

Her face softened. "Congratulations. I guess that means I'm going to lose you. Just when we were really getting to know each other, too."

"I'll be here until the first of August, anyway."

"That all? That's mighty quick." She cocked her head. "Is it a good position, Jim? Is it what you wanted?"

"Frieda, it's what I'm meant to do." He patted her arm. In such a short time, she'd become like a mother to him. "The interview I went on first would have been just a job to me. This one—well, I felt like I was home."

"I'm glad then," she said. "I'll miss you. The kids will miss you." She perched her glasses on her nose and pulled several sheets of stapled paper toward her, computer generated calendar with big squares for each day. "Wait a minute. August first. Our summer reading program will be over by then."

"Yes, barely."

"The kids have really taken a liking to you. I think it's the different voices you use for each of the characters."

Jim laughed. "I'm a frustrated actor. Listen, I really gotta run."

"See you tomorrow night then." She pushed the calendar

back under the lip of the counter and sat on a stool as he hurried away.

When he was seated before a microfilm machine, Jim pulled out his notepad with the list of names. He made his notes next to the ones he had called the night before, having finally tossed the piece of paper Wannamaker had given him. Not knowing when to start, whether any of the deaths—for he assumed all five of the men were dead—were before or after Madison's, Jim decided to begin with Madison and work his way forward. If he didn't find the others, he could always go back.

The microfilm system was simple and, with the advent of computers, outdated in most places, but worked well for the preservation of newspapers. A spool of film in excess of an inch high was threaded into the machine. The person viewing the film simply had to press a button one way to go forward or the other way to go backward to view negatives of newspapers recorded in chronological order. Holding the button down would result in weeks of newspapers flying by at a time.

Jim dropped the spool marked January 1 - March 31 onto the spindle, threaded it, and spun it up to March since that's when Olivia had said her father had died. He scanned through the newspapers until he came to a headline that said FIRE-BALL ON HILLSIDE ONE CAR ACCIDENT. On his mental score-board, he chalked up a second strike under fiery one-car accidents. Not very creative of the perpetrator or perpetrators, but effective, so far.

Just as Olivia had said, the article confirmed that Tom Madison had lost control of his truck, missed a curve, rolled down a hill, and the truck had exploded into flames, some-thing Jim thought only happened in the movies. Witnesses stated that it was too late to pull him out by the time they had arrived. There were actually no witnesses to the accident itself.

It occurred at approximately eleven at night on a poorly lit section of the farm-to-market road which included a hilly and curvy stretch of highway.

Authorities would know more after the medical examiner released his results.

It sounded unreal. A vehicle didn't really just burst into flames, did it? Had someone helped it along? He went into the restroom and splashed water on his face before taking up the next name. His eyes were blurry and ached. His head had begun to pound. Reading from those machines was one of the worst experiences of his life.

Backtracking another quarter, he popped the spool for July through September into the machine. Nothing in July, but at the end of the previous August, there it was. A very succinct article about Quincy Clark. And how his car was found in the river, with him in it. The conclusion at the time of the accident was that he'd lost control of the car, it had gone off the hill, down the hillside, perhaps rolled over once or twice, knocking him out, and ending up in the river whereupon Quincy Clark drowned.

After studying the copies of the articles for a few minutes, Jim realized there was a time pattern also. One death approximately every quarter. Quincy Clark the previous August. Roberto Melendez on the first of November. Tom Madison in March. Albert Johnson on May 15th. Approximately every three months a man died. Was that by design? Or if there were a killer or killers, were they getting braver? Had there been others earlier and at longer intervals? And why hadn't anyone ever noticed it before now?

Well, Noel did, but how about the police? Was it because each death appeared to be an accident? He knew there were a lot of one car accidents and head-on collisions in the hill country because of the road conditions, but come on. How come no one else noticed? Were they too far apart? Were people's memories too short?

Jim remembered one year when the infant mortality rate seemed higher than usual to him for their county. He had been a regular subscriber to both daily newspapers back then as opposed to now. Every day he read the obituaries, and it seemed that all too frequently there was a baby listed. After some investigation, he had discovered that the teen pregnancy rate had skyrocketed. Jim was able to write a series of articles that caused a task force to form that eventually led to the opening of a teen health clinic across the street from the high school.

Kids began to get more information on sex. Health care improved. The birth rate dropped over a period of several years, and the infant mortality rate dropped. So, why hadn't he noticed a pattern to these men's deaths? Because he didn't regularly get a paper anymore. Why hadn't anyone else noticed? He didn't know. Maybe they had. Or maybe an accidental death every three months out in the country is just not noticeable. They weren't the only deaths of men. They weren't even the only accidental deaths of men. And men weren't the only ones to die in highway accidents. Perhaps it was only a pattern because he fit it into one. But he felt sure it had to be more than coincidence.

He had one more name to go: Frederic Wink. Sighing, Jim finished the quarter he was working on and replaced that spool with one for the previous quarter. It was getting near lunch time. His stomach had rumbled a couple of times. His eyes were past being tired. The top of his head felt like it was going to blow off. He was ready for a break. There was nothing in the previous quarter.

Thinking that somehow, he'd missed it, Jim ran it again. April, May, June of the previous year. There were a lot of dead people, but not Wink. So, much for Jim's quarterly murder theory. Pulling that reel out, he replaced it with the January through March one for the previous year. Nothing. Thinking that perhaps he was going too quickly, Jim went through it again. He drew a blank. Okay, so it wasn't a sound theory. Then again, maybe Wink hadn't died in town. Perhaps he'd moved to a neighboring county. It was possible. His child support probably went through the Attorney General's office as most everyone's did. The local clerk and the AG worked together, the court files being kept by the clerk. Noel would have still seen that he'd died when the Suggestion of Death showed up in the court's file.

Jim thought about giving up. There was a sharp pain in his skull right above his eyes. His vision blurred worse and worse. His eyes burned. He stomach made demands. Now it was past lunch. But he forced himself to stay. He made a deal with himself. If he couldn't find Wink in the three previous years, he'd go to lunch and return to the library later in the afternoon. His neck and back ached from hunching over the machine anyhow.

Popping in the next reel, Jim took a deep breath and began reviewing pages again. He knew generally the newspaper placed the obituaries on page four and gory accident reports on page two so he began with those pages. If he found nothing there, he'd scan the whole newspaper. He found nothing in October. Nothing in November. December came and went. And the next one. He drew a blank. Finally, June, two years ago.

MAN KILLED IN TRAFFIC MISHAP

An accident Tuesday night may be the target of a grand jury investigation, police said, after finding Frederic Wink dead at the scene.

Angeles police Officer Ivan Denholt discovered that the driver of the car in which Wink was a passenger was Wink's ex-wife, Elizabeth "Bitsy" Wink. The couple had only been divorced two weeks.

Jim slapped himself. What did he have, congealed oatmeal for brains? How had he not realized that? How many Winks could there be in a small town? He re-read the paragraph. Officer Ivan Denholt, two years ago. Now Sergeant Ivan Denholt. No wonder the guy had seemed interested in what Jim was doing. Maybe he already suspected Bitsy himself and was looking for support for his case. Maybe Jim would have had—could still have—an ally if he'd trust Denholt. He finished reading.

Bitsy Wink, who was seriously injured, was taken by ambulance to County Memorial Hospital where she is listed in serious condition.

Witnesses reported that Wink ran a stop sign, causing her car to be directly in the path of an 18-wheeler driven by Alan Steele. Steele refused to make a statement, but police reports show that Steele had the right of way.

Bitsy Wink is the bailiff for Associate Judge Lucia Maria Lopez, but she is officially in the employ of the Sheriff. Officials have indicated they will request a grand jury convene to investigate the matter.

Wink is survived by a son and a daughter, his mother, and grandmother.

Jim wondered whether Noel had read any of the newspaper articles or whether he had put the thing together himself. If Noel Wannamaker knew Denholt, why didn't he go to him? It didn't add up. He could see now, though, why Wannamaker seemed scared to death that someone, like Bitsy Wink, would see them talking. If Noel had put something together, he probably had been sitting on it for quite a while, not knowing what to do. Jim happened to come along, asking questions, and presented Noel with the ideal opportunity to pass the buck—or at least the names on his list of suspicious deaths. But either Noel had somehow already given himself away, or somebody saw them, and that was the end of Noel.

A whispered voice said, "Find what you're looking for?" Frieda stood behind Jim's shoulder.

Jim lurched forward, a shiver tickling his shoulders. He switched off the machine and turned in his chair, wondering whether she'd read the article over his shoulder. He whispered back, "Hey, how're you doing?" He stood and stretched. "It's killing my eyes, not to mention my neck and back."

"Maybe someday we'll get some more modern contraptions that'll be easier on the body."

Jim wondered if she had a reason for being up there where people only went for research, or whether . . . no, just because she was female didn't make her part of a deep dark plot. He jerked his head toward the machine. "Computers have replaced this process for all the large newspapers and the wire service."

"Yes, like *The New York Times*. Then there's *LexisNexis* to do your research, if you can figure out how to find what you're looking for. And if you can afford to pay."

Jim wished she'd disappear back downstairs, but she had been good to him, was Ethan's sister, and really, a dear lady. "Nothing like digging around the old-fashioned way."

"Did you have lunch? I have half a sandwich with your name on it."

Now, he really felt guilty. "Thank, Frieda. I appreciate the offer, but I've got to get this done and then a million other things. Some other time."

"Okay," she started away. "But if you change your mind, come on down."

As soon as she left, Jim went down to the restroom, used

the facilities, and splashed water on his eyes before hurrying back up to the microfilm machine. In the back of his mind had been a worry that the reel of film would be gone when he got back, but it was still there. He chastised himself. But then chastised himself again for not taking the reel with him or printing out the article. Well, enough of making himself nuts with his inner dialog.

It had to be that bailiff Bitsy Wink was central to what was going on. It didn't seem to fit into the same category with the others. All of them were single incidents or accidents involving only one party. In Frederic Wink's, there were two other people involved, Bitsy, the driver of the vehicle in which Wink rode, and the driver of the eighteen-wheeler.

Jim turned to the next day's paper for the obituary and to see if there was a follow-up article. There was. Further investigation revealed that the driver of the eighteen-wheeler had no stop sign and didn't see the Wink car until it was too late to miss it. He claimed that it was as if the driver of the car in which Frederic Wink rode pulled out deliberately in front of his truck. Police were unable to interview the driver of the car, Bitsy Wink, who was also seriously injured in the accident. She was taken to County Memorial Hospital where she was still in serious condition at the time the paper went to press.

Ordinarily, Jim would have thought the driver of the eighteen-wheeler was just trying to deny liability. It seemed far fetched that Bitsy, the bailiff of Judge Lopez's court, could be involved in anything so sinister. Ugh, Jim hated that word. It seemed so melodramatic. Bitsy Wink. One of the original members of WiNGS. Another shiver ran across Jim's shoulders. The woman who was now president of WiNGS. The ex-wife of the decedent, Fredric Wink. God almighty. She must have really hated him to risk her own life to kill him. Jim shook his head. How irrational would a person have to be to risk their own life in order to get back at someone they hated? She would have to be deranged to set herself up to be injured, perhaps killed, like that. Jim didn't even want to think about it, much less dwell on it. But the fact remained, the woman was president of WiNGS. He went back and printed the original article and the follow-up, placing them in his file.

Turning back to the newspaper for the day following the accident, Jim found that there was no obituary for Wink. He forwarded to the next day's paper. Another follow-up article on page two. Bitsy Wink had made a statement. She and Mr. Wink, who were divorced, were on their way back from dinner. They were attempting a reconciliation but had gotten into an argument.

She was driving because Fred had too many drinks at dinner. It was nighttime and the road was not well lit. They were in the middle of an argument when she entered the intersection and heard the truck's horn. It was too late to avoid the accident. She never saw the stop sign.

Police were continuing their investigation.

It was possible, Jim thought. Even plausible. She could have been so involved in arguing with her husband that she drove right through the stop sign. Who in this world hadn't at one time or another been so involved in a conversation with a passenger that they missed their exit or made some other stupid move. Who hadn't day-dreamed their way home on a route they regularly drove?

He turned to the obits. Finally, Frederic Wink. He read through all the man's affiliations and got down to the bottom line where it listed the two children. Jim shook his head. Would she have killed her children's father? Were Bitsy Wink's children better off now that he was dead?

Jim spun through the following pages, looking for more follow-ups. There was a little more detail the next day and then a statement that the grand jury had been impaneled. Since Bitsy Wink was a county employee, both the regular judge, not Lucia Maria Lopez, and the sheriff insisted they wanted the grand jury to give Bitsy a clean bill of health, so to speak. Neither wanted anyone to think there was a cover-up.

Jim read further. Within two weeks, Bitsy had been no-billed by the grand jury. They had not found probable cause to indict her for the death of her ex-husband. According to the reporter, Bitsy would be back at work in the family district court when the doctor released her. At present, she had been released from the hospital and was at home, recovering from her injuries.

Jim sat back and stared at the last article. So, Bitsy Wink had gotten away with murder. That was how he saw it. That was how Noel must have seen it. Something had snapped in the woman's mind. She had formulated the perfect crime and had gotten away with it. Since then, she had taken it upon herself to form the WiNGS group to help other women. Boy, was she helping other women. Jim, convinced that he was on the right track, printed the article, put away the spools of film, and then heeded the growling of his stomach and went down-stairs to take Frieda up on the sandwich.

CHAPTER

SIXTEEN

Alarms rang in Jim's head as he left the library. He wished he had someone to talk to about everything. Sergeant Denholt would be the most likely candidate, but Pat was the first on the list. A nagging voice in his head said that he should have gone through additional newspapers. Perhaps he would discover more, but if there were any other bodies, he'd just as soon not know of them just now. Stuffing the photocopied papers between the pages of his notebook, Jim found a pay phone outside the back door of the library and called Pat again. "Where in the hell have you been?" he yelled when she answered. "I need to talk to you."

If she was surprised at the angry tone of Jim's voice, Pat didn't let on. "You had lunch yet?"

"Not really." He checked his watch. Way after one. His head felt like someone had struck with a hatchet between his brows. "You?"

"No. Where are you?"

"The library."

"Okay. Meet me at the Wendy's. I'll be there in about five minutes."

"We could go to my place." He was thinking that a little privacy would be good if he was going to confront her.

"No way. Meet me at Wendy's in five or so minutes." She hung up.

Jim had parked in the back of the library, on the sloping parking lot on the other side of the alley that was added a few years earlier so people would have a drive-up book drop. He liked parking back there. His emergency brake hadn't worked in ages. He always looked for a space where neither the front nor back of his old Mustang faced downhill.

Women with children preferred the front lot that was centered around a huge sculpture. It was better lit at night and closer to the front entrance and the kids liked to climb on the sculpture. When he came out, next to him was another vintage Mustang in much better shape than Jim' own. He would have remembered the Mustang if it had been there earlier, but he didn't. There was no one in it. He didn't know why he thought there should be. If someone was going to threaten him in some way, they wouldn't do it in the middle of the day. And they wouldn't do it in a Mustang. They'd use a van or a truck. He was growing paranoid.

He glanced through the windshields of the other cars in the lot. The two vans were too far away to contain anyone that wished to do him harm. They probably belonged to families, the mothers and older children inside at story time or some other summer reading program. He was becoming mentally deranged. Satisfied that he was safe, Jim decided to leave his car and walk down to Wendy's. He needed to work out the stiffness that had settled in his limbs anyway.

Wendy's parking lot and interior were packed with mothers and small children. It was loud and cluttered and dirty, as most fast-food restaurants were around lunchtime in the summer. The odor of frying fat was so strong he could almost see grease clouds hanging in the air. Jim stood in line and ordered when he didn't see Patty. He had come right down. It was less than a five-minute walk, all downhill, so she was likely to get there after him.

He found a table in a corner where he could see both entrances. Although he wasn't quite sure what he was going to say to Patty, it was time for a confrontation. She either knew about the men being killed, or she didn't.

Keeping one eye on the entrances, Jim bit into his chicken sandwich. He devoured it in less than half a dozen bites. He had stuffed fries into his mouth and was washing them down with a large Coke when he saw her. She waved but did not smile. She wore jeans, a sleeveless top, a pair of running shoes, and had a windbreaker tied around her hips. She got into the food line. A few minutes later, after she had filled a Styrofoam plate with salad, she slid into the seat next to him.

Jim had planned to let her eat before he questioned her, but he couldn't contain himself. "What in the hell have you been doing?"

"Shh. Keep your voice down." Pat squeezed salad dressing onto her salad and mixed it with the plastic fork.

"I've been trying to reach you all morning. Are the kids all right?"

"Sure, why wouldn't they be?" She plunged a wad of lettuce and tomato into her mouth.

"You want to tell me what the hell is going on?"

Patty watched his face as she chewed.

"In regard to what?"

"Are you deliberately being evasive?"

"God. Give me a break, will you? You yell at me on the

phone. I come to meet you and immediately you begin yelling at me in public. I haven't had time to be evasive."

"I'm not yelling."

"Well, it sure sounds like it from this end."

"Okay, I'm sorry." Jim breathed in and out. He sat back and spread his arms across the back of the chairs, drumming his fingers along them. He kept quiet a few minutes while she ate. Finally, he said, "Did you see in the paper where they found a man's body in a car trunk?"

Pat shook her head and swallowed from her drink.

"I knew him." He twisted his sandwich wrapper.

"I'm sorry."

"What I mean is, I knew him from the courthouse. Hey, you probably knew him, too. He worked in the district clerk's office."

"Really? What was his name?"

"Noel Wannamaker. The tall, young fella who used to sit near the front counter."

"Oh. Yeah, I remember him."

Jim didn't think that she sounded too shocked or sorry either for that matter.

"Do they know who did it?"

Why was he not surprised by that question? He weighed the answer he wanted to give before settling on a different one. "Apparently not."

She watched him while she unwrapped a package of crackers, her face drawn into a scowl. Crumbling them over her salad, she mixed again, careful not to spill it over the side of the Styrofoam platter. Jim wondered if she was stalling for some reason. Everything she did seemed to take so long, but then, she wasn't the one who felt a sense of urgency, of panic, he was.

"I've been doing some research."

"About your article thing? Child support?"

"I guess you could say that." He wanted to scream accusations at her. He wanted her to scream denials back, but somehow it wasn't happening. "Pat. Men are dying. I mean, fathers who owe back child support."

She didn't blink an eye. "What do you mean they're dying?"

He knew he should choose his words carefully, but somehow, they just slipped out. "Somebody is killing them, and I think you know something about it."

"Me?" She choked on her food. It took a few moments for her to get where she could speak. "What, you think I'm killing them?" She laughed and ran the paper napkin across her mouth.

"All of them are related to your women's group—WiNGS. There's a connection. There's got to be."

"Oh, that's crazy. How could WiNGS have anything to do with it?"

"Someone in your group—"

She looked down at her food, her head shaking.

"It's possible they're doing it. I've thought it all out."

"I don't know what this is really about—" She sipped from her drink. "Where did this come from?"

"I think the judge is involved in it, too."

"Judge Lopez or the real judge?"

"Lopez. There's something about her. Remember the first time we were there she told Mr. Johnson his kids would be better off if he were dead?"

"I don't remember that." She kept her eyes on her food.

"Well, she did. I think they're all a bunch of man-haters up there."

"Well, I think you're losing it. You'd have to be out of your mind to believe Judge Lopez could be involved in anything illegal." She wiped her nose with her napkin and sipped from her drink again. "She's a very honest and honorable woman."

"Hah. From what I've seen in that courtroom, I'm convinced that she's somehow involved. I can't believe you haven't noticed the way she talks to some of those people."

"Get off it, Jim. You're dreaming."

He reached across the table and pulled on her forearm, forcing her to look at him. "Listen to me. I'm serious."

"I don't know what's happened to you. If we can't talk about something else, I'm leaving." She pushed back from the table and stood up.

"Why are you being evasive?" Jim jumped up and leaned into her face. "You do know something."

"Shh," she whispered and glanced about at the people seated nearby. "You don't know what you're talking about."

Jim grabbed her by the shoulder. "Am I in danger? Are they after me because I'm on to them?"

"Who else knows about this?" She wrenched away.

Jim felt a hard knot in his stomach. She was confirming his worst fears. "We can leave town. It's not too late. Pat, if you'll get the kids, we can move to Dallas. I got the job. The one I wanted. We could go right away."

She began backing away. "I feel like I'm being confronted by the ravings of a lunatic. Something's happened to you since Tuesday morning. You don't know what you're saying, Jim." She looked at the people sitting at the tables on both sides of her escape route and then turned and made for the door.

Jim cut through some tables and caught up with her in the parking lot. "It's true, isn't it? And you're involved."

"Get away from me, Jim." She took long strides toward her car, close to running.

"Stay and talk to me, Patty." He followed close behind. "We can talk it out. I can help you." He grabbed her hand.

Fumbling with her keys, Pat finally got the door open and jerked her arm away. "Just get away from me," she yelled. "I can't believe you think that I or Judge Lopez would be involved in such a thing."

She got into her little red sedan and slammed the door in his face. Jim tried to open it, but Pat locked before he could pull it open. He banged on the window as she started the car. "I just want to talk to you. I can help you before it's too late. I can protect you."

Pat backed out the space, pulling Jim along since he wouldn't release the door handle. He heard her muffled voice through the rolled-up window. "Get away." When she drove forward, he ran along side until she was going too fast for him.

He stopped and watched her drive away. He did sound like a lunatic. No one who hadn't done the research, no one who hadn't seen Noel's body, no one who hadn't been on his side of the courtroom and seen the look in Bitsy's eyes, would get it.

Where would she go from there? Who would she tell? What would she do? Deciding to follow her, he ran up the hill to the library as fast as he could. He hoped he wasn't already too late. If he could catch her before she told Bitsy or whoever was behind it that he was on to them, he could—what? He didn't know. But something.

After he got the Mustang turned around, Jim could see the back of her car far in the distance at the bottom of the hill. He wished he'd driven down to Wendy's instead of walking. He raced after her. Maybe she would talk to him if they weren't in the public eye. He'd approached it all wrong. Been too direct. Tactless. Too abrupt. He should have eased into a discussion about it rather than directly accusing her.

Maybe someone was watching her. Maybe she had been threatened. Maybe she was afraid of them herself. Maybe they'd threatened the kids.

Jim drove down the hill after her and braked as he went around a curve. His brakes didn't seem to catch right. He pumped them. After a couple of jerky movements, Jim thought they were going to catch, but they didn't. Fear wrapped it's fist around his throat.

A fleeting thought that Patty had set him up crossed his mind. Surely, she wouldn't have tampered with his brakes. Did she arrange for him to go to Wendy's just so someone else could? No time to think it through. His car gained speed as he went down the hill and there was nothing he could do about it.

His emergency brake hadn't worked for ages. She knew that. He'd intended to get it repaired after the time he came out of a convenience store where he'd had to park on a slope and found his car on the other side of the street. He'd been lucky it hadn't rolled back and hit anyone. But he hadn't. Too expensive. He stomped on the brake pedal again. It went to the floor.

What to do? There were no hills going back up the other way steep enough to slow him down. A few slopes but basically sloping curves. And he was gaining speed every moment he spent thinking about it.

He could steer into a telephone pole. A car. Something to stop his momentum.

Swerving into the left lane, he narrowly missed rear-ending a young kid in a Toyota pickup. He ran a red light at the bottom of Mueller's Hill, but it had just turned green the other way, and no one jumped the gun. He was fast approaching the center of town and shops and tourists and children.

One chance. A turnoff before the main drag. He'd try to make it. There was a mild slope and a curve and a small bridge over the river, which was almost as small as a creek at that point than others.

Thoughts raced through his brain like his car did down the hill. He prayed no one would be sitting on the side of the bridge, dangling their feet in the water. It was prohibited and there were signs, but locals liked to see the river rush under the bridge and didn't give a damn about signs.

And tourists. Tourists walked around the downtown area —or what Angeles's residents considered the downtown. Tourists would hang off the side of the bridge and gather along the grassy embankment to rest.

There was a small picnic area on the other side of the bridge. A patch of grass and a patch of gravel for parking and, if Jim remembered correctly, a couple of telephone pole sized logs separating the parking area from the picnic area. If that didn't stop his car, he'd careen into the picnic area, a baseball field, and lots of trees.

As he grew close, Jim spotted a city truck parked by the side of the road where often people sprawled to rest. He would steer across the bridge and swerve over the curb and onto the grass into the parking lot and, hopefully, come to a stop before he hit the logs. At any rate, he was sure he would be stopped by the logs and, if not, God help anyone picnicking in his path.

And if there were, he'd honk so they'd run out of the way. And if they didn't, well, he couldn't think about that. This was his only hope.

As he came around the bend, adrenaline shot into his hands like sparks as he gripped the steering wheel. Jim made the curve on the approach to the bridge. The side of the Mustang scraped a post but he was able to maintain a straight line across.

Twisting the wheel, Jim pointed the car toward the picnic area. The Mustang left the road going so fast Jim didn't believe the logs would stop it, but it was his only hope. Up ahead was only more slope—down another short, steep hill before the road started up again.

No people sat at the tables. As the car bumped over the

rough grassy embankment, Jim bounced and lost his grip on the steering wheel. As he shot toward the parking lot and the logs, he was glad he'd buckled his seat belt. He had a feeling he was going to wish he'd been able to afford a new car with a driver's side air bag.

Covering his face with his arms, he felt the impact, more than saw it. The car slowed considerably, haltingly, but did not cease its forward momentum. For a moment, Jim didn't understand what was happening, then he realized his car was pushing the log along in the front of it. Since he had long ago cut off the ignition, Jim just had to wait for the car to run out of steam. The car went up on its front two wheels, throwing him forward, and fell back again. It finally came to a complete stop with a dull thud as it hit the dirt.

CHAPTER
SEVENTEEN

When he opened his eyes, he peered at two small reflections of himself in someone's mirrored sunglasses. Looking past them, he realized they were on the face of a woman. Her finger made small circles in the air. "Roll down your window," she said in a muffled voice.

He didn't know who she was, but being in no condition to argue, he did as he was told. His body rested in the cradle of his seatbelt. He wasn't quite sure, after all the bumping and bouncing and battering, he was all in one piece. Dropping his left arm, he cranked the window down and felt a warm gust of air on his face.

"Are you all right, sir?" Her breath smelled of the faint aroma of coffee.

She wore a uniform. A police uniform. Her nameplate read Pratka.

Jim took a quick inventory of his body parts. "I'm not sure yet. I may have passed out." In addition to his aching hands and arms, his shoulders felt stiff, his neck throbbed. He eased back in the seat until he sat upright.

"You probably shouldn't move until the medics get here." She squatted down, holding on to the edge of the window. "Where does it hurt?" She pulled her sunglasses down and peered over them. Her eyes were a startling pale blue. Her blond hair was swept back from her face. A wrinkle of concern creased the middle of her forehead between her eyebrows.

Jim grunted. "I'm all right." He rolled his head around even though he knew he shouldn't and instantly knew that it would feel worse later. "Just shaken up a bit. I feel claustrophobic though. I need to get out of the car."

"I would advise against it, sir."

"Naw. I'll be fine if I can just get out and walk around a bit."

"It's your body." Her voice held a warning. She stood up and backed away a few feet. She wore the same blue uniform as the male officers, down to pants with a black stripe down the outside, gun, and billy. "When you're ready, I'll help you, but I think you probably should wait. An ambulance is on its way." Her stance was that of a woman who is accustomed to getting her way, legs spread, hands on hips.

"My neck will probably be stiff tomorrow, but other than that and a few bruises on my chest and forearms from the seatbelt, I feel okay. Really." He was lucky he had worn his seat belt, otherwise he could easily have been thrown through the windshield. He tried to breathe evenly but began to feel the fear of the situation all over again. Leaning his head against the headrest, Jim closed his eyes for a few moments and tried to calm his rapidly beating heart. There would be time to relive the event for the rest of his life. He knew he was going to have to tell it to this officer in a few moments.

When he opened his eyes again, he saw that the car had come to a halt at the backstop of the baseball field. An upturned picnic table and bench were jammed between the front of the car and the chain link fencing. If the backstop hadn't been there, no telling how far the momentum would have taken him.

Several people stood watching him, their faces looking like they'd seen the rapture. Could any of them have had a hand in his accident? Though he scrutinized especially the women's faces, he didn't recognize any of them.

He unsnapped his seatbelt and opened the car door. Easing from under the steering wheel, he turned in the seat. Officer Pratka watched in an attitude of readiness should he need her assistance. As Jim stepped onto solid ground and started to rise, his knees buckled. He grabbed the door while Pratka sprang to help him.

"You'd better get your land legs for a minute." Pratka had a strong grip on him, stopping him from hitting the ground. "Sit back down."

He sat sideways in the driver's seat with his feet upon the ground and hung his head between his knees. Life was good. To be only shaken and stirred, not hurt, was good. Breathing was good. His literary side thought his feelings were trite, clichéd, but he didn't mind. He could have been killed. Instead, he was there in a park of green trees, arid summer air, sweat beginning to flow down from his pits, cop studying him, and how glorious it was to be there. He grinned at Pratka who was not grinning back. "How'd you get here so fast? Or have I been here for a while?"

"A city crew working under the bridge called it in when you went crashing by. I was the closest."

"Oh, because this is the fastest I've ever heard of a cop responding to a call."

"You got something against cops, mister?"

Jim could have bitten his tongue off. "No, ma'am. I'm really glad you showed up. I just mean that your getting here so quickly was a good thing. Well, anyway, when I get my foot out of my mouth maybe I'll be able to apologize better."

She finally smiled. Two small wrinkles appeared on each side of her mouth. "Maybe you want to tell me what happened?"

"Lost my brakes."

"Hey, that's no good in this town. All the hills and valleys. You could have been killed."

"I'm aware of that, ma'am."

"Pratka," she said, pointing at her badge. "Esther Pratka. What's you're name, sir?"

"James Dorman."

She swiped at her hair. "Why is that name familiar?"

"I assure you I'm not wanted. Used to be a reporter for the paper."

Pratka chewed on the inside of her lip. "Right. Read some of your stuff. It was pretty good. What happened to you?"

"I'm unemployed, Officer Pratka. After the evening paper went out of business I couldn't get on with the other paper and haven't been able to find another job until now."

"So, where are you working now?" She was down on her haunches, looking him in the eye.

"Well, as soon as I can get out of town, I've got a job lined up in Dallas."

"Great. For a paper?"

"A magazine. Dallas Downtown Magazine."

'Never heard of it." She stood up and stretched. "Can't do that very long. You want to see if you can make it to one of the benches?"

"Okay." Jim took a deep breath and put his weight solidly on one foot. "I think it was just the—what, adrenaline? I don't know what makes you shaky right after a scare. I should be all right." He flexed his muscles as he stood.

"You need my help?"

Jim clutched the top of the car door. "I think I'll be okay if we go slowly. Which one are we headed for?"

"If you can make it to the one nearest the clearing—that way the ambulance can just pull in there next to the table.

"I'm sure I'm going to be okay." He began putting one foot in front of the other, taking baby steps. By the time he got to the picnic table, he felt better.

When the ambulance showed up a few moments later, Jim was embarrassed that they'd had to come out. The two attendants had him lie down inside their vehicle on a stretcher while they checked him over. "You're going to be all right," the yellow-haired male EMT said. "Can't say the same for your car."

Jim could see the front end of the Mustang had distinct problems. "Sorry for all your trouble, but thanks for coming out."

"Hey, you shouldn't even have moved out of your car 'till we got here," the young, red-haired female scolded. She assisted him in sitting up.

"I'm sorry. I felt all right though." His mind was a whirlpool of thoughts about the accident. He wanted nothing more than to get away by himself and think things through.

"Next time, stay put. You could do injury to yourself."

"Yes, ma'am," he said. "Thank you." He inched toward the edge of the stretcher.

"And if your neck is stiff tomorrow, see your family physician, but I think it's probably just going to be temporary. Take a hot bath as soon as you get home. Soak. Apply moist heat to your neck and shoulders."

"I will. Thanks." He maneuvered his way out, sat back

down on the picnic bench with Pratka, and watched the fiery paramedic as she backed out of the clearing.

Jim glanced at his car and back at Pratka. "Would you call a wrecker for me?"

"Sure. You got one you prefer?'

When he shook his head, Pratka traipsed over to her police unit, spoke into the microphone, and returned. She sat across from him and picked up her pen. "Done. Now, when are you supposed to go to Dallas?"

Jim drank out of a large bottle of water the paramedics had left with him. He was glad the table sat under an oak tree to block the sun. "Whenever I can get there. I just landed the job today, in fact."

She jotted something on a note pad. "When do you plan to leave?"

"I've got to tie up a few loose ends first."

"Like?" She twirled the pen in her fingers.

"There's my wife and kids."

"Your wife work? I mean does she have to give notice?"

Jim realized what he'd said. Not that it mattered one iota to this officer. She didn't know the difference. She didn't know what he was into. Now, Denholt, the one who was investigating Noel's murder, he'd be on him like a flea on a rat. "My ex-wife and I were discussing getting back together."

"Oh. When was this that you were discussing it?"

"Yesterday."

"And you aren't sure yet?"

"No, ma'am. I haven't even had time to explain the offer from Dallas, but I thought I might get the job when I asked her to go with me."

Her eyes flitted across his face, her brow wrinkled, she licked her lips. "Why do you think your brakes went out, Mr. Dorman?"

Jim reared back, surprised at the abrupt change of topic. He hadn't had a chance to think the thing out. Pratka had caught him off guard and now he didn't know how to answer. Pratka didn't know what was going on and he wasn't sure whether Patty was involved in it or not. And why was Pratka asking him about his brakes? Didn't people's brakes go out sometimes? Or did Pratka know something about his involvement in Noel Wannamaker's murder?

Angeles was a relatively small town. Pratka could know something. Would she believe him if he told her his suspicions? He didn't know who to trust. "The car is old. My emergency brake hasn't been working for a while."

"You think someone tampered with your brakes?"

"I'd need a mechanic to look under the hood to answer that."

"Mr. Dorman, I didn't just come in on the hay truck. Even considering your situation—that you almost had a terrible accident, you act like something is going on. Are you involved in something you want to tell me about?"

Jim again wondered what she already knew. "My big aim in life is to reconcile with my wife and make plans to move. Hey, and I sold my novel too, Officer. You're the first to know."

"Why is that? Why haven't you told your ex-wife?"

Jim studied Pratka's face. Was she goading him? "What do you mean?"

Pratka's blank expression was hard to read. "I would just assume that selling a book would be a big deal to a writer."

"It is." Jim smiled in spite of the seriousness of the moment.

"So, why haven't you told your ex-wife or your mother or someone like that?"

"I see what you mean."

"So, Mr. Dorman, you ready to tell me now just what the hell is going on?"

Jim hesitated to give her the whole story. It sounded preposterous even to him. The woman's sunglasses lay on the table between them. Her oddly colored blue eyes roamed Jim's face through her regular glasses as she waited for an explanation.

What seemed even more absurd to Jim was the inkling that Officer Esther Pratka already knew what he was involved in. Knew because she was involved. And what if she was questioning him because she was sent to find out what he knew? He wanted to shake that feeling out of his brain like he would shake out a shirt before hanging it on the clothesline, but it bloomed into a real fear. He stared into the woman's eyes, wishing they were really the windows of the soul. Could he trust her or not?

He wiped the corners of his mouth. "It sounds so ludicrous. I hate to tell you. I don't want to sound like a fool."

"Just try me, buddy. All cops aren't as dim-witted as you writers make us out to be." She beat her fingers on the table-top. Her unpolished nails were cut short like a man's.

"It's not that I think you're dumb, Officer. It's that the whole thing is so unbelievable. If it made any real sense, I'd have brought the whole mess to the police a long time ago."

"I'm not getting any younger." Her voice had taken on an angrier tone.

"All right." He studied Pratka's heart-shaped face. Her eyebrows were plucked into a thin line. She colored them in with brown pencil. Her tanned skin was leathery like the turtles in Town Creek that sunned themselves on the rocks. Her face was as expressionless as a mannequin's, but her eyes fixed on his.

The dry wind blew through the trees. The air had a dusty

smell from the vehicles stirring up dirt in the parking lot. There hadn't been much rain that summer. He knew that by the evening it would be cooler if the breeze kept up and a good time to take the kids to the park. To walk down to the river's edge. Dip their feet in. To listen to the small rapids downstream. He heard a twitter and looked up. A little bird was chasing a larger one and giving it what for.

Pratka continued to stare at Jim. Fear nibbled at him like fish on bait. She seemed nice enough, but she could be as deadly as whoever was involved in what he now thought of as a conspiracy. Should he go down to the station and give a statement to a male officer?

Maybe Pratka was all right. Maybe Pratka wasn't involved. Maybe Pratka would believe him. But Jim wasn't sure.

He finally answered. "I don't know where to begin."

"Okay, sir. I'll make it easy. Do you think your brakes going out was an accident? Or do you think someone tampered with them?"

Jim ruminated on the second question. He peeled the wrapper from the water bottle. "I hate to say until a mechanic looks at them, but yeah, I think someone did something to them."

"Who do you think it was? Your wife?"

Jim jerked his head and something in his neck snapped. There was a burning sensation right below his skull. He rubbed the spot with two fingers. It would take a little while for the ibuprofen that the paramedics had given him to take effect.

"I don't think my wife did it. What made you say that?" He couldn't meet her eyes.

"The way you were talking about her in the past tense."

"Listen, I really haven't had time to think about the brake thing. It just happened. I was in Wendy's with Patty—that's my wife. We had a fight. She couldn't have done it. She was inside with me."

"She could have fixed them while you were waiting for her inside."

"True. But she didn't have time. Or, I guess, while I was at the library, but she didn't know I was there either."

"You were there today?"

"All morning."

Pratka grunted. "And went straight to Wendy's?"

"I called her from the library, and she told me to meet her there. So, I guess she couldn't have done it if she was at home when I called her. Besides, she knows nada about cars. I don't know much more."

"Okay. But she did name the place for you to meet. She could have had someone else fix your brakes while you were either at the library or at Wendy's."

"Yeah, but if she knew someone had already tampered with them at the library, why would she agree to meet with me so close in—you see what I mean?"

"Wendy's is not far enough away for you to have to use your brakes much."

"Right. Besides, I really don't think Patty would do this to me. We were just talking about getting back together." He deliberately left out the fact of their sleeping together. It wasn't any of Pratka's business and probably wasn't relevant anyway. Somehow, though, he didn't want Pratka to think ill of Patty or to think himself lecherous.

"So, is there someone that wants you harmed?"

"Okay. Okay, Officer. The deal is, that . . . I think it could be a group of people." Jim knew that telling her that much might confirm any suspicions she might have about his knowing about the conspiracy, if she was involved. On the other hand, if she didn't know diddly about it, he wouldn't look too stupid for words if he didn't tell her much.

Pratka poised her pen over her pad and peered at him, waiting. "Like how many?"

"I'm not sure." He figured each lady whose ex-husband had been killed was involved and possibly some whose ex-husbands were targeted for the future. "Maybe five or six." And then he thought about Mrs. Peterson. "Maybe seven." And possibly Judge Lopez. "Or eight." I don't really know."

"A conspiracy against you."

"Me and some other people."

"And why would a group of people want to kill you?"

"See, it is hard to believe, isn't it?"

"Just answer my question." Her lips rolled back and forth.

"Because I'm on to them. I could expose them. They could all go to jail for life or—now that I think about it, perhaps they could get the death penalty."

Pratka's right eyebrow arched toward the sky. "I see. And what could you expose them for?"

He wasn't about to tell her who it was that he thought was involved. "I'm not sure that I want to get into that just yet."

Her other eyebrow shot up. "So, how am I supposed to help you if you won't tell me what this thing is all about?"

"Look, Officer, I don't have enough evidence yet. If I told you anything more, you'd just laugh and I'd look like an idiot."

"I hate to tell you—"

"I already look like an idiot?"

Tsk. Tsk. Tsk. She snapped her tongue. Her nostrils flared. 'So, you have no hard evidence?"

"No. But circumstantial. Yes."

"What have you got?"

Jim shook his head. "Can't do it."

"Look, Dorman, if somebody's trying to kill you, don't you think it's time you leveled with me? Come on."

"Just as soon as I have something concrete, I swear."

"Am I going to have to take you downtown?"

Fatigue began to plague Jim. It took a lot of energy to spar with the cops. He'd used his up on the ride down the hill. He just wanted to go home, lie down, rest, take a hot bath, and lie down again." Let's not get melodramatic, Officer. Why don't you give me a ride home and as soon as I have one solid iota of proof, I'll call you."

"Let me ask you this, Mr. Dorman, is there any history of mental illness in your family?"

He shook his head. "No and I'm not surprised you asked that question." Pratka was pretty sharp. If she was involved, she had just given him the suggestion that he was imagining everything. Shrewd. Very smart of her. "So, no, ma'am. And I'm not free at this time to discuss the matter any further."

She looked at him like she wanted to stretch his legs between two chairs and bounce up and down on them. Her frown was so deep it looked like it had fallen into a crevice. After staring at Jim silently for a few moments, she appeared to reconcile herself to the fact that she was getting nowhere. "Promise you'll report it as soon as you've confirmed your suspicions?"

Jim saluted her. "Absolutely."

"Come on, then." She pulled her legs out from under the picnic table and stood, her shoulders up around her ears, and walked stiff-legged toward her police unit.

Before they could reach the car, Jim remembered his notebook and the newspaper copies he'd left on the front seat of his own vehicle. "Let me get my things from my car."

He wished he could tell Esther Pratka everything and get it off his chest. He was sure she'd laugh at him right now, if she wasn't involved. As an alternative, he could call Denholt, but, again, he would probably laugh at what Jim had so far. It was a pretty preposterous story. Wouldn't he just love to turn the whole mess over to the police and get out of town. If he could get them to give him an exclusive when there finally was enough evidence to make an arrest, he could get safely away. It would get the heat off him. And just as soon as he could, he would do it. But not yet.

He didn't really think his life was at stake yet. Jim figured they were only trying to scare him. They just wanted him to lay off. He didn't figure they were really trying to kill him—but he could be mistaken. There was Noel, for example. Assuming Noel Wannamaker was one of their victims and not involved in something else entirely unrelated. After all, he didn't know Noel. The young man could have been involved in any number of shenanigans. Drugs. Human trafficking.

He reached his car, but his notepad wasn't on the seat. He leaned way inside. Got in. Groped under the seats. He got out and opened the rear door. Got in and searched under the seats. His notepad was gone. So, were the newspaper copies. Now he really had nothing to show Pratka or Denholt. His anger grew.

They, whoever they were, must have stolen everything while he was in Wendy's. There was no other time. Unless Pratka had taken it out of the car while he wasn't looking. Had she left the table when he was inside the ambulance being checked over? He didn't think so, but he wasn't sure.

Thank God he hadn't said anything. Pratka would really be laughing, either way. He bit his lip as he walked back toward the police car. It wasn't like he couldn't duplicate everything. It was all at the library. All of it could be copied again. It would just slow him down. The list. He'd have to try to reconstruct the list of names from memory. He'd thrown away the one

Noel had given him and now his notepad was gone. He shook his head in disgust. He could do it. It was pointless for whoever it was to take his notes. Unless it was supposed to serve as a warning.

"You all right?" Pratka asked as Jim returned to the car. "You look like you're feeling bad again."

"I'll make it."

"Find what you need in your car?"

"My notes aren't there."

"You sure you had some notes?"

Jim glanced at her but didn't answer. The only person who had faith in him was him. He got into the front seat. If she had taken them, they weren't in plain view. On the way to his apartment, Jim couldn't find it in himself to engage in small talk. He wanted to trust Pratka to help him. He wanted to tell her the whole story. And he would go to the police as soon as he got reorganized. Just not her. Even if he was wrong, he couldn't be too careful. The best thing he could do at this point was play the rest of his cards close to his chest. He'd reconstruct his notes. He'd do some more investigation and immediately report his findings to the police.

In the meantime, Jim had to worry about where he was going to get the money to pay the wrecker that was going to tow his car. And for repairs to his car. And what would he do for transportation until then? The advance for his novel wouldn't be forthcoming in the next twenty-four to forty-eight hours.

After thanking Pratka for the ride, Jim clomped up the stairs to his door. Once inside, he popped the top on his last generic beer. Gulping it down, he checked his answering machine. Again there were several hang-ups, but no messages. He climbed up to the bedroom. Stripping off his clothes as he went, he made it to the bathroom where he ran a hot bath. Weariness seeped into his bones.

Not until he went back into the bedroom to get some clean underwear and a t-shirt, did he feel uneasy. A chill ran through him. Something was wrong. A subtle difference in things. His underwear was not quite stacked the way he liked. His t-shirts looked rifled. He spun around and saw other things. Small things. Furniture barely moved. Bed not quite as messy as he'd left it.

A knot the size of a baseball formed in his stomach. Looking under the bed, he found no one there. He brushed off his knees. Course if they had been, he'd be dead already.

He checked his closet. Couldn't tell if his shoes had been moved. Ran his hand through the hanging clothes. No one there. Nowhere else to hide. He perched on the edge of the bed. Whoever it was didn't want him to know they had been there. They didn't want him to alert the police or they had some kind of plan. There could be any number of reasons.

His computer! Jim jumped for the stairs and could see his desk before he reached the bottom. Gone. Nothing but wires left. WTH? His stomach turned over. It might have been old and out of date, but it was the only one he had. He sank to his knees in front of his desk and yanked open the drawers.

The thumb drive was gone. All his thumb drives, new and old, missing. He had one for every novel. One for his short stories. One for his essays. One for his articles. They were all gone.

The asshole had taken his disks, as well. His old backups of his old stories and articles. Everything he'd ever written, gone.

So much for his theory of their not wanting him to know someone had been in his home. Unless it was two people. Two people with unrelated motives? Not very likely. He crumpled onto the floor like he was fatally wounded. And smiled like someone possessed.

Thank God he had a job to look forward to. Thank God he'd have a salary with which to buy another computer. Thank God, he always emailed himself a copy of what he was working on. All his work was perpetually floating in cyberspace.

Even so, his right of privacy had been violated. Anger nipped at him like a rat dog. Someone tampered with his brakes. Tried to kill him. Burglarized his house. Stole the one possession that meant more to him than any other object he owned—the device with which he made his living. What was he going to do about it?

He lay there reviewing his options. He was tired. So tired he couldn't get up off the floor for a few minutes. The rush and ebb of adrenaline left him feeling like he'd just climbed out of the spin cycle of a washing machine.

After a while, he did get up. Shot the bolt on the front door. Hooked the chain even through he knew chains weren't worth much as a security device. Propped his desk chair under the doorknob. Pushed the sofa up against the chair. That should slow down anyone who tried to break in while he was taking his bath. They probably wouldn't be back, but he wasn't taking any chances. He also got the hammer out of his toolbox and took it upstairs into the bathroom with him.

He stripped and stepped into the tub. In spite of everything that was going on, he was going to soak so he wouldn't be so sore the next day. He laid back and tried to get comfortable. After some sleep, he'd be able to think more clearly.

Closing his eyes, Jim tried to think of other things but his brain kept going back to WiNGS like a nail to a magnet. He wanted to go to a meeting. See all the women together. See them in action. Let them know they hadn't scared him off.

What day was it? Thursday? There was a meeting that evening. And in spite of his resolve to get some sleep, Jim knew he had to be there no matter what it took to get a car. Was that, in fact, the plan of the person who'd burglarized his house? To draw him to a meeting? If so, they were going to get their wish.

CHAPTER

EIGHTEEN

Unless he stole one, getting possession of a car might be impossible. Jim lay for awhile on top of the comforter, though he couldn't sleep. He was mentally making a list of all the people he might be able to persuade to loan him a set of wheels. The list wasn't very long. In fact, it was downright short. His main trouble was that he'd more or less severed his relationships by his failure to cultivate them.

But he needed a car, so he was going to have to call. Or better yet, he'd hitch a ride down to the Shy Ann and see if any of his old buddies were there. It was Thursday. Who used to be there on Thursday nights? Thursday. Oh, shit. His night at the library. He picked up the phone to call Frieda.

"Angeles public library," Frieda's said.

Frieda, it's Jim. Now don't get worried, but I've been in an accident."

"You just left here a few hours ago."

"My brakes went out after lunch when I came back to get my car."

"I'm so sorry. Were you hurt?"

"I'm bruised and my neck is probably going to need a lot of attention from a chiropractor, but otherwise, I'm okay. Just wanted to let you know."

"That's a relief. What about your car? Is that what you called to tell me? Is it out of commission? Oh, dear."

"Front end smashed. The only way I could get there tonight is if I hitch a ride." It was the truth, but he felt bad all the same. She depended on him. But his situation was more important. He'd have to make it up to her somehow.

"You should probably be in bed," she said. "Hold on a minute." He could hear her talking to a library patron. "Jim? Don't worry about coming in to work tonight. I'll be fine. After all, I used to get along without you."

Jim's stiff neck ached when he chuckled. "I know I'm not indispensable. But here's the thing, Frieda. I wanted to ask you a favor. I can't tell you what is going on, but I need a car to do something tonight. Is there any way I could borrow yours? I'm pretty sure I could return it before closing."

"Borrow my car? Oh, Jim. Well, I don't know."

Her reaction was no surprise. He'd hated even asking her. "I'm a good driver, Frieda. It wasn't my fault I had the accident. The brakes went out."

"Listen, Jim, I've got a line here at the counter. Let me think about it and I'll call you back as soon as it lets up."

He hung up. Who else was there? Patty? No way he'd even ask her now. If he could just get to the Shy Inn. He had enough money to buy a round of drinks. He had good news to share with the guys. He thought he could persuade one of them after they saw him. After all, they used to be good buddies. It was six-thirty. He had an hour.

He dressed in a pair of jeans, running shoes, a short-sleeved sport shirt, and a blazer. If he didn't hear from Frieda in a few minutes, he'd walk to the road and see if he could pick up a ride. He couldn't just sit there. He wanted to get to that WiNGS meeting. He'd ask the women at the WiNGS meeting for interviews for his articles. See what was up with Bitsy. Some of the others. Even Patty.

They couldn't bar him from the meeting. It had to be public. There might even be other men there. Men who had custody of their children. Men who were on the receiving end of child support. Checking himself in the mirror, Jim thought he looked writerly, except for the running shoes, but that couldn't be helped. He might have to do some walking before he picked up a ride.

The phone rang as he was about to leave. "Jim, I have it all worked out." Frieda sounded breathless. "Sandy was just leaving. She'll stay long enough for me to come get you. I'll drop you at the Shy Ann. Ethan will loan you his car. I called him on his cell. I'm sorry, Jim. I just have this thing about being stranded here at the library at night with no way to get home."

"You're a doll." Relief washed over him. "And I can just take the car back to Ethan at the Shy Ann when I get through with what I need to do?"

"Sure. I'm leaving now. Be ready."

While he waited for Frieda, Jim dug around in the kitchen for something to eat. He found a can of beans in the closet that passed for a pantry and ate straight out of the can. He was about to go outside when the phone rang again. Patty's voice came on the answering machine.

What could she want? To set him up again? He grabbed the phone. "I'm here. Hold on a minute." He turned the machine off. "Okay, what do you want?" His anger rose to the surface like scum on a pond.

"Are you okay?"

SUSAN P. BAKER

"Why shouldn't I be? Or are you going to claim you know nothing about my brakes?"

"What are you talking about?"

"If you don't know, why did you ask me if I was all right?"

"Uh, your voice sounded funny, that's all. What about your brakes?"

"You know nothing about the brakes on my car going out?"

"Heavens, no. When was that? Are you hurt?"

Her sincerity was almost believable. "This afternoon after you ran away. I was following you and suddenly I had no brakes."

"Oh, Jimmy, are you okay? What happened? How did you stop the car?"

"I managed to steer into a park where the only thing that got hurt was a picnic table and a baseball backstop. And my car, of course. I'm mostly bruised."

"I'm so glad you weren't injured."

"Are you?" He couldn't keep the ire from his voice.

"Of course I am. What's wrong with you? What do you think happened to your brakes? Have you had them looked at yet?"

"I don't know what happened, Pat. I had the car towed. I expect I'll find out tomorrow. Unless you'd like to enlighten me now."

"What do you mean? You don't think I had anything to do with it?"

"Should I?"

"Jimmy, what's going on? I should be really angry with you for that remark, but after what you said this afternoon, I can't help but wonder if you're all right. We need to talk."

"Uh huh. That's what I tried to do this afternoon, and you ran out on me."

"Can you meet me tonight?"

222

Jim pulled the receiver away from his ear and stared at it for a moment. "Tonight?"

"Yes, in about an hour. Say 7:30 or so?"

Now he was sure something was going on with her. After a long silence, he said, "Can you come over here?"

"Mmm, no. And you can't come over here either. Have you had dinner? How about meeting me at *Butch's Bar-B-Q*?"

"That's way out on South Junction. How the hell am I supposed to get out there?" Why would she want to go to a place on a hillside on the opposite side of the county from the West County Christian Church? "Are you going to pick me up?"

"No. I thought you could borrow a car.

Evidently, she had more faith in his connections than he did. "You thought I could borrow a car, from whom?"

"Well, what else were you going to do for transportation, honey?"

Honey? "I was just on my way out to see about borrowing one. It would be so much easier though if you'd just come and get me." He knew she wouldn't but couldn't help baiting her.

"Where were you going, your old haunt, the Shy Ann Inn?"

"Now, don't start. Where else would I go?"

"I trust you, Jimmy."

Jim wished he could say the same about her. He didn't reply, he merely took a deep breath and let it out.

"You will try to meet me, won't you?"

"I'll try. I can't guarantee I'll get a car. Want me to call if I can't make it?"

"You'll make it" She chuckle. "I'll be waiting for you." She hung up.

Jim locked his door and waited on the stoop for Frieda. It was beginning to cool down a bit. He hardly broke a sweat. He wondered if he had bean breath but decided not to run back upstairs to brush his teeth. He didn't want to keep Frieda waiting after she did this big favor. Frieda drove up in her little Honda and minutes later dropped him back off, wishing him luck with whatever he had planned that she insisted she didn't want to know about.

The Shy Ann was a sore point between them. How many hours had he spent out there with his buddies when he could have been home with Pat and the kids? It had been at the Shy Ann that he'd first heard rumors about his wife. If he'd been home where he belonged . . . ."

Now, he admitted to himself and anyone who would listen, after what he'd been through the last months, he knew he had been in the wrong. It was he who had not been paying enough attention to Patty. And the kids. And their home. What on earth had he been thinking? But he'd grown up. He only hoped it wasn't too late.

That same neglect was very likely to have been the catalyst to his present situation. That could likely lead to his demise at the hands of the WiNGS people if he didn't get the thing figured out and fast. All because he thought his career, his buddies, his shoptalk had been so all-fired important. If not for his behavior, Jim wouldn't be where he was today—divorced, behind on child support, and scrambling to stay out of jail and out of the clutches of murdering women.

There he articulated it. The 'M' word. And in his mind, that's what they were.

Jim's stomach tightened as he mulled over his visit to the WINGS meeting. If he hurried through dinner with Patty, he could still catch the tail end. And just exactly what did he intend to do? Should he continue his charade about the series of articles? Okay, not really a charade, but not number one on his list of reasons why he was going there. Would it be appropriate to show up, uninvited, and ask for a chance to address the group in order to line up interviews? What would he do if they threw him out? Or if they shut the door in his face before he ever got inside? He was assuming it was a public meeting, and anyone could attend. Would those who had been violating the law uphold their facade, maybe even give him interviews? Jim didn't know what he expected to find but was hoping that someone would make a slip somewhere.

As he had bid Frieda goodnight, the wind blew up from the north, dust flying in the air. During the ride, gray clouds had clustered overhead. The temperature had dropped several degrees, and the sun had begun to set. It was darker than usual for the tail end of summer at that time of day. He hoped the bottom didn't drop out of the sky, though probably not yet, since the smell of rain hadn't permeated the air.

Only a couple of the cars in the lot next to the Shy Ann looked vaguely familiar though it was more than possible that every one of the reporters he had known had moved off or purchased newer models. Pushing through the doors, he was relieved to see through the dim, smoky atmosphere two faces he knew at the bar. Ethan was in a ribald conference at the small circular table in the corner, though in the distance he noted something different.

He strode to the corner table and hollered out at Ethan who did a double-take. Laughing, Ethan stood and clapped Jim on the shoulder.

"Come out of hibernation at long last, eh, Jimbo?" Ethan crushed Jim's hand in his own. "How the hell have you been?"

Ethan had dropped a number of pounds since Jim had seen him at Tex's. Did Ethan have cancer or AIDS or some other illness? Torn between wanting to snatch up the keys and make a run for it or catching up with old friends over a drink, Jim thought he could squeeze in a little of both. His spirits immediately lifted. There was something about seeing old friends. Something akin to unconditional love—he guessed it was unconditional friendship—that made one feel uplifted. Jim grinned and shook Ethan's hand. "I've been great, how about you?"

"Never better." Ethan turned to the man across the table. "Let me introduce you to William Crumb. He's a new associate professor. Like me, he decided to live in the country. Bill, this is Jim Dorman. He used to be a reporter before his paper folded."

Bill Crumb, a small man that came just to Jim's shoulder, stood and shook his hand. "My pleasure. Heard some stories about you."

Jim glanced at Ethan. "All exaggerated, I'm sure."

"You can have my seat." Bill moved away from his chair. "I have to be going anyhow. My wife's got me on a short leash."

Jim could still feel the warmth from Bill's body when he and Ethan sat down. There was an awkward silence for a moment and then Ethan called out for a short beer. He looked at Jim.

Jim waved his hand. "Nothing for me but a Coke but put it on my tab." When the man looked skeptical, Jim said, "I can pay, Luke. Trust me."

"So," Ethan said, raising his fur-like black eyebrows, "what have you been up to lately? You haven't been in here. No one has seen you at Tex's."

"Got some good news. I'd been selling a few short pieces occasionally, but now I've got a real job starting soon."

"Congratulations." He stroked his folded ear. "Where?"

"Dallas Downtown Magazine."

"I've read it. A pretty good rag—trying to give Texas Monthly some competition, I understand." Ethan held out his beer mug as a salute to Jim and took a long swallow.

"I snared an investigative reporting job. I can start as soon as I can get there. I also sold my novel." That, almost shyly.

"Well, you're in tall cotton. When did all this come about?"

Jim glanced at the calendar behind the bar. Seemed like days ago after everything that had happened that day. "This morning. You're almost the first to know."

"Both on the same day?"

"Yep—well, I sort of figured on the magazine job, and my book's been at the publishing house for months. I just happened to get the word on both of them like that."

"I'm honored that you came here to share this with your old buddies." Ethan took another swallow of his beer. "Even if you do have an ulterior motive."

Jim held his Coke glass up to Ethan in a toast. "So, how have you been doing? You feeling well, Ethan?"

Ethan glanced at Jim and then down at himself. "Oh—you mean my weight loss." He laughed. "Uh—you know I hit fifty last spring."

"Say, that's right."

"Suffice it to say that I've decided to reform. I've got a two-beer limit now and I work out every other day. How do you like the new me?"

"You look great. Feeling good?"

"Terrific. But then I've been this way for several months and I'm used to it. Gad, I just can't believe it. Got a fancy magazine job and sold your book in one day."

Jim grinned, feeling like a boy being praised by his dad.

"And come to share it with us here at the old Shy Ann." Ethan's voice grew deep as it always had when he was emotional about something. The old cowboy professor often acted like a father to the younger men, even those who weren't very much younger.

"Well, to be perfectly honest, Ethan, I was going to tell you all about my good luck, it just wouldn't have been tonight. I appreciate you agreeing to loan me your car. I didn't even know Frieda was going to ask you."

"No problem. You know when you're in need you can always come to your old grandpappy."

"I'm sorry. I didn't know who else to turn to."

"Aw, that's all right, amigo. Must be important. You were never one to mooch. Besides, I appreciate the time you've given Frieda at the library. It was a nice thing for you to do."

"She's such a nice lady, your sister. I'm going to miss her. And you, too. You'll have to come to Dallas for a visit."

"I'll do it. Not that Dallas is my favorite town, but I'll let you buy me a beer and put me up sometime."

"Sure you don't mind about the loan?"

"No—it's okay. My old Ford Taurus is across the street." He dug into his pocket for the keys. "Tom can take me home when I'm ready." He gestured toward the bar where two men were watching television.

Jim took the keys. "I hate to just run in here and buy you a beer and borrow your car after not having seen you for so long. I know that's rather crass."

"You better quit while you're ahead, boy." He grinned and leaned forward conspiratorially. "Seriously, I know you wouldn't ask like this if you didn't really need it, Jimbo. Get going."

"Thanks, Ethan. I'll get it back to you as soon as I can." They shook hands. Jim dug in his jeans for a few dollars. Laying the bills on the bar as he went out, he said, "That should cover it, Luke. See you."

As Jim stepped onto the sidewalk, he picked out the Taurus on the opposite side of the street. It was a deep blue almost nondescript vehicle. The sky had grown darker. People had already turned on their headlights. The scent of rain was like a spritz in the air. The wind had increased. He'd better hurry or Patty would think he wasn't coming.

He wasn't halfway across the street when tall bright headlights flew in from nowhere. Jim found himself directly in their path. He dashed back the way he'd come, but that seemed to keep him lined up with the lights. He sprang toward the Taurus. The lights were almost upon him. Making a mad dive, Jim hit the pavement and rolled over until he was between two parked cars. The lights flashed past and when Jim got to his feet, he was only able to make out the tail lights of the truck and one letter on what looked like personalized license plates, the letter W. The remaining letters were covered by mud.

Jim brushed himself off. Was that near miss intentional? Who knew where he would be tonight? Who else except Patty? Determined to get some answers right away, he started up the Taurus. He knew exactly where he was going to get them. And she'd better be there.

CHAPTER
NINETEEN

Distant thunder rumbled as Jim drove to *Butch's Bar-B-Q*. An occasional bolt of lightning lit up the sky far away. The storm could still pass right by them or stop and give them a light and water show. It didn't seem to have committed itself one way or the other. It was pretty, though, and so far, nonthreatening.

Butch's was past *Dead Man's Curve*. That very thought made a shiver dance across Jim's shoulders and down his spine. He kept expecting to glance up and see glaring headlights in his rearview mirror or hear the grate of metal upon metal as the Taurus was hit from the side and pushed over the edge of the cliff. Nothing happened though.

Jim exceeded the speed limit, but only slightly. One accident per day per person was his limit. He didn't intend to push his luck. He also wasn't in a hurry to find out if Patty had betrayed him. In his gut, he knew she had. His heart, however, was still hoping for a plausible explanation for her recent weird behavior. His dream of their reconciliation, of his success as an author and investigative reporter, and of a happy little family in a warm, loving home seemed more fairy tale-like with each passing moment.

He wasn't kidding himself. He knew they had problems that would need work. The whole family needed counseling. There would have been a lot of good times and bad in the future that would have needed tending to, that is, if the reconciliation had worked out. The kids would have had their share of childhood tragedies. Those were the very things that he'd been looking forward to experiencing together. Jim shrugged and decided to concentrate on his driving. It was dark. The air was thick with moisture. The road glistened under his headlights.

It was eight-thirty by the time he arrived. *Butch's* was the most popular barbecue joint in the county. A night didn't go by that it wasn't packed, except major holidays when Butch insisted on closing in spite of his customers' protests.

Driving slowly up and down rows of parked cars, Jim searched for Patty's little red Ford. When he didn't find it the first time around, he figured it was probably squeezed in between a couple of pickup trucks and that he'd missed it. He made the rows a second time. He knew he was late, but somehow, he'd thought she would wait.

Jim parked in the fire zone and ran inside to see if Patty was waiting. He asked the hostess if she had seated a lone woman at a table. Maybe Patty had some other mode of transportation. Maybe she had gone ahead and gotten a table and ordered for both of them.

Shaking her head, the hostess replied in the negative. Jim described Patty to the woman. Maybe Patty had arrived earlier but hadn't waited. Was she sure a woman of his wife's description hadn't been there? Stepping past Jim to beckon to a waiting party, the hostess shook her head. Yes, she said. She was sure and would he quit bothering her and go away?

As he climbed back into the Taurus, Jim felt like the biggest sucker of all time. Patty had only had to crook her little finger, and he had come running like an adolescent with his first crush. What had she been up to?

Starting the car, Jim put it in gear and headed back the way he'd come. He was still going to try to catch the WiNGS meeting on the other end of the county. Something must be going on there she didn't want him to know about.

Or Patty had been trying to pinpoint where he was going to be so whoever was in the truck would be able to run him down. Whichever it was, Jim was still going to finish what he'd started. He was still going to get enough evidence on the WiNGS group to hang them.

The storm was now at Jim's back and closing. It had apparently made up its mind to pay a visit to Angeles. Jim only hoped to outrun it and get his business taken care of before the downpour. He could see some of a fantastic light show in his rearview mirror as the sky was illuminated by lightning every few minutes. On any other evening, he would have pulled over and watched for a while. Now, he was in a hurry. Now, he drove well above the limit.

The radio blared out a heart-rending country tune interspersed with static. The thunder rumbled. The wind blowing in through the window ruffled Jim's hair. He clutched the steering wheel so tightly that his hands began to ache as they had earlier in the day when he'd gone crashing down the hillside and into the park in his Mustang. He didn't even want to think about what it would take to repair it and get it back in good condition.

The drive to West County Christian Church took about twenty-five minutes. The building was a small wood frame in the middle of three lots. It looked brand new.

Jim passed the building and parked in the shadows of a

tree a little more than a block away. Keeping under the cover of the trees and the darkness, he approached the building from the rear. There was less exposure for him than through the cleared parking lot. The wind had picked up and felt cooler than earlier. Lightening flashed. He hoped no one was looking outside. The sweet smell of flowers and the sounds of night creatures were all around him.

He didn't know exactly what he was going to do except make a list of the cars and license plates in the parking lot so he could ascertain who the members were. He'd brought a camera but wasn't sure it was safe to use it. He wished he had a special one that would take pictures in the dark without a flash.

When he got close, Jim could see movement inside the building but couldn't make out any detail. He had to leave the relatively full cover of the trees, cross a ditch, and enter the clearing where the church was in order to see anything distinctly. He crept up and peeked through the screen. About two dozen women sat with their backs to him. There was a long, rectangular table at the front of the room. Patty sat at the table and faced the other women. Now he knew why he hadn't seen her car in s *Butch's* parking lot.

She was saying something—making some point to the group—he recognized her gestures *Ooooooooooooh,* the wind howled as it blew through the trees, making it impossible to hear what was being said. Two other women sat at the table with Patty. Jim didn't know either of them.

Jim flinched like something jammed in his ribs. It did.

"See what you're looking for?" said a disembodied female voice that sounded a great deal like Bitsy Wink's.

CHAPTER

TWENTY

J im came out of his skin. When he collected his senses, he realized the thing stuck in his ribs was the barrel of a pistol. He felt temporarily fortunate it wasn't a knife. And wasn't inserted.

"Turn around slowly, please."

He was not surprised to find Bitsy Wink. And she did, indeed, have a gun, though Jim noted it was not the large caliber revolver he'd seen in her holster at the courthouse. The exterior lights of the church illuminated the outside of the building enough for Jim to see this one was a small, chrome-plated derringer which fit easily into her large, meaty palm.

For the trace of a moment during a flash of lightning, he glimpsed her hard expression.

"What the hell you think you're doing?" Her voice was as mean as the look in her eye.

Jim felt like his chest had caved in. His breath wouldn't come. His arms felt like lead weights hanging by his sides. He tried to read Bitsy's face, but couldn't. "I-I wanted to make sure I was in the right place before I came in."

"Bull. Shit." Her teeth were clenched together like synched gears. "I've had enough of your antics. Now turn around and get moving." She prodded him with the gun barrel.

Jim didn't budge. He was stalling for time. "Where do you want me to go?" He hoped to find a means of escape.

"Just start walking and I'll tell you when to stop. Head for the parking lot." She pressed the gun up against his shoulder blade.

"Yes, ma'am." Jim took baby steps and glanced inside the building as they came even with some windows. He could make out Patty still saying something to the group. As they approached the corner, he thought about making a run for it. He guessed that derringers weren't very accurate and probably couldn't hit a distant moving target. The thing was, he needed to get some distance from her before she got off a shot. How he was going to do that he hoped would come to him any moment.

"If you're thinking of running, forget it. I'll shoot you down like a coyote in the hen house, make no mistake."

Jim shook his head. "Yes, ma'am. I have no doubt about it."

"Don't get smart, either."

They rounded the corner and ran smack dab into a woman coming from the other direction.

"Excuse me," she said after she laughed and straightened up. "Bitsy, we were wondering what happened to you."

Jim turned around just soon enough to see Bitsy pull her gun hand from her pocket. He wasn't sure the other woman had seen the derringer. "Excuse me, ma'am. I didn't see you coming."

They stood under an outside light on the corner of the building. Bitsy's jaw flexed and he could imagine the wheels and pulleys working in her mind.

"We was just coming inside, Carol Ann. This here's Mr.

Dorman, and he wants to make a speech to the group. Ain't that right, Mr. Dorman?"

His heart climbing up his esophagus, Jim cleared his throat to force it back down where he could speak. He didn't know what to do except go along. Some of the women might not be in on the murder scam, Carol Ann being one of them. She looked fresh-faced and naive.

Jim held out his hand to shake Carol Ann's. "Yes, ma'am. I wanted to talk about my articles. I'm writing about child support."

"Why that's just swell, Mr. Dorman." Carol Ann took his hand and somehow ended up hooking her arm in his. "Come on inside and when our speaker gets done you can be next. Hurry up, cause the sky is going to fall at any moment and we don't want to get caught in it, now do we?" She patted his hand.

"It's exciting having a real author, ain't it, Carol Ann." Bitsy walked so close behind Jim he could feel her breath on the back of his neck.

He felt like a mouse with one leg caught in a trap. The cat was toying with him. His only choice, as he saw it, was to play along. He let them lead him to a chair. He caught Patty's eye. She looked stricken and started to rise but apparently thought better of it and slid back down and clasped her hands in front of her.

A woman speaker stood beside the table. Her topic seemed to be about having a live-in when one has custody of the children and how that's frowned upon by some judges.

Several women stared at Jim and whispered to their neighbor. Most of them eye-balled him like he was a giant cockroach.

Jim wished he'd told someone where he was going. Even

his friend, Ethan, who would want to know what happened to his car.

Bitsy Wink stood beside Jim's chair with her arms crossed like a military guard. From time-to-time he glanced up at her, but she appeared to be intent on listening to the woman's speech. Patty made eye contact with him. He wished he knew what she was thinking. Rain began pelting the tin roof. Within moments, torrents of water rattled the glass. Rumbling thunder was so close it sounded like it came from the ceiling rather than the sky. It seemed to have a deleterious effect on some of the women's peace of mind. A low murmur like a softly playing melody permeated the room.

It was clear when the speaker began taking questions that she had not expected to hear complaints about her comments. One woman thought it was none of the court's business if she wanted to live with one man or fifty men so long as the children were fed, clothed, and educated. A murmur of agreement arose from the audience.

The few times he'd been in the courtroom recently had illustrated the fact that there were attitudes too numerous to list when it came to childrearing. He listened to the questions and answers and prayed it would take all night for them to exhaust the topic. If he had long enough, he could come up with some way to get out of the stupid mess into which he had gotten himself. He didn't know what they intended to do with him but supposed that he would find out soon enough.

There was light applause as the speaker took a seat at the table next to Patty. Bitsy left Jim's side and walked quickly to the front of the room. Jim briefly thought about running but realized it would be futile. There were many of them and only one of him. Ethan's car was not close by and in the lot, instead it was a good distance away and under a tree. And then there was the small problem of Bitsy having the derringer. Was her larger gun not far away?

"Thank you, Ms. Thornton," Bitsy said, beaming like Little Mary Sunshine. "That was a very enlightening talk you gave us and something for each of us to keep in mind when we are trying to decide how to live our lives." She turned to the entire group. "Now is there any other business that we ain't taken care of?" Bitsy made an obvious sweep of the room with her eyes. "If not, I have a surprise guest who would like a few minutes of your time. Mr. Dorman is an author and a reporter who is writing a series of articles about child support." The murmur of voices grew louder. She held up her hand. "But, he is writing the articles from the ex-husband's side, I believe. Ain't that right, Mr. Dorman?"

Jim stood and pushed at the creases in his pants legs. "Yes, ma'am."

"Who cares," one woman called out.

"Yeah, like we haven't already heard every reason in the book," another said.

Other women grumbled to each other. The mood grew steadily worse. Jim had the feeling he was participating in a dark comedy, and he was the butt of the joke.

"Ladies, calm down. Let's have quiet," said a somber-faced woman sitting on Patty's left. She pounded on the table with her fist as a sergeant-of-arms would.

When the women settled down a bit, Bitsy continued, "Mr. Dorman wants to make a short presentation to y'all and perhaps interview one or two of you afterwards. Ladies, welcome Mr. James Dorman." Bitsy began clapping and took her seat as Jim walked up to the front of the room. He felt like a royalist making his final approach to the guillotine. Bitsy Wink was his executioner, Patty was his accuser, and the chattering women before him made up the mob of revolutionaries.

He stood looking out at the faces of the all-female audi-ence. There were black ones, white ones, and brown ones. Some were very young, appearing hardly old enough to be mothers. Some were very old and Jim wondered if they were the grandmothers, forced by difficult economic times to raise their descendants. Most of them were in-between, a nonde-script middle-age.

He would keep his talk brief though it might be better for his health to filibuster. Not having prepared anything, it wouldn't be very difficult to explain what he was doing and ask for volunteers. As he studied the faces that stared back at him, Jim wondered which of them were part of the conspiracy and which were innocent victims of a ruse.

"I'm not going to take a lot of your time this evening." Jim's voice came out like a croaking fish. He cleared his throat. "I appreciate you're allowing me to speak to you at all. You see, I'm also one of the errant fathers, if you will." Jim glanced over at Patty and pointed to her. "This lady sitting at the head table is the mother of my children."

There was a murmur throughout the audience. Jim waited until it had died down a bit and began speaking again. "You probably didn't recognize my last name, because Patty changed hers. It was one of the saddest days of my life." He tried to catch Patty's eye, but she studied her cuticles.

"You see, I made a mistake, and my mistake cost me my wife and children. I've asked her forgiveness, but I'm not sure she's ready to give it." Jim let his eyes meet several of those watching him. He found it very difficult to look into their faces for very long.

"I'm here tonight because I'm investigating the *why* behind fathers not supporting their children. I know why I got behind, but I don't think I'm typical. I lost my job and had very little money to live on."

A woman called out, "Yeah, well that's all we ever have to live on, Mister."

"I hear you out there. I hear your rumblings. I may be wrong. I may be typical. At any rate, what I propose to do is study five families and I'd like five of you to volunteer. The article will be written from the father's viewpoint, but it will also show the difficulties of raising a family without support from the other parent. I'm hoping to get families with as many different circumstances as possible."

"Why should we?" a woman called out. "What's in it for us?"

Jim shook his head. "Nothing. I'm just hoping that it will promote clearer understanding between parents of the troubles divided families have. I can't pay you anything. All I can do is acknowledge your assistance if you want your names used or protect your privacy if you don't."

Bitsy stood up after a few moments when there were no other questions. "Thank you, Mr. Dorman. If you'll sit at this here table, the ladies can come up and speak to you if they want. Okay, ladies. Quiet. The executive board will meet for a few minutes in the Sunday school room. Otherwise, the meeting is done. Coffee and cookies in the kitchen as usual. Don't forget to pick up your kiddies in the day care room. Ha ha. Good night."

Bitsy headed for the back of the room. Patty approached him but seemed to be watching Bitsy warily as she did so.

"Jim, I need to speak to you," Patty whispered as she brushed by him. She patted him on the shoulder. "Don't leave without me."

He started to get up, but a woman plopped into a chair adjacent to him. "I'll let you interview me. I like to do stuff like that," she said. The woman had red, rosy cheeks, and the biggest breasts that Jim had ever seen peeked up at him from a round neck, fitted t-shirt. Although he was interested in looking at them—amazed that she found anything to cover them—he was desirous of catching Patty to hear her out.

He looked over his shoulder at Patty, but all he saw was her back. She didn't turn around. Bitsy stood in the doorway that led to the meeting rooms. She was giving him the Medusa eye. She wore an artificially brilliant smile, but her eyes clearly sent a message to him not to move. She said something to Patty and then followed Patty into the hallway.

"Mister, I'll be a guinea pig," the woman at the table said loudly and pulled on his sleeve. "What do I have to do? Got some forms for me to fill out?"

"Uh, no, ma'am," Jim said as he turned back to the woman and was again confronted by her breasts. "I just need to get your name, address, and phone number and I'll call you and set up a time that would be convenient for us both." He pulled his pen out and poised it over his notepad.

"It's convenient now. I don't mind staying. I don't like to drive in the rain anyhow." As she spoke, a bolt of lightning struck nearby, illuminating the trees blowing in the wind.

"I can't right now. I wanted to sign up as many of you as I could, so you see, I need to speak to a lot of your friends tonight, too." He was trying not to stare and focused on the lady behind her. She was a redhead with well defined freckles covering her face and arms.

"Oh, well, they won't mind waiting." The red-headed woman standing behind her with a rolled-up newspaper under her arm was leaning on every word. "You don't mind waiting, Mary Beth, do you? Mister—"

"Dorman."

"Dorman wants to interview me right now."

The red-headed woman said, "I thought you was going to interview everyone tonight."

"Well, that's what Bitsy said anyways," the first woman said.

"It's such a lengthy interview process that I couldn't possibly get it all done this evening," Jim said. "You understand, don't you, ladies?" Jim wanted to sneak out while Bitsy and Patty were in the executive board meeting if he could get past the other women. He didn't like the idea of their possibly conspiring about what to do with him in the next room like kidnapers with their victim.

"I mean, I have to get all the information about yourselves, your children, your divorce, the amount of child support, when he first quit paying—you do understand, don't you?" He smiled into the eyes of the big-bosomed woman and took her hand, shaking it. "You aren't afraid to see me later at your home, are you?"

She grinned and swiped at the thin blond bangs brushing her forehead. "No, I am not." She turned to the line of women behind her. "What about the rest of you? Any of y'all afraid to have Mr. Dorman come to your house to interview you?"

Laughter rippled through the line of women behind her. Now the ice was broken, way more than five women lined up. He wrote down a name and address and looked for Pat. Took down a name and address and looked for Pat. He promised each one of them he would call and every time he looked for Pat. But she was never there.

Jim finally decided not to wait. He hurried the women, ushered them in and out of the chair, cut the conversations short, and rose. Heading for the front door over the protests of the last two women who wanted to ply him with coffee and cookies, he rushed through the rainstorm. He was soaked but safe and saw no sign of Bitsy, or Patty, as he raced away, breathing a sigh of relief as the church grew smaller in his rearview mirror.

CHAPTER

TWENTY-ONE

T he drought having dried and cracked the earth, the plants having withered and died, the road being old and rutty and unkempt, the rainwater was slow to be absorbed. Standing water forced Jim into the left lane of the four-lane highway, the highest part. He rounded a sharp curve and felt the car plane for a few moments. His heart hammered from a combination of events, the dangerous road conditions being only one of them. Putting distance between the church and himself became less important than careening off the hillside. Reducing his speed as he approached a particularly hilly portion of the highway, he gulped a breath several times to calm himself.

Though he couldn't relax under such conditions, the high level of tension eased up so the shaking of his knees ceased. He shifted about in the driver's seat, trying to get support for his back instead of hunching over the steering wheel. His mind kept targeting the point at which he realized Bitsy held a gun on him.

Carol Ann's coming outside was literally the luckiest break

of his life. Now out in the countryside in a thunderstorm, rain crashing down like the storm that wrecked the Herperus, in a borrowed car, not in possession of a cell phone, what should he do? He needed a plan. He needed to get off the streets. He needed to be where Bitsy couldn't find him.

He couldn't go home. He could go to the police, but would they believe his story? Bitsy would say she was a certified peace officer—and everyone knows cops are cops 24/7—and he was a peeping Tom. He was the one snooping around in the dark looking in the windows at a bunch of women. Yeah, he'd really get a lot of sympathy from the cops.

An enormous bolt of lightning burst overhead, lighting up the sky like the Fourth of July fireworks. The highway ahead of him was desolate. He glanced in his rear-view mirror and saw nothing but empty, glistening road behind him. He slowed the car a little more, falling under the speed limit and feeling himself physically loosen up.

Moments later, a glare lit up the inside of the Taurus. There had been no additional crash of thunder. No lightning.

In his rear-view mirror two enormous, glaring lights approached at a speed that would break the sound barrier. Glancing to his right, Jim saw nothing in the right lane and moved out of the way. A white Ford dualie—a gigantic four-wheel drive pickup truck with double rear tires and a huge iron grill guard on the front—closed the distance between them and came alongside.

Jim's hair bristled and goosebumps covered his arms when he realized the truck bore a striking similarity to the one that tried to run him over. The truck began crowding his lane. *Bump. Ee-raaa-ch.* It sideswiped him. Scraped the side of the Taurus.

Shockwaves jolted him into action. He jammed the pedal to the floor. The Taurus lurched and sped up but had no get up and go. The truck had little trouble keeping up with him. They ran parallel down the rain slick, potholed road for several minutes.

It was like deja vu except the memory was real. This was exactly what he'd been afraid of on the way out to *Butch's*. The Taurus careened close to the edge of the road. Jim hit his brakes. The Taurus spun around on the slick highway and faced the way he'd come.

Jim accelerated and cut across two lanes, heading back in the other direction. In his rearview mirror, he saw the brake lights of the white truck before it made a wide U-turn and came after him. The Taurus didn't have a big enough engine to get any real speed out of her. Jim knew it was just a matter of time until the pickup caught up with him.

As the truck sped closer, Jim moved to the outside lane. The truck remained on the inside lane. At the last moment, before it caught him, Jim jerked the steering wheel and turned across the highway in front of the truck. The truck swerved to the right. As Jim reversed his direction once more, he watched behind him. The truck planed on the water and crashed into a tree.

Jim accelerated, going as fast as he could, which wasn't very fast. He talked to the Taurus, coaxing it, urging it. When he got little traction, he yelled, "Move. Move. Move you rattletrap!"

In his rearview mirror he saw the powerful truck backing away from the tree and turning to come after him like a single-minded monster. He had only hoped to slow them, whoever was inside, down a little. He wanted to find a turnoff to civilization before they caught up to him again. They—whoever it may be. He suspected it was Bitsy behind the wheel. He hadn't really focused on who was driving. He'd been too busy trying to outsmart them.

As the bright lights rushed up to his rear end again, Jim calculated that he was still a good couple of miles away from the closest turnoff. The road rose as he approached a hill. He'd have to top the hill and get down the other side before it was too late. "Come on, baby," he said aloud. At that moment, the lights seemed to envelope him. The truck smashed into the Taurus' rear end, causing it to leap forward.

A balloon burst in his chest as he tried to get a breath. Another smash. A sensation of helplessness came over him as he swerved into the next lane. The truck did the same. It was as if the driver was inside his mind and could anticipate his every move.

The next time, the truck crawled right up onto the back of the Taurus and with its greater power began pushing the Taurus up the hill toward the peak. Jim knew there was a cliff of sorts off the side of that particular hill but was defenseless against what was coming. The gas pedal was all the way to the floor, and the Taurus could not break away.

Who was behind the wheel of the truck? He couldn't see but felt sure it was not Patty. Patty could never do this. Even if she were a party to planning it, deep inside Patty was too kind. She would never be able to kill him. He would take that with him to his grave.

The Taurus was like a hood ornament on the front of the truck. Jim tried to swerve into the left-hand lane, away from the steeply sloping sides of the hill, but the car wouldn't move sideways. They were being propelled in the direction the truck wanted to go. It didn't matter whether he accelerated or braked, he had no choice in his destination.

As they reached the top of the hill, the Taurus lurched again as the truck quit pushing. Instinctively he hit his brakes and screeched to a halt just over the crest. Glancing again in the rearview mirror, Jim saw the truck backing up. He jammed his foot on the accelerator, but the engine had died. Turning the key in the ignition, Jim heard the starter grind, but the engine failed to catch.

The truck made a wide turn and was coming toward the driver's side of the Taurus with everything it had like a bull toward a matador's cape. The truck's grill and grill guard looked like the gleaming teeth of a giant white monster. Jim felt like David in the shadow of Goliath but knew his story would not end as well.

He twisted the ignition switch over and over and pumped the gas pedal but never got a response. When he looked up from the truck's grill, he glimpsed the wide, glazed, fish-like eyes of Bitsy Wink just moments before impact. His body rattled like a dried-up old skeleton. Refusing to let her take pleasure in watching his pain, he turned his head away and took a deep breath, reaching for the armrest on the passenger side of the car. It was just a bit too far out of his reach.

The whole situation was just about incomprehensible, but he couldn't think about that just then. His immediate concern was survival. He pressed the release on his seatbelt and gripped the steering wheel with all his strength. The Taurus crashed against the guard rail and stopped for what seemed an eternity. Jim was thrown to the passenger side of the car. He feared that if the guard rail held, he was about to be squashed between it and the truck, a human sandwich. He cranked the window down, but it stopped after a couple of inches. The passenger door was smashed flat; no chance of opening it.

Bitsy—her lips spread across horse-sized teeth—backed the truck up. Jim searched for a way to get out of the car. There was no escape route. The roar of the diesel engine exploded in his ears as the pickup aimed at the Taurus again.

In lieu of escape, he clipped on the seatbelt on the passenger side, hoping if he wasn't squashed, if the car bounced down the hill, he wouldn't be thrown. Gripping the armrest, tensing his body for the impact, he glanced down the highway, amazed no other vehicles had come along. A flash of lightening lit up a huge cavity between hills. Valley, really.

As the impact smashed the Taurus through the guard rail and threw it sideways over the edge, Jim turned upside down and heard a man agonizing. Recognizing the voice, he realized it was his own. He uttered a prayer.

TWENTY-TWO

B y the next morning, the river swelled like an old lady's varicose veins. No one minded because the drought had caused it to dry up and had withered the plants on the banks. The rain bath made the town of Angeles squeaky-clean and shiny, the streets still glistening wet when it was time to go to work. The air smelled like fresh flowers. The birds sang. People seemed more cheerful than they had over the past intensely hot months of summer even though the day was heating up to be a scorcher barring any more thunderstorms.

At the county courthouse, it was child support Friday. Associate Judge Maria Lucia Lopez was in a good mood. The rainstorm had made her feel reborn. Yards would turn from brown to green again. Shriveled plants would be replaced with new ones. Flowers would spruce up gardens. Now that there had been a break in the weather, everyone would be more optimistic that Autumn and cooler weather would be coming soon.

"Cause number 75,628, Dorman versus Dorman," Judge Lopez called. Everyone watching could see her scan the courtroom in search of the writer and the schoolteacher. No one said anything. Not even a sheet of paper dared make a crinkling sound.

Judge Lopez frowned at the faces before her. Her pleasant mood soured when there was no response to her case announcement. "Dorman versus Dorman," she said louder. "The rest of you people pipe down."

As if anyone had uttered more than a breath. The courtroom was packed. It was always like that on the Friday nearest the first of the month. More people were scheduled because of paydays.

Judge Lopez glanced at her staff. "Am I going to have to issue a capias for Mr. Dorman's arrest for failure to appear?" She muttered something else, something about lawyers under her breath. No one understood what she said, therefore, no one responded.

"Ms. Reinhart here?" She cupped her hands over her eyes and peered toward the back windows. "Ms. Reinhart?"

Judge Lopez licked her lips and scanned the faces in the courtroom. "Mrs. Peterson," she said to the clerk. "I'm going to give Mr. Dorman the benefit of the doubt. Maybe he's just running late. I'm going to put his case at the back, take up the next one, and only issue the capias if he doesn't appear by the end of the call."

"Yes, ma'am," Mrs. Peterson said. The clerk sat in her usual place in the box-seat next to the judge's bench.

The court reporter wrote down what the judge said and smiled up at her, awaiting her next words. The bailiff stood solemnly next to the jury box and stared at the audience behind the bar.

Mrs. Peterson cleared her throat. "Excuse me, Your Honor," she said.

"What is it?" Judge Lopez rolled her chair over toward the woman and looked down at her.

"One of the clerks just brought me this." Mrs. Peterson handed up two sheets of paper.

Judge Lopez quickly read over the two pages. Again, she leaned over the bar separating her from Mrs. Peterson and whispered, "Who filed this? It doesn't have an attorney's name and address on it."

"I don't know, Judge. One of the clerks just handed it to me and left. Want me to call downstairs and find out?" The woman adjusted her glasses and stared up at the judge.

"That's all right, Mrs. Peterson. I'll just read it into the record. My secretary can call down later."

Lucia Maria Lopez called out the cause number and the style again to the court reporter and then said, "Let the record reflect that a *Suggestion of Death* was filed this morning with the clerk and it reads as follows: *Be it remembered that on this day the Court was duly notified that James W. Dorman, Respondent in the above styled-and-numbered cause, met his demise as a result of a traffic accident on the evening prior hereto. That a certified copy of the death certificate will be filed herein as soon as one is available from the county medical examiner.* Let the record further reflect there is no signature on this document, and the Suggestion of Death was filed in this cause by some unknown person along with a Motion to Dismiss the Motion for Enforcement of Child Support Order by Contempt."

Judge Lopez sighed and studied the people sitting in the audience. They stared back, quiet. "The court finds that upon presentation of a duly certified copy of the death certificate, this cause shall hereby be dismissed with costs assessed against the movant." She pounded her gavel on its block and handed the file back to Mrs. Peterson.

A man in the back of the room muttered to the man sitting next to him. "That's pretty cold-blooded, ain't it?"

"What do you mean?" the other man asked.

"She don't believe he's dead. She ain't going to close his case until she sees the death certificate with her own eyes.

"Oh. So that's what she was saying?"

"That's what I mean. I guess she thinks that guy will do anything to get out of paying his child support."

"I would," the other man replied. "Say, have you been here before?"

"Sure. Been coming up here for about ten years." He held out his hand. "My name's Richard Cook. What's yours?"

Judge Lopez called out, "Order. If you want to talk to your neighbor, take it outside. Otherwise, sit still. Nelson versus Nelson, come on up." The judge peered at the audience and scowled. The clerk handed her the next file folder and a man and woman stepped forward.

THUMP. Something banged against the rear door of the courtroom. The door was flung open, and Patty Reinhart held the door wide. Behind her came a nurse pulling on the back of a wheelchair with a bottle of glucose hanging down from a metal rod. A man with a neck brace sat in the chair. Bandages wrapped his head. One arm and one leg were in a cast. The nurse turned the wheelchair to face the front of the courtroom. It was Jim Dorman.

Jim saw Richard, the man he usually sat next to, staring at him, wide-eyed. "Hey, Buddy. How's it going?"

"Man, they said you were dead."

Jim looked at the front of the courtroom and met Judge Lopez's eyes. Then Bitsy Wink's. Bitsy's flitted from him to

Patty at the rear door. Then her eyes strayed to the door behind herself. The door into the hall.

Jim turned to Angeles police officer Esther Pratka who was walking in behind him. "That's her," he said, pointing with his good arm at Bitsy.

At about the same time Jim fingered her, Bitsy spotted the officer and charged into the hallway. Pratka ran out before the door could close.

Bam bam bam. Judge Lopez banged her gavel. *Bam bam bam.* "What's going on here?"

"Push me over to that glass where I can see into the hall," Jim told the nurse.

Patty and the nurse wheeled Jim to the window. As they looked on, Pratka was struggling with Bitsy who had a good fifty pounds on her. The second officer, Ivan Denholt, was trying to cuff her. They weren't having an easy time. People on other business in the hall had backed up, glued to the walls like posted notices.

Bitsy had her hand on her weapon and was trying to get it out of her holster as they shoved her up against the door. The rest of the people in the courtroom crowded behind Jim and Patty. Jim was dimly aware of the judge banging her gavel and hollering for order. He didn't care if he was held in contempt or not. He was going to watch Bitsy get what she deserved. He'd told the doctor that and threatened to check out of the hospital AMA if the doc didn't let him go to court.

A few moments later, the marble floor was cooling Bitsy's cheek. Denholt had his knee in her back and held her wrists as he cuffed her. Pratka had disarmed her and shoved her gun in her own belt as she spoke into the walkie-talkie on her epaulet. Bitsy's stony eyes stared into space.

Denholt jumped up, pulling Bitsy with him by the hand-cuffs. Her face was red, and angry words spewed from her mouth like vomit as he led her away. Jim could hear most of she said, and she was not making small talk. Just before she was out of their range of vision, she turned and stared Patty down. Then she turned her hard eyes on Jim. With his free hand, Jim grabbed Patty's arm and squeezed it. "Don't be afraid. We're going to be okay now."

Patty patted his cheek. "We are as soon as we get this case against you thrown out and get you back in bed where you belong." She turned and faced the judge as the rest of the people went back to their seats. "Your honor, may we come forward?"

Judge Lopez rested her cheek on her palm, her fingers entwined in her hair. She rolled her eyes at the ceiling. "If you must. Come on up. The rest of you people sit down and be quiet before I have all of y'all thrown in the hoosegow."

Jim covered his laugh at the judge's expression. She was the biggest control freak he'd ever met and for once events were totally out of hand. Her piercing yellow eyes roved over his injured parts as the nurse pushed him forward.

Patty said, "Do you remember us, Your Honor? We're the Dormans."

"And the ones responsible for turning my courtroom into a circus side show."

"I apologize, Judge," Jim said. "It was my fault. Please don't blame my wife."

"Your ex-wife, you mean," the judge said. "And I suppose you have an explanation for your actions this morning."

"Yes, Your Honor," Jim said, for once not feeling nervous speaking with her. "Could we tell you about it in chambers instead of here on the record? I'm not sure the authorities are ready for it to be made public yet."

"Come around then." In a loud voice she said, "We'll be in recess for fifteen minutes." She picked up a stack of papers and put them under her arm as she stepped down from the bench.

Jim, Patty, and the nurse went out the side door and into the judge's office where the secretary worked on the computer. When she saw them, she smiled and waved them in. "How are you, Mr. Dorman?" she asked. "Bitsy said you were in an accident the other day."

"I'll wait out here," the nurse said. She sat down next to the magazine stand.

Just which accident had Bitsy told her about? Plainly, she knew of both of them. *Caused* both of them. "I survived," was all he said with a look at Patty.

They found the judge with the telephone to her ear. She waved them into chairs and said into the phone, "I don't give a rat's ass how short of personnel you are, get me a bailiff over here and I mean right now. And you can have someone come over here and pick up Bitsy's personal effects, too." She paused, then, "I don't care whether she gets out on bond or not, which I doubt, but I will not, I repeat, not take her back, not now, not ever. Never. And if you know what's good for you, you'll suspend her without pay pending grand jury indictment. All right. See that you do. Thanks." She hung up. "Y'all have a preference for coffee or a Coke? I can send Clarice down to the machines."

"Nothing for me," Patty said.

Jim shook his head. He felt a bit guilty now for thinking that the judge might be involved in the killings. But he didn't say anything.

"Well, Mr. Dorman. Miss Reinhart. I hear you're responsible for busting my bailiff."

Jim studied the judge's face. He couldn't tell for a moment whether she was angry or joking, then she smiled.

"Why don't you tell me about it?"

Patty sighed. "It's rather complicated, Your Honor."

Jim said, "You know she founded a women's support group called WiNGS."

"Yes. I'm on the advisory board. They've provided a much-needed service to divorced women in this county."

"Yes, but it was a front for her killing spree."

Patty said, "Well, it wasn't exactly a spree. It was more like a revenge thing. We think she killed about six or seven men."

"By herself?" Pointing at Jim's head, she said, "And you must have been next on her list. Concussion?"

Jim nodded.

"As far as anyone could tell no one else was in on it, but the police are still investigating. Jim thought I was part of it."

"Well, you could have told me that you had been approached by the authorities." Jim gave Pat a look.

"I was sworn to secrecy, honey," Pat said.

Judge Lopez said, "Hold on. Miss Reinhart, you were working for the police?"

"Not working for them exactly. After I joined WiNGS and got on the board, they asked me to keep an eye on Deputy Wink. They didn't think she'd be suspicious if I made friends with her. That way I could hang out with her and report to them." She ran her hand down Jim's arm cast. "The trouble was, Jim started investigating WiNGS. Bitsy got nervous."

Jim watched Pat as she spoke. His brave little wife. Pride filled him at the thought of what she'd done for him—for them. Jim rubbed his lips with his knuckle. "I just wanted a story at first. But Patty kept acting so strange that I wondered what she was up to. And lately every time I turned around, something happened—like my brakes going out."

Pat glanced from Jim to the judge. "I'm sure Bitsy must have been listening to our conversation. We'd been in a special-called board meeting. She must have heard our discussion and knew your car would be around there someplace while we were in Wendy's. She had to have been the one who did something to your car." Patty snickered. "I kept trying to get rid of you and you kept showing up at all the wrong times."

"Bitsy is very mechanically minded," Judge Lopez said. "Her father owned a garage. That's where she met her husband. Tsk. Tsk." She shook her head. "Too bad they couldn't have gotten anything on her back then."

"Did you suspect something when her husband died, Judge?" Jim asked.

"Yes, we all did, but the grand jury didn't indict. Bitsy testified and they believed her."

"Weren't you worried that she might come after you?" Patty asked.

"No. She liked me. She was very protective of me. But I could tell she hated men. I just didn't know how much."

"Enough to kill one every time the opportunity arose," Jim said.

"And you were almost her next victim."

A little shiver ran down his back at just the mention of it. He reached for Patty's hand. "I would have been if Patty hadn't come along. She called for help and stayed with me until the ambulance came. I'd be dead by now if she hadn't been so heroic."

"You should have seen it, Judge," Patty said. "We were in this meeting and Bitsy got up and left all of a sudden and didn't come back. Jim had shown up earlier and was supposed to be waiting for me. . . ." She pushed her hair out of her face. "But he left and Bitsy left. When she didn't come back, I called the police and headed home in my car. I came around a curve and spotted her pushing him off the highway in her truck. I killed my lights so she wouldn't see me." She turned to Jim. "I'm sorry, honey, but if she could push that Taurus off with no

257

trouble, she could have gotten me in my tiny little car. Anyway, as soon as she drove off, I hurried over and left my flashers on so the police could find us and climbed down the hill after Jim."

"She was wonderful," Jim said. "The last thing I remembered was rolling down the hill. The next thing I saw was Patty. My angel. I knew then that she couldn't have been in on it."

The judge huffed a deep breath and let it out loudly. "You two are pretty brave if you ask me. Bitsy could scare the bejesus out of anyone she didn't like." She made signs of getting out of her chair. "Well, I'm glad it's finally over."

"Judge, there's something we'd like to ask you," Patty said. "Would you waive the three-day waiting period and marry us today?"

"You want to marry this bum again?" she asked, mirth in her eyes.

"Yes, ma'am." Patty stepped beside the wheelchair and took Jim's unbroken hand. "You see, we're moving to Dallas to start a new life. Jim's got a new job there and he's sold his book and we're buying a house."

"Well, congratulations. And I suppose you'll be selling that article about child support now, too."

"In a slightly different version, Your Honor."

"I suppose it will be more than slightly different. Tell you what. Go get the waiver and I'll have my coordinator see if she can find the district judge to sign off on it and marry you. That's one of the things I'm not allowed to do as an Associate Judge."

"It's a deal," Jim said. "And even if you can't marry us, we'll like to have you be with us at the ceremony."

"And Judge," Patty said, holding a hand out to her.

The judge had stepped over to the door leading to the courtroom. "What is it now?"

"Would you please dismiss the charges against my husband?"

"I guess a death certificate won't be forthcoming from the medical examiner." Judge Lopez studied the serious faces of the couple before her. "Kidding. I'll go right in and do it on the record." She doubled back and went out to speak to Clarice before going into the courtroom. They followed her and stood in the doorway.

"Mrs. Peterson, you want to give me back the Dorman file?"

She read the cause number and style into the record again. "Upon oral motion to dismiss made this date, this Motion for Enforcement of Child Support Order by Contempt is hereby dismissed without prejudice."

Judge Lopez added, "And the Suggestion of Death is hereby disregarded. Mr. Dorman is alive and well."

Several people clapped. Lopez banged her gavel. But she didn't look angry.

A male deputy sheriff passed by Jim and Patty and entered through the side door.

"You my new bailiff?" Judge Lopez asked.

"Yes, ma'am. Sheriff just assigned me."

"Very well. You stand over there," she said, pointing to the spot where Bitsy always stood. "We'll have a brief orientation after I get through with my morning cases."

"Yes, Your Honor."

"Nelson versus Nelson. Let's finish this up."

Patty, Jim, and the nurse, headed for the elevator. Downstairs to get the waiver, upstairs to get it signed, downstairs to get the license, upstairs to get married, and downstairs again so they could go home to their children.

THANK YOU FOR READING!

If you enjoyed *Suggestion of Death,* I would appreciate it if you would help others to enjoy this book, too.

Share it with a friend.

Recommend it. Please help others find this book by recommending it to friends, readers' groups, and discussion boards.

Please tell other readers why you liked this book by reviewing it wherever you purchased your copy. If you do write a review, please send me an email at **susan@susanbaker.com** so I can thank you with a personal email.

If you'd like to receive news of events and publications, please go to https://www.susanpbaker.com

ACKNOWLEDGMENTS

For their critiques and assistance, the author would like to thank the (first) Galveston Short Story and Novel Writers' Group, especially Katy Farmer, Richard Ferguson, and Geoffrey Leavenworth. And the SWMWA online critique group, especially Jonnie, Carol, Nancy, and John Foxjohn. And Bob Stewart, deceased. And, lastly, J.E. Taylor.

BOOKS BY SUSAN P. BAKER

NOVELS:

The Light in the Barn, A Domestic Thriller

Is the person behind the mysterious light in Aurora's barn the serial killer who is victimizing women in her neighborhood?

My First Murder

No. 1 in the Mavis Davis Mystery Series. A cafe owner hires Mavis as a last resort to discover who murdered his mysterious waitress.

The Sweet Scent of Murder

No. 2 in the Mavis Davis Mystery Series. Mavis' search for a missing teenager turns into a murder investigation in Houston's Ritzy River Oaks.

Murder and Madness

No. 3 in the Mavis Davis Mystery Series. Mavis takes on the cold case of a grisly ax murder of a cruise ship captain in Galveston.

Not Murder

No. 4 in the Mavis Davis Mystery Series. Mavis is hired to locate a lawyer's deadbeat client and finds a Pandora's box of problems, including a dead body.

Defensible Murder

No. 5 in the Mavis Davis Mystery Series. When twin babies are stolen from a church nursery, the parents hire Mavis to *assist* the police and then to clear the father of murder of the prime suspect!

The Underground Murders

No. 6 in the Mavis Davis Mystery Series. Was the widow's husband's death a suicide or murder? What Mavis uncovers is a conspiracy of epic proportions right out of the current headlines.

Death of a Prince

No. 1 in the Lady Lawyer Mystery Series. Sandra Salinsky & Erma Townley defend the alleged murderer of a Galveston millionaire plaintiff's attorney who was Erma's best friend.

Death of a Rancher's Daughter

No. 2 in the Lady Lawyer Mystery Series. Sandra & Erma defend a family friend for murder while fighting gender and racial prejudice in a small Texas town.

Ledbetter Street

A Novel of Second Chances: Not just the story of a mother fighting for custody of her disabled son, but one of love, tragedy, and the relationships of the women of Ledbetter Street.

Suggestion of Death

An investigative reporter who can't pay his child support searches for the killer of deadbeat dads, before he becomes the next victim.

UNAWARE

Attorney Dena Armstrong wants to break out from the control of the two men dominating her life, unaware that a stranger has other plans for her.

Texas Style Justice

Judge Victoria Van Fleet aspires to the highest court in the land, but is she willing to pay the price?

NONFICTION:

Heart of Divorce

Divorce advice especially for those who are considering representing themselves.

Murdered Judges of the 20th Century

True stories of judges killed in America.

Fly Catching

An eclectic collection of short pieces.

www.susanpbaker.com

ABOUT THE AUTHOR

Susan P. Baker, a retired Texas family court judge, presided over everything from divorce to murder for 12 years. Afterward, she traveled around Texas as a visiting judge for another 12. Prior to being elected to the bench, she practiced law for nine (9) years, and was a probation officer for two (2) years. Susan's works are derived from her experiences in the justice system and/or events in and around courts in Texas, *fictionalized*, of course!

She is the author of 13 novels of mystery and suspense set in Texas, two nonfiction books, and an eclectic collection of short pieces. Her novels include six featuring Mavis Davis, a private detective; two Lady Lawyer mysteries starring criminal defense lawyers Sandra Salinsky and Erma Townley (3rd in the works); and five stand-alones with court participant protagonists (including judges and lawyers).

Her two nonfiction books are Murdered Judges of the 20th Century and Heart of Divorce—Advice from a Judge. The title of her collection is Fly Catching.

Susan has two children and eight grandchildren. She loves dark chocolate, raspberries, and traveling the world (and has lost count of the number of countries she's visited). An anglophile, Susan most enjoys visiting her cousins in England and Australia (where she was finally able to visit in September of '22). She hopes to drive Route 66 someday. She is at home in Cypress, Texas.

Read more about Susan at www.susanpbaker.com. Find her books at <u>books.by/judge-susans-bookstore.</u> Like her at http://facebook.com/legal writer. Follow her on Bluesky@ baksp2.bsky.social and on Instagram@suewritesandreads.

www.ingramcontent.com/pod-product-compliance
Lightning Source LLC
Chambersburg PA
CBHW060308260626
47160CB00007B/2536